YELLOWSTONE

A Novel By William J. Hughes

ISBN: 978-1093621419

This book is for my Mother,
and with thanks to Mr. W. Somerset Maugham

"Go west young man." Horace Greeley

Once upon a time there was a fairly handsome prince. The time was about 1972.

Upon a lifeguard stand sat Paul Barnes-Pauley, if you were his family, Paul to everyone else. He was the prince of all he surveyed.

He surveyed Long Beach, Long Island, New York. The time now was just after 4:00 o'clock, late August, almost Labor Day. Almost the end of the season.

The sun would be a sailor's delightful red tonight. The fairly handsome prince surveyed the gold and the peach of the sun.

Yes, a delightful red. A seasonal lifeguard tried to know these things. He had come to know these things.

"Good night," from below on the sand took him away from his surveillance.

"Oh, hi. Yes, good night." She said "good night" each weekend. "Good night" to her prince up there with his trim brown hair, his trim waist, his brown all-over tan; his soft brown eyes, his full brown eyebrows, his thin, serious, sun-worn face; his throne.

She wasn't for him. She was nice but not princess enough. He had to not encourage a lot of "hi, good night."

"See you later," she offered up from below.

"Sure, take care. Beautiful day tomorrow?"

"Hope so," and she looked back over her shoulder at him, folded blanket on her arm, books under the other arm.

A little too old for me, he reminded himself. Too old? He kidded himself with a laugh.

Today another young one, a teenager, called him "sir."

"Sir?" She's not that young, is she? I'm not that old, am I? Of course not, the handsome prince reminded himself.

Twenty-seven's not so old for a lifeguard? Or is it? Now when he surveyed the setting sun and the long stretch of nearly empty beach he included himself. "Sir?" Smooth sand, the weary stone jetties breaking the surf, the wire trash cans and the sentinel lifeguard stands. Now when he, he included himself. "Sir?" Am I? Too old for this? He wasn't a captain of a crew, or a boss of the whole lot-- just a guard.

Free to partake of the summer, free to partake of the ladies-in-waiting. Free to substitute teach the winter away. Free to return each season.

Free to start wondering, pondering a career? A plump, red and white Coast Guard helicopter came in low along the tide line, reminding him of the one career he'd had.

Three years. College had to end and that little Asian war had to begin. The Coast Guard seemed the safest place.

Long Island life meant a constant use, a constant love of the water. So did the Coast Guard, right? Right. They put him on a cutter out of south Florida. Young, fairly handsome prince.

Free to scuba dive, and tan and back again.

The coffins were coming home from Asia while he tanned. Free to stay alive, stay in one piece.

That piece of him that heard, that felt that "sir" interfered with the final, daily ritual of enjoying the end of a work day, especially a work day that was ending in a golden butterscotch light, quiet enough now so you could hear the incoming waves breaking on the beach.

Maybe I'll mention it to him, Paul Barnes suggested to himself, as he raised his binoculars to look for him. This was his usual time. Maybe he'll get a kick out of the "sir" thing.

He focused the binoculars down the beach two stands down where the boardwalk ramp came down onto the beach. "There he is."

CHAPTER

Paul hadn't seen him for three weeks. He was like that. He'd be gone without a word, and then one evening he'd be back. Same time, same place on the beach.

This was his time, each evening--when the crowds were gone.

Paul got him clear in the binoculars. The focus gave him a tall, thin man--in his what? Paul guessed at it--60's, early 70's? He never did say did he? with a short smile. And I never did ask, with another short smile.

The man in the binoculars was chestnut brown from the sun, his hair the bright white of Caribbean beach sand. The binoculars couldn't get in that close to see the dark eyes, bright with life, bright with interest. White eyebrows made his eyes clearer, brighter.

His face was thin and hard, but soft at the lips, white and even at the teeth, pleasant in the smile.

He wore what he always wore. Tan shorts, a web belt, a white, short sleeve shirt, India's sandals, a short, plain walking stick.

He rested his hand on the shoulder of a younger woman, older than Paul, jet black hair in two long braids, a simple, white muslin dress that heightened the native darkness of her plump brown face and arms. She was barefoot.

They walked easily together through the sand. Paul Barnes always anticipated him, looked forward to seeing him. Larry.

Larry Darrell with this companion.

This woman with him had a straw mat rolled up under her arm-his straw mat.

Paul watched him, the evenings he appeared. Sometimes with someone, sometimes alone, he'd spread out the mat on the sand, just in the dry sand above the tide line. He'd fold his two pieces of clothing neatly beside him, and then sit in his bathing trunks, on the mat, and what? What? Paul wondered. Soak in the soft, setting sun? Tonight he went the same distance on the sand. Paul didn't need the binoculars now. Larry and his companion rolled out the mat near enough to where Paul could have yelled a greeting to him.

Yelling a greeting to Larry didn't, wouldn't sound right from off the lifeguard stand. Something more personal, more important was the way around this man.

Lots of hippies still hip-hopping through society. Paul liked his little joke, his little thought of the day, the evening he coined it.

Larry, though. The genuine article? Made in India wasn't stamped on him. It was more like written on him. Paul liked that little phrase the same evening as that little joke.

Larry Darrell folded his clothes; black swimming trunks from a by-gone day--a 1940's day.

He had the waistline of a youth. His smile, young and wise, at the same time, pearl white, at the same time. Turning away from the surf, using the smile to say hello to Paul.

Paul waved a hearty hello from atop his post. Larry sat down, his companion on a short blanket beside him staring out to sea-the worn jetties, the white waves, the white spray.

"Pauley? Are you going to close up?" The handsome prince had a handsome princess--his sister, Kate.

Seventeen, working the concession stand--a sturdy, stucco block house dropped on the sand alongside the sturdy, stucco, lifeguard H.Q.

The rest of the beach was closing shutters, taking down flags, tipping over lifeguard stands recoiling life-lines, hauling up boats, calling it a day.

Kate Barnes state high jump champ. A gazelle in a yellow tank top and blue shorts. She looked out towards the surf to see what was keeping her brother.

Oh, his friend out there. Mr. Darrell? Right.

"Your friend's back," to her older brother as he climbed down from his perch.

"Yeah. It's good to see him again." They tipped over the wooden lifeguard stand together.

"You in a hurry?" he asked his sister. A ride home.

"I'd like to get going." She could see that Mr. Darrell came first right now.

"Can you catch a ride? I want to stay for a bit." She adored her brother. He could do no wrong, not to her anyway.

"Oh, sure. Let me run and catch Susan." She yelled to

"Susan!" down the beach. "Susan!"

"Thanks, Champ. It is good to see him again."

"He's got a new friend."

This Mr. Darrell's routine was well known to this section of the beach. So was Paul's interest in him.

"I know," Paul answered her. He zipped up his red windbreaker. "Thanks. I'll get you at home in the morning."

"O.K., bye. Tell him I said hello."

"I will."

CHAPTER

Paul filled in his time card and put his official windbreaker in his locker while the other guards made plans, laughing plans for the evening, laughing young jokes around him in the compact headquarters building. Youth wasn't being wasted here. A party was always being offered.

"No thanks," was his laughing reply. He changed into khaki shorts and a blue sweat shirt.

"His buddy's back," came a yell--a yell from Junior Collin, wrestler, future hard head.

Paul only smiled and left them to banging their lockers shut.

The evening was moving slowly into night. A star in the light purple sky. The sky with the rose, orange, red sunset. A dog barked far down the beach. If you listened closely, you could hear the ringing of some winning game bell--a Kewpie doll game up on the boardwalk.

His buddy, Larry, was in the surf now, swimming just beyond the crest of the waves. Paul walked out to the straw mat.

"Hello." The dark woman with the braids answered from a mouth of teeth white as paper. "Hello?" as if she'd known Paul for some time.

Like Larry, Paul noticed. He noticed she was native. To where? India, Wyoming, Polynesia? I think so. She was barefoot, a small book on the sand beside her. Larry's friend. One of a few. Paul had met a few. How old is she? I have no idea.

"He's out swimming?" he said to her.

"Yes." She looked up at Paul. "You are a friend of his?"

"Of course," is what he almost said. "Yes," is what he did.

She just smiled, as if she knew something about Paul.

"Here he comes now," she said.

They both watched the lean, partially wrinkled, browned-over man, with the white hair, come dripping from the surf. He stopped to nod a "good evening" to a couple walking ankle-deep in the desert-painted surf.

"Hello, Paul," genuine, glad, pleased as he toweled off. His handshake was that of a man--genuine, sincere, firm, soft.

"I'm glad to see you again, Larry." Paul was.

Larry stood with the red ball of sun at his back. Always, Paul thought. Calm, collected, assured, genuine.

Larry pulled his shirt on and knelt on the straw mat.

Paul was anxious. "Where have you been?" It had been India, Peru, Kenya, New Mexico, Bali, and many more through the three summers Paul had known him. Paul could sit here, or in Larry's stark apartment and listen.

Larry told without ego, without I, I. He took you there, told you of it as if his trip was a place you were planning to visit.

"We've been to Paris, Paul." Now he sat, facing the ocean.

Paul sat on the sand beside him, like a pupil.

"It's been a long time since I was last there, Paul," with a voice like his handshake.

Paul enjoyed the way Larry used his name, a name. Always sharing with you.

"When was that, your last time there?" like they'd seen each other the night before.

"Oh, when I was much younger."

"I'd love to see Paris."

Larry smiled. "You will, Paul."

There, that again. As if Larry knew for sure, certain.

I wish I was as certain of so much. Paul watched a man in a sweat suit tossing a chunk of wood into the surf for his black dog.

"Where will you go next?" he asked Larry, watching the dog loving the stick.

"Yellowstone," without hesitation, without doubt.

Now Paul looked at him. "Old Faithful?"

"Part of it," Larry smiled. "I'll need to put the cab to work for awhile." Paul knew that meant earning money. Enough money, as Larry always noted.

"Where is it, Yellowstone?" Paul asked. "Montana?"

"Wyoming. Under the big sky. An American big sky. I read some things on it in Paris." Not a word from his companion. Not a word about his companion.

Paul knew that the time, his time with Larry could expire--not into indifference, but into some other place where Larry would take himself. Someplace it seemed more pleasant than your company.

Paul felt it now, Larry stretched out on his stomach, head on his hands, into that other place.

"Time to call it a day, I guess." Larry turned his head to face him. "I'm glad to see you, Paul. Come by the apartment." He never tells you when he'll be there.

"I will. Yellowstone sounds great." Larry's companion said, "Good night." It would be. Larry always left a glow, a reassurance, comfort.

Paul took those with him.

CHAPTER

Larry's apartment. Paul's would qualify. A rug, a couch, a lamp, a chair, a refrigerator, a bed, a table, a stereo, an indifference to accumulation.

Paul's present live-in, on and off again, was home before him.

"Paul?" Terri called from the table and chair kitchen.

"Yep. The old man is home." Old man? Puzzled, with boy length brown hair, an even, lean body, a girlish, green-eyed face that would never be older than her 20's.

They kissed hello in the kitchen door frame. Paul could taste what he started to taste about two weeks ago. Indifference? "Yeah," he answered from the kiss. "I got another sir from somebody today." Terri wasn't going to say, "see, Paul, it's time to settle into something, permanent." She just said it in her indifferent kiss.

"Larry was back today." He went to the back door and opened it onto a tiny back deck above a long, wide canal, star bright with boat dock lights. Paris, Yellowstone were bright out there right now.

"Oh?" Terri answered from afar--a far away from the back deck.

"He's been to Paris." Sea gulls made shadows across the canal.

The word, that word, Paris, caught Terri's attention.

"Paris this time?" not too soft, not too, "what, Paris this time?" Not too, "when is he going to? When are you going to?" She came up beside him and put an arm around his waist. Terri knew. Life with Paul meant interludes of this Larry Darrell.

"Glad to see him?" He tried to hold her real close. But that kiss. "I am." A one-man boat with a sputtering engine came up the canal, red light, green light bow and stern.

"You know I am," he smiled at her.

I know you are. "What is it about him, Paul?"

He was never too sure. Something Larry had said brought it all close. "Living is occupation enough, Paul. Emily Dickinson." Terri, Terri Crowley was a county recreation director, with a husband and a house on her mind. A career was occupation enough.

Paul had it in him. Terri had it in her to get it out of him.

Once upon a time ago? Now? "Now he's off to where again?" she asked.

"Yellowstone," with a reverence reserved for reverent people and places.

"Ever been there?" he asked her.

"As a kid." She could hear it in his question. "Want to go there?" in there.

He could hear it in her answer. "As a kid," sounded a period.

Paul went away from it--not very far. "Want to go for a swim?"

"Sure." She couldn't resist the just living of that. They were still very good to each other.

CHAPTER

Water, water, everywhere--and a place to hide.

Paul knew the public, as well as the private water. Private lifeguards, at the private clubs, gave him a look the other way.

Stars and a moon and a short stretch of Atlantic beach. A large, white clubhouse, its view of this surf cut off by the walls of the handball courts. Paul had a key to a gate.

Nothing on the beach between two jetties but two pairs of shorts, two shirts, sandals, a blanket and a worn pair of tennis shoes.

Terri was trim and firm, soft and moist where it mattered most. Her mouth, her tongue, her ears, her breasts, her thighs, her moist hair.

Their legs were moist together. The salt water and themselves, floating, bobbing in the calm water just inside the breaking waves.

She felt him where it mattered most.

"Pauley," is all she said. "Pauley," was why she was here, again.

Paul turned her in the water and felt her from behind. Not a care in the world. Not a world, just this, here. Living.

He pushed away from her and stroked, hard, glad to be glad.

Terri followed in as he swam into a breaking wave, riding it, glad of it, feeling the smooth sand on his stomach. Standing now, dripping from the moist places.

Terri ran from a running wave, beautiful, all woman.

Moist tongues and wet limbs made them remember to always bring a blanket. Paul laid there waiting for her.

She came down to him and made him glad to be firm and throbbing. Terri made him glad with the palm of her hand. With her mouth.

With her mouth. More and more until Paul made her glad in her mouth.

"Umm, Pauley." He took his hands from her hair and lifted her head to his.

The kiss was a taste of all things here in the night. The waves, the stars, the woman. The woman.

Paul found the woman's thigh, the woman warm between the thighs. Glad. Glad, very glad. Always glad, always. Ahhh, glad.

Terri was glad. Terri was very glad until she was glad by biting his shoulder.

The waves rolled in and ran out. They lay on the blanket, two warm cats, dry, warm.

"Look at all the stars," Terri whispered.

"I wonder what the sky's like over Montana? Wyoming?"

He's wondering. She had him full all over her, almost in her.

That's how she wanted him, them. All the way in her. He's wondering? She loved the taste of him. She'd love to have him. Not like this. This part time life of his.

"This sky suits me," she told him.

"Yes, beautiful. Beautiful." He surprised her with, "let's make love in Paris sometime."

"Paris?" surprised.

"Sure. Larry says I'll go there someday." Suddenly she was cold. "I'm cold, Paul. Can we get going?"

"I guess so." He looked at her under the starlight. "You all right?" They got dressed and rolled up the blanket in silence. They walked up the beach the same way.

"Good to have a day off tomorrow," Paul offered.

"What will you do?" Terri offered back.

I don't want to say it. Why don't I want to say it, all of a sudden? He said it. "I want to see if I can catch Larry at his apartment."

"Oh." All the other tastes from just before. They both felt a bad taste in their mouths.

I hope he's home. I wonder how he does it without a telephone? Paul stopped wondering about Larry not having a television long ago.

I wonder what he's going to do in Yellowstone? I wonder how long he'll be gone? I wonder if he's home? The apartment house wasn't much, wasn't more than it needed to be: red brick, twelve stories, four blocks from the beach, a bit musty, used, in the lobby: a bit creaky in the elevator, a bit narrow in the low-lit hallway, worn carpets. Bits of sounds from the green doors along the hallway.

Larry's was No. 12, 8th floor. Paul knocked. I wonder if he's home? "Come in," from inside said he was.

He never locks his door. Paul shook his head in "how about that" admiration and went in.

"Larry?"

"Paul? Oh, hello. Come in. I'll be right out," came from the bedroom.

The bedroom was as sparse as this room--with a worn couch, Santa Fe patterns, two deck chairs, a rocking chair, a battered Santa Fe rug, absolutely nothing on the walls.

"Hello, Paul."

That smile, that ever genuine smile. Paul savored it and looked for Larry's companion from the beach. They were alone.

Two wide windows looked out on Atlantic Avenue below, and out over the rooftops to the Atlantic Ocean. One window had a window seat. Larry sat there in his usual shorts and shirt. Paul sat in a deck chair. He would have agreed if someone said, "At Larry's feet."

"No beach today?" Larry asked.

"No, day off. How about you?"

"Perhaps. Later on I'll take the cab out." Paul never heard Larry say, "I need to make the rent. I need a few bucks." Never a word of a grind towards a pay day.

"How have you been?" Paul asked.

"Sad, Paul. This Vietnam war has hurt me." He never does say all that much, but when he does, it's like this. Paul followed his gaze out the window.

"I was in a war, Paul."

"When? You were?" he sat down.

"Yes. Many years ago."

"The second world war?" Larry turned and offered a parental smile. "No, Paul, the first one. The war to end ... " and he didn't finish.

Paul tried some instant math, some instant birth dates. His surprise interfered with his calculations. "The first world war?"

"I was there. For a while," and he turned back to the window.

A few clouds gathered in the blue, the sun summer bright. "I was a pilot ... " Paul wouldn't push. "Vietnam stinks." He wouldn't need to say more.

"All those parents, both sides ..." Larry didn't need to say any more.

He's using that coin to calm down. Paul could see him turning it in his hand. The large, smooth, gray coin, with the head of Alexander the Great flat on it. I think it's Alexander the Great? From India? Yes, I think so. How it intrigued him. It seemed to be from the time of Alexander. Couldn't be, could it? Larry put the coin in his pocket.

Paul took them to what intrigued him now. "How will you go to Yellowstone?" Larry was quick to smile. "By train, Paul. I've read that the trains used to pull, right up to the gates of the park. Bozeman, in Montana, is as close as possible now."

"Bozeman."

"Yes, a bus from there? Seventy odd miles?"

"And then you'll walk, hike?" He knew a bit about Larry by now.

"Most likely. Should we do that for a bit now? Walk?"

"Sure," very glad.

CHAPTER

"Renoir would gladly paint this. Larry and Paul walked along the boardwalk; enough people, enough children with balloons, enough noise from the carnival rides; enough ocean, enough sun, enough time to stroll.

He couldn't have known Renoir? He's known enough, seen more than enough. Paul went back to before Larry's Renoir comment had changed the subject matter. "Grizzly bear. Must be some animal."

"Yes, Paul. A king. Yellowstone will feel good around me, knowing the great bear will be there." They walked. Heads of hair as hippies passed them. Paul didn't give them any attention. Larry.

"Have you ever seen a grizzly bear?"

"Only in my dreams," was his answer.

Paul liked that. He wasn't exactly sure why, but he liked that.

He knew Larry and his walks. You could find yourself with a long way back. He had something he wanted to mention to him.

"Want a soda or something?"

"No thanks, Paul." I never see him eat, or drink. "Be right back." Larry waited by a boardwalk bench, the ocean, the gulls, the warm end of a summer day free of charge.

"Want some?" Paul had a coke.

"No." Paul got to it as well as he could before Larry started moving.

"Ha. I wanted to tell you that a teenager on the beach called me sir yesterday. Happened before." Tell me what you think about that, Larry.

"You love being on the beach here, don't you, Paul?"

"I do."

"In some way, I've loved all the places I've been." He turned and looked at Paul. "All the places, Paul," and he smiled, warmly.

"Should we walk back, sir?" Paul laughed at that, with a slight pinch in his brow about the rest of it.

"When will you come back from Yellowstone?" Larry dodged a running child, its mother in giddy pursuit. "I can't say. When this war is over?"

"Yes? I hope it's soon."

"I do too, Paul. I do too."

"Oh, I read the book you loaned me. A little tough going for me. Didn't you say you knew him?"

"Mr. Maugham? Yes. We were friends, in Paris. Sorry to say I've outlived him."

"When did he die?"

"Oh, I've outlived him by quite a few years." Larry stopped walking.

Two young women said, "Hi, Paul." Paul followed their bikinis away. Two little girls tried to out-think their hay bales of cotton candy.

Larry hadn't moved.

"Everything all right?" Paul asked.

"Fine, Paul." Larry put his hand on Paul's shoulder. "I was remembering India, Paris. Mr. Maugham listened to a young man. He was very gracious, courteous, listening to my tales."

"I'd like to hear more about it." What was it he'd say? The "light" he found there? "I have to be getting home, Paul," and he walked briskly, Paul with him.

At the front door of the apartment house they said so long.

Larry didn't say goodbye. He left you with the hope that you'd see him again, soon.

"Have a good trip if I don't see you."

"I will, Paul." They shook hands, and he was gone.

Paul missed him already.

CHAPTER

Ice. Chunks of ice like barnacles on the jetties. Cold Atlantic wind spinning the beach sand into dust devils.

Terri kept Paul warm, naked, on top of his back, covers off, floor heater helping out. Ice on the apartment windows.

She kissed his hair. "I love these winter Saturdays. No work, all play." Paul rolled over under her. "Especially the no work."

"And the play?" She slowly, warmly, began to jerk him off, her nipple between his teeth.

"Come, come up here," he begged her. She did, spreading herself above his nose, his mouth. Both enjoyed her warmth.

The wind blew the bare tree branches. Terri was warm in his arms, quiet, content, glad of her man, proud of him. Work.

Teaching full-time--substitute full-time anyway. Next year we'll see him with a position. The spring will see us – she left out the rest for now.

For now, he was content. Now had been a few months. A few months closer to another birthday. He lay warm in her arms, content with his woman.

They both needed a drink from the orange juice on the lamp table beside the bed. The glass made two round stains on two postcards beneath it.

One card showed a great winter waterfall, encrusted in snow and ice. The other was a grandfatherly bison crossing a steaming river. Yellowstone. Larry.

In that lamp table, in a drawer, under some books, under some magazines was something else Larry had sent--a job application, with a note attached. "No one calls me 'sir' here." Paul filled out the application and forgot it--while Terri was in the apartment.

Terri was in the shower. The postcards were out from under the juice glass.

"I've seen the track of the great bear. ." one of them read. The other read, "Here, there are almost no wars." And no one calls you "sir"? Paul told himself.

"What are you smiling at?" Terri asked, a towel in her hair and nowhere else.

"Larry's postcards?"

"Oh." She finished drying off.

It's still "oh" with her. But oh, man, she's beautiful.

"Love me?" She sat on the bed and rough dried her hair.

"Yes."

"Marry me?"

"Probably," and he laughed. "Get a full-time teaching job? Probably. A little house with a picket fence? Probably." She grabbed him by the throat, jokingly. "Probably, probably?" I probably won't ever go to Yellowstone. I'll probably never see Larry again.

"Uh, the sun's coming out." Terri went to the window and stuck her face in the bright gold. "Warm out. Let's take a walk?"

"Sure." They looked good walking in the remains of yesterday's light snow. Down Clark Street, where the oaks and the elms were bare, and the sun bright, icicles melting in the branches.

PASSAGE

Sun. A frisbee skipped off the jetty and into the rolling ocean. "Get it," was the yell from the beach.

A stick and a dog, its owner throwing, the dog kicking up the beach sand, kicking up its heels. Early April. Everyone kicking up their heels.

Terri was. Paul would be a county park supervisor this summer. Away from that beach, finally; away on the way to each other, seriously. "Pauley. I practically live here now."

"I know. I'm glad to keep finding your underwear all over the place." He was in the front room, she was in the kitchen.

"Maybe we can look for some place bigger?"

"Sure." Why? Seven o'clock and the day done.

"Did you mail the cards today?"

"I did." Parents, both sets, in Florida for spring training.

Mail made him remember. He'd done it. Mailed the Yellowstone application--over a month ago. Why? Why not? Terri came out and sat on the couch with him, as strong as a rock climber, as feminine as a lady.

"I have to go to my home for a bit. Come by and get me later? Have dinner?"

"I will. You look terrific."

"Why, thanks." He looked like he did all summer--neat, trim, denim shirt, minus a tan.

"Bye, I'll see you in a bit." A short, sweet kiss.

A short, sweet nap, he told himself. He heard her VW bug pull away. He closed his eyes and saw Terri--clearly, confidently. He smiled and slept.

Someone's knocking at the door his nap told him. Wake up, someone's knocking at the door. He got up to see who it was.

CHAPTER

It was a stranger. No it isn't, Paul. Native dark, braided hair, muslin dress. Larry's companion.

Almost as good, almost the surprise as if it was Larry.

"Well, hello? Come in, come in. I remember you. You were with Larry." She nodded and came in.

"My name is Sophia. Your name is Paul?"

"Yes, yes. Please, sit down. Is Larry back? Have you seen him?" She doesn't want to say much.

"What are Larry's plans? Will he be back soon?" She sat down in a worn deck chair.

"Have you been in Yellowstone with him?"

"Yes. Until the heavy snows came."

"How is he? I got a few cards from him."

"Yes," and she smiled, weakly.

"How do you know him?"

"I know him from Egypt." Egypt? When? Never mind. "What are Larry's plans? Will he be back soon?"

"No."

"Oh. Staying on in Yellowstone?"

"Yes. Always."

"Always?" He has a job there or something? Always? What.

She looked straight at him. "Larry has died, Paul. In Yellowstone." I knew that. God damn it. I knew that as soon as I opened the door. I knew she was going to say that. That "always." He hung his head. He held his head in his hands. He held his face in his palms.

"How?" from his palms.

"Easily, Paul. Asleep in the snow, near the clouds." Paul lifted his head. What the fuck do you mean, near the clouds? Shit. Sorry, sorry about that. This woman here wasn't someone he'd meet in the teacher's lounge.

"Near the clouds?"

"Yes."

"Uh, huh." He had a hundred questions to ask. He picked one.

"Was he sick?"

"No."

"Just went to sleep on some hill?"

"A hill or a mountain."

"Yes? When?"

"Weeks ago." How do you know? Paul left it unasked. Larry was dead.

Seemed too young to die. Paul, he was old. He was.

"Where is he? Where is his body?"

"In Bozeman, Montana. I will go there soon now." I want to go with you. "You'll take care of him?"

"Yes."

Mind if I leave you "Damn. I'm sorry I won't see him again."

"You will."

"What?" Never mind, Paul. He stared at her. Larry said I will see Paris. Never mind.

"Could I rest here?" she asked.

"Sure, certainly."

"I'm sorry," she said.

Paul stood up. "Yes. He just went to sleep? No pain?"

"No, nothing."

"Well, sure, make yourself at home. I'd like to walk a bit."

"You'll need to see his apartment."

"Oh, yes, sure. I'll be back."

He took his bicycle. Spring was on its way, beginning. Hard to imagine snow. Not too hard to imagine Larry asleep in it.

Dead.

No, dead is not the right image. Paul shook it from his head as he pedaled, pedaled slowly along. Gone to sleep is the image, Paul.

That felt better, under the broad trees, along the broad street.

Am I going to cry? Yes. He was a friend of mine. Am I going to weep? No. He was a different friend of mine. "Larry," he said, softly, gently, quietly, sadly.

No, not right, Paul. We were different from him. Right.

That stopped his eyes from watering, his nose from dripping.

He came to a near sudden stop. Railroad tracks and a grand old maple tree set his scene. Am I going to go? There? Am I going to go? Is there any question? Of course I'm going? Of course.

A freight train took its time going by, giving him time to reconsider. The reconsider was in the affirmative. Larry. Yellowstone.

I've got to. I knew that. "You will, Paul." I will.

The freight train ended. He turned around and pedaled home.

Yellowstone. He didn't stop to consider anything, anyone else.

Outside his door he wiped his nose and pushed the door open with the bike's front wheel.

"A young woman phoned." Oh right, Larry's friend Sophia is still here.

"Just now?"

"Yes." The phone rang. Paul got it this time. "Hello?" He knew it was Terri.

"Paul? Who was that?"

"A friend of Larry's." He let the "Larry" sink in. "He died, Terri."

"Oh, Pauley. I'm so sorry. I am." She let that sink in. "I know how much you cared for him. How?"

"Went to sleep in the snow Sophia, uh, the woman here, tells me."

"Where?" Terri asked through the phone.

"In Yellowstone," quietly, gently, sadly.

"Can I come over?" came quickly through the phone.

"Uh, sure." She hung up, quickly.

"He cared very much for you, Paul."

"What? Oh. Well, thanks. I guess he sort of cast a spell over me." No, it wasn't a spell. It was more, more reality. "Yes," something like that."

"Yes, a spell."

"Come to his apartment," she said, getting up to go.

"Sure. When?"

"Sometime soon."

"I will," and he kept from smiling at the unusual set of circumstances of it.

"Thank you for telling me."

"Larry is glad you know," and she stroked his cheek with the back of her hand.

Paul closed the door behind her, easily, quietly. Soon after he opened the door to Terri.

"Oh, Pauley. I am sorry." She embraced him.

"Thanks. Thanks." Terri held him, tight. He held her, not so tight. They let go.

"Is that woman here?"

"No, she just left. She went to his apartment. She wants me to come by."

"Are you?"

"Sure."

"Why?"

"Why? To see what's there. Respect?" They hadn't moved.

"Want to come with me?" he asked.

"No." She took a few steps further into the apartment.

"Aren't we going to have dinner?"

"How about tomorrow? I do need to go to his apartment."

"Were you that close to him?"

"Close? Close enough."

"Why don't you go tomorrow?"

"I'd like to go over now." He stepped to her.

"Problem?"

"No problem." I've heard the way you speak about him. I'm afraid of him. I'm afraid? "Yellowstone is where? Wyoming?"

"Yes."

"Oh."

Paul was quiet, very quiet.

"What are you thinking about?" She bit her lip.

"Oh, just a little sad. I can see him on the beach. Always so, so calm, assured. I envied him."

"He was just a cab driver, wasn't he?"

He forced a smile. "I guess so." A real smile. "He said there weren't any wars in Yellowstone."

"Maybe we can go there someday?" nearly a plea.

"You bet. But right now I've got to go. Sure you don't want to come?"

"I'm sure. I'll wait for you here."

"O.K. I won't be gone long."

"Don't be?" and she kissed his neck.

"What's that woman's name?" as she zipped up his jacket.

"Sophia."

"I'll wait for you."

"I'll be back soon." He closed the front door and she was alone.

CHAPTER

Just a box of books, a shoe box of papers. Sophia sat on the floor with them. There wasn't much to remove from Larry's apartment.

The afternoon sun made shadows through the windows--short slants, like the light through church windows.

"What about his cab?" Paul asked.

"Someone will take care of it." Paul didn't ask "who, what or where?"

"This, I think, is for you." She took a heavy brown envelope from the shoe box. Paul's name was written across it.

"For me?" He knelt on one knee to her, puzzled, excited.

The envelope had something of weight in it. Paul opened the flap. A heavy gray coin slid out.

"It's the coin he carried," wonder, privilege in his voice, on his face.

The coin filled his palm, rough around its edge, smooth on its face. A worn, smooth face made one side of the coin.

"Is this someone historical, someone significant? Is it Alexander the Great?"

"It is," was her answer.

Now he couldn't have known Alexander the Great, could he? Paul? "Oh." It felt good and firm in his hand. "India?"

"Persia." He didn't want to ask. It felt lousy to ask. He asked.

"Uh, what will become of Larry? His body?" She stood up and came close to him. She smelled like fresh wood, fresh grass.

"There are great mountains nearby. Nearby this Bozeman. His ashes will go to the wind from there."

"I see. Does he have any family?"

"There are notes to be sent to Chicago."

"I see." He didn't. "Will you need any money for this, for Bozeman?"

"No." He didn't have much else to say. "Will you be here very long? I'm going to walk for a bit."

"No. I must be going." Where? He didn't ask.

"O.K. Well, then, goodbye?"

"Goodbye, Paul," and she stroked his cheek. "You will." and she clasped her hands in Hindu reverence.

Paul left the apartment with that as his final image, the coin in his pocket.

He saw seagulls flying, gliding, among the white clouds floating on the blue lake. He saw his way down two blocks. He saw a yellow cab rush by. He felt the coin in his pocket. He felt good. He walked up the wooden ramp to the Long Beach boardwalk.

He'd been with the ocean for several years now. He went to a bench on the boardwalk and was with it again, it curling in, salt white waves.

I wonder how it is in the mountains? Not the Catskills, but the Rockies, the American mountains, the American big sky? I should go and find out. Find out what Larry found there.

He rubbed the coin. Find out what I need to find out. There? There.

The ocean wasn't great, snow-capped peaks. But it had its power, a power.

I'll do well in the mountains, he decided.

He stopped rubbing the coin as he started back home.

Terri.

CHAPTER

"Oh, Christ, Paul! When are you going to grow up! Run off to Wyoming! For some make-believe what? I'm right here now, right now. You leave to run after some fairy tale and I'm not going to be here, right now, right ever.

"I love you, Pauley. Doesn't that mean anything to you? What about a life, our life together? "Don't go. Get your head out of the clouds. There's nothing out there like me. Nothing.

"Please don't go. For your own sake. Stop, Pauley. What is it you want? What?"

One duffel bag packed, another filling up as he listened to Terri, from a memory--a memory from a week ago now.

"What is it with this man? Larry?"

"That's what I'm going to find out, Terri."

"Oh, Christ. Find out right here." It was black and white vs. all misted-over with tales of India, Paris, grizzly bears, tall mountains, coins, yearnings, yearnings, excitement.

"I may be an asshole, Terri. I'm sorry, sorry. I have to go."

"You are an asshole!"

"I can't explain anymore."

"Don't need me anymore." No answer.

"And don't say come with me! I'll scream if you do!" No answer.

"You're breaking my heart. And I think your own."

"Terri. I'm not doing this on purpose. I've got a need to go stronger than a need to stay."

"By all means go then! Go!" She caught her breath. "One thing, though. I just hope someone fucks you over the way you've done me!" It was a slamming door vs. his face.

He remembered the slamming door part.

He made himself forget it while he cleaned out the back seat of the car. Empty beer cans, an empty Jack Daniels bottle.

Some of the beach guys said so long with a few cold ones.

They hadn't been as enthusiastic as Terri. They were glad for him; a shrug the shoulders glad. They were New Yorkers. They believed the world was flat beyond metropolitan New York. Why would you want to leave? Leaving was taken care of. Boxes packed, stored in dad's basement. I wish I was going with you. Thanks, dad. I wish you weren't going. Thanks, mom. I'll miss you. Thanks, sis.

Now I'm going. He went back into the apartment and made one last check. Empty.

He took Larry's coin from his pocket. It felt safe, secure, heavy.

So, Paul. Yellowstone? Yellowstone it is.

Let's go.

CHAPTER

Dairy cows and tall silos and working tractors. Green and blooming, and hay stacks. Exits for Clearfield, Du Bois. No Montana, Wyoming license plates yet.

I've enjoyed every place I've been. Paul heard Larry. He enjoyed these Pennsylvania places.

Unnamed lakes and meandering rivers. You know, Paul, you're going to cross the Mississippi on this trip. Remember Larry, the Ganges? Wonder if there'll be a spirit water out west? He drove across the Allegheny, running full, brown and silver.

New York was now another river behind him.

Where will I stop? What's next? He had the map spread out on the seat beside him.

Ohio? Maybe in Ohio? Or Indiana? The American continent was spread out on the front seat. I'm glad I left. Not just for Larry. I'm glad.

Where will I sleep tonight? A tent and a sleeping bag were stuffed in the trunk.

Ohio? Maybe Indiana? A train caught up with him and ran on ahead--freight cars in the late Indian summer sun.

Larry took the train west. I haven't been on a train in how long? Since I was a boy? He chased after the train into Ohio.

Youngstown out there off the interstate. Smoke. Work. Chimneys. Labor. Industry.

This is some big dose, Paul. Look at it out there. Like New Jersey refineries. Ohio like a son of a bitch. I'm glad.

Industry crowded down to the banks. 1-80 flowed through. Miles per, his foot steady and stiff on the pedal.

Gotta get some gas. He exited down into the industry.

Gas stations like casinos in the desert. Great, lighted shouts of attention.

Rounded gas pumps smooth as artifact Coca Cola machines. He rolled into the short station crouched in the freeway's shadow, ivy from the concrete wall of it crawling in with the ivy of the brick walls that made a two-car bay and a one-man office.

The one young man came out when Paul's car rang the wire bell.

"Howdy," he said through the driver's window.

Howdy? The New Yorker got a kick from that hick stuff. Ohio must be full of hicks. He tried to beat back the New Yorker in him.

"Hi," he said to the greased-over Huck Finn.

"Fill 'er up?" he asked.

"Yeah, please. Yeah, and could you check the oil?"

"Sure thing." The pleasantness of the place, and the place's curator, gave Paul a pleasant pause.

"New York, huh?" came from under the hood. The Huck Finn stuck his head out.

"Yeah," Paul answered.

"The Big Apple?" without sarcasm.

"Sometimes."

"Headed back?"

"Nope, away."

"Oil's good," slamming the hood shut. The gas nozzle clicked itself off.

"Where you headin'?"

Headin', I like that.

"Out to Montana, Wyoming, Yellowstone."

"No shit?"

"No shit."

"What's up out there?"

"Well, somebody I knew died in the park."

"Hey, sorry." They leaned on the gas pumps.

"No, it's O.K. He went O.K. Not so young anymore. He was lucky."

"Better than Ohio." Paul sort of gave him a smile of encouragement, agreement.

"This guy a close friend of yours?"

"Close?" Paul didn't have a ready answer. "Close enough."

"So, you gonna work out there?"

"Yeah. Tour bus stuff."

"Got room in the trunk for me?"

"Ha. Don't you have to keep this place going?"

"Screw it. I'll take Montana."

"Me, too." A new customer rang the service bell.

"You take care," Paul told him.

"Wish I was goin' with you. Climb a mountain for me."

Paul left him there outside Youngstown.

CHAPTER

Akron. Take this exit. Take it and it will take you to Akron. Paul kept on for Cleveland.

Akron. Making tires? Yeah. What's the other place, Toledo? Yeah, I'm going by Toledo. The big factory idea of Ohio.

Maybe I'll sleep in Indiana. Back in the dairy farms? Signs, signs, signs, commercial and directional. Cleveland coming up. Next 2,000 exits. The day was warming down into a daylight saving time. Cleveland was a great shipyard on a daylight saving Lake Erie.

Traffic appeared from out of everywhere. It went well with the scenery.

Paul steered and cut himself a slice of salami, a slice of cheese from his provisions. Absolutely greasy. Wonderful.

The Ohioans hurried home, at a snail's pace. Paul paced with them, picking it up around Olmsted.

The gas was good, the road was open again. He rolled down his window and let the open air come in.

Chicago too, he thought. Sophia. She said that Larry had someone in Chicago? I wonder who? Family, friends? Maybe I could stop. Put an ad in the paper? I knew Larry Darrell. Did you? Please call the nearest campground? Come on, bub. A camp ground in Indiana.

Norwalk, Bellevue, Fremont, Ohio. Sandusky off to the right by the ocean lake. Farther from New York.

Purple sky now, preparing for black, for stars. Torches light the purple. Tall, flaming torches far across the level fields.

Toledo, still hard at work. The exits for the hard-at-work.

Larry worked in a coal mine once? God. For the work of it he said. Larry. A surprise package.

How many work in the coal mines? Paul drove beyond them, watching them disappear in his rear-view, glad for beach work, glad for what was ahead.

Ahead was Indiana. Indian with ana attached. I wonder if I'll see any Indians out west? Our Indians. Our Paul? Come on, since when do you have any connection to them, or the other way round? Easy answer. Since Larry.

Beautiful calm evening. Perfect for a tent and a sleeping bag. On to South Bend, Indiana. Bulla, bulla. The golden dome.

There were golds and reds and oranges and blues at the top of the sky as night came to take it all.

CHAPTER

Not the great plains, but the pretty good plains of northern Indiana.

Farming was the factory here.

Do I know anyone from Indiana? Did I ever know anyone in the service? A blank space.

Gas was getting low, night was getting dark. Brighton, Howe, Scott. Lots out on the flats, house lights on the landscape.

Tired. Long day, if driving to Yellowstone could be considered such.

I want to see Notre Dame in the light of morning. Paul, a true subway alumni. How about a stop at Elkhart? First campground. Paul agreed with himself.

Big country, our country. He felt an attachment to the history of those who had trekked across. A slim connection seeing as how his covered wagon was stocked with rocket fuel and rocket foods.

Fuel and foods were running low. KOA called to him, yelled to him from a high, wide and ugly roadside advertisement. He knew that KOA shade meant any available awning. Camping meant driving a tent peg into ground as stiff as a parking lot, and water could mean a nearby drainage ditch, but when in Indiana, or anywhere in the dark ...

He exited and it was green and lush in the few street lights, a Chevron station lighting a road that rolled with the soft hills it rolled through.

The K, the 0, and the A pointed an enormous arrow. Right here, a gravel road between a post and wire fence.

A minor miracle, a major surprise. There were trees, there was a clear creek, there were tents up around the A-frame office.

Well? and he drove in.

Not the season so not too many folks. Retirees taking a break from wherever they were wandering to, and, and a pale white VW van.

Pale white in splotches between the Grateful Dead stickers stuck all over. Post all bills.

Paul picked his site. It had a tree, a bush, some stones, some Uncle John's Band playing nearby.

"Hi. I'd like to get in site thirty-four?" The plump, pleasant manager popped out from behind the beefjerky, the cigarette lighters, the key chains, the Frito Lays.

"I think we can do that," pleasantly. "Not a big rush," from a pleasant red face.

The folks from the pale white van came in. Yep, Dead-Heads.

Paul knew enough to know.

"Hi," both of them to the manager.

"Hello, ladies." Paul noticed. Ladies all right. Hiking boots, cut-off jeans, warm brown legs, each in a vest and a worn long-john shirt, patched and beaded, open buttons all the way down each throat, neck, breast, curly black hair, straight, straw blonde hair, the sun and the wind and about twenty-two years on their handsome faces.

"Hi," for Paul.

"Hello," he answered. "Your van?"

"Uh-huh," from the straw blonde. A warm smile from the curly hair.

"Going or coming?" he asked them.

"Both." They spoke in a tongue the manager didn't have, or know.

"Saw them in Colorado," the blonde announced.

"On to Philadelphia," from her companion.

Paul would have winked at the manager and said, "Dead Heads," but it would have fallen on blank eyes.

The two ladies got a six pack of Pabst.

"Want to join us?"

"Sure," the fairly handsome prince answered.

CHAPTER

"What's this?" Brenda, with the curly hair, asked.

Paul had to shake his head a bit, remind himself that he was in Indiana, in a sleeping bag with soft, brown Brenda, a taste of deep, dark hashish still in his mouth, the taste of a warm, moist woman still on his fingertips and lips.

Her van to his tent went easy, went with her ease, her desire, his desire, their on top of, oral of, under of, tongues of, cream of, shadows of on the tent.

"Wha?" and he pushed himself up on an elbow. The contents of his pants pockets were spilled out on the sleeping bag.

"This?" Brenda held the coin.

First he kissed her neck and eased his tongue into her ear.

She felt him hard on her leg.

"Everyone's asking," he joked.

"Everyone?" She nearly moaned, him against her pubic hair.

"Oh, just somebody back in Pennsylvania."

"Mmm, Pennsylvania," like the state name could make you come, as her come met his coming.

"Ahhhh, shitttt," not in chorus.

Early evening, chill air, naked, sleeping bag, coming, enjoying, chorusing.

The coin lay on his sticky belly.

"Why don't you join us?" Brenda asked, unsticking herself.

No question. "Nahh, thanks."

"Sure?"

"No, but I have to go the other way."

"The other way's O.K. We went into Yellowstone."

"You did?" He dropped the coin onto her stomach.

"Saw the geyser. All we had time for. Oh, we saw some buffalo." She took hold of the coin. "Maybe I'll go back there with you." They both knew that wasn't going to happen. Neither one of them was new at this one night stuff of standing open to what felt good, right then.

"Couldn't disappoint the Dead?" he laughed.

"No," answering his laugh. "I can feel something here. She had the coin to her cheek. "Some spirit. Some ancient thing." Paul kissed her. "A compass." He surprised himself by saying that.

"Compass? Maybe. Takes you to good things?"

"Took me here." That was his thanks to her.

"Thanks," was her thanks to him.

"Here, send me a postcard." She pulled on her jeans.

She had a rawhide medicine pouch. A narrow green note pad and pencil. "Here's my name and my folks' address. Write yours here."

"Sure." Paul Barnes, Yellowstone. That looked awfully good.

"I'm sorry you're not coming along."

"Maybe we'll see each other someplace else."

"I hope so."

"Me, too." Taking down the tent was good work, everything clean, clear, physical, compact.

The ladies and their van honked and Brenda waved out the window.

She felt good, from a distance. He felt the distance between himself and his departure, his destination. He felt as plump and as full around as the brand new sun.

CHAPTER

The golden dome, the temple mount. Notre Dame. No scenic turn out, but the scene, the upper parts of the campus could be had from the interstate.

All former lifeguards, all men, are once upon a time dream athletes. Notre Dame, Mecca. Touchdown passes on the beach, a softball home run. Knute Rockne out there. America's out there.

Americana wasn't a term Paul Barnes used too frequently. Now he did. I'm in it, moving along through it.

An all-male school. Ugh. The golden whistle stops disappeared in the trees.

And speaking of sports. Up ahead, Wrigley Field, Paul.

Chicago. Should I? Let's wait and see. Let's wait and feel.

Man, feel that semi going by. Feels like a supertanker and a sail boat.

The eighteen wheels of the semi made its own wind. It's next stop, the Windy City? Paul re-checked his map to make sure the earth hadn't shifted in the last eight minutes. Yep, Chicago is still in Illinois.

South Bend, Indiana flashed from a roadside flash card.

Smaller, tinier, quieter with Chicago on your mind.

Is that where Larry is really from? Of is a better word.

Where was he really of? So many places. Of them. Like he belonged, everywhere.

I belong where? I wish he was with me. He is, where I'm from, where I'm going? Paul, he is.

Where am I right now? Michigan City coming up. Flat, pleasant Indiana needed to be gone now, done with, behind. Gary, Indiana and then into Illinois.

Isn't there some song about Gary, Indiana? Some musical something? He tried to hum it. The car tires hummed. Nothing special to note, only America at its most normal.

The closer to Chicago, the closer to a history of Larry. A line from here to there, to the beach on Long Island. To Yellowstone.

No, I won't go in. Keep moving, keep on.

Like road signs. Farming became buildings, buildings became homes, homes became communities, communities became towns, towns to cities, cities to suburbs, suburban, urban Chicago.

Lake front, like the front of an ocean. The first view of it.

There, that looks like stock pens. The second view. Hog butcher to the world? Who said that?

He lived, grew up near here? He, Paul? You make him sound holy, saintly. Well? Well?

This metropolis made itself clear, a skyline shorter than New York's. He had to compare. It was in his DNA.

It felt good to be with a great city. This great city, compact, easier to hold than Manhattan. But cold? The ice man liveth, Paul. Snow. Out west snow. West away from Chicago.

Cicero, Oak Park, the Cubs, the Bears, the tree-lined neighborhoods, the unnamed buildings. I wonder if Sophia is nearby? I wonder how it went for her in Montana? Can you see her, Paul? Up on some peak with his ashes? The wind comes, blowing the snow, taking his ashes. He put himself on that peak.

He put himself in the lane for 1-90. North now. Into Wisconsin, Minnesota, the Dakotas. Go to those peaks young man.

Wisconsin was coming. Something changed. Not altogether, but something. Wisconsin was coming. Chicago city gone. Not exactly wilderness, but. Pastoral, like a shawl, like a scarf, like a state preserve, preserved. Green grew around the lilacs.

Wisconsin had Milwaukee. Beer. Ahhh, beer. He had to.

A mom and pop gas stop shouted "Coldest Beer in America!" How could anyone resist? Why would anyone?

Two Asian-Americans kept the coldest beer in America in a glass and ship iron reefer. They were right. They did; the beer at the exact liquid moment before it becomes ice.

On the wall behind the wooden counter there hung a plate with the faithful geyser going off. Elvis was alongside it. So was an American eagle.

"I'm headed there," as the pop and the mom put a cardboard insert between the frosty gold bottles in the bag.

"Yes, yes," the pop answered after a look over his shoulder. "I went, uh, nineteen-sixty, uh, seven. Ha. Lotsa bears. Many bears. I am a citizen in Wyoming," making change. "Railroad family. Way back."

"Thanks." Thanks for the history lesson.

Thanks for the coldest beer in America. He stretched out, foot off the pedal a bit, cold beer in a cold cup. Ahhh, watching for the highway patrol.

Larry said something, about Emily Dickinson? Another swallow refreshed everything, including his memory. Living is occupation enough? Yeah, that's it, I think. Now this is living.

Life in Chicago would carry on without him. Life in Des Plains. Up ahead. Church steeples in the trees weren't factories and rail yards. Communities weren't pork and grain. Milk and cheese, and the honey, beer, were coming.

A second beer made it the life that Reilly sought. Milwaukee up there, Paul. Brew. Too bad, I'm headed for Beloit on the map.

All the way up and over to La Crosse. French for trappers up that way? Mountain men? The Rockies. Their home park.

The Illinois that remained was an Ohio, an Indiana, another fence, another farm.

At La Crosse we cross the Mississippi. A Huck on a metal raft.

The raft drifted towards Beloit, Wisconsin, the fella at the tiller sayin' to himself, "you know he's dead, Paul. You won't ever see him again. That's a cryin' shame." So he did.

Something in the air though. Something about not Illinois, and being Wisconsin got him sniffing the air, sniffing away some of the cryin' shame of it.

Raw? Rawer? Is that a word? The state felt bigger, closer up to high places.

Still farms, though. What's that we all say? Just like a postcard? No, I don't think so. Postcards are cartoons of this.

Everything plump. The silos, the cows, the machinery, the forested hills, the plowed earth. The cheese, the cheese.

Big blocks of it on big blocks of billboards. Big chunks of it just off the road. "Ours is best," they all pleaded.

What's the best place to stay tonight? I'd like to stay … with my little Dead Head friend again. Just thinking about her got him. Keep going? No. Got to stop, camp. No. I think I'll loaf in a motel tonight. Tonight would be beyond Madison, Wisconsin.

But first, a beer in a bar from a glass.

CHAPTER

The bar, with the glass, with the beer, was made from logs, lacquered-over, inside and out. The road up to it was trying to return to dirt. The town it ran through, Lair, Wisconsin, plowed the dirt, milked it for all it was worth.

Here it was worth a John Deere dealership, a Ford truck dealer, rusted train tracks, church, buildings, homes, home to 1,265, with their low level elevation noted.

"Buck's" was the bar. "Of course," was Paul's assessment.

A Green Bay Packer pennant hung from a moose antler. Anything with antlers had its head stuck through the wall as if they were posing in some Coney Island bar scene cut out; all of them with that content, Mona Lisa laugh on their lips.

Paul took a barstool, a lacquered-over log stump barstool.

His late afternoon drinking buddy was a coyote frozen in mid-run on the wall behind the bar, and two Coney Island buck deer.

When in Rome, Lair. He ordered a Schlitz.

A blonde, buxom, beyond fifty in the light blue bib overalls took his order. Mrs. Buck? She went to a cooler down the bar--in the forever fish section. A row of trophy trout were mounted on the wall above the cold beer. A school of them. Any fisherman would weep with envy.

Paul was a swimmer, not a fisher. He couldn't help but be impressed though by the concentrated carnage in Buck's.

"Here you go," Mrs. Buck said. Good and cold. "Want a glass?"

"Yes, thank you." He left out the "ma'am."

"Some fish." He indicated the captured catch with his beer glass. He almost half expected it.

"You bet. Got 'em in Yellowstone. Keepers." He half expected. "Oh?" There were only two other customers, content with their drinks.

Mrs. Buck didn't mind talking. "Are you a fisherman?"

"Not much."

"Well," checking the other two, sort of making sure they weren't listening, sort of lowering her voice. "There's this Slough Creek," and she stopped talking, letting the secret reverence seep in. "Not too deep off the beaten path. A catch 'em and release 'em place. But." That stayed put because someone called her from the kitchen. But she added quickly, "and there…"

And there what, Paul found himself wondering. Slough Creek.

Make a note of it.

"O.K. I'll run out for a minute," he heard her telling someone.

She was pulling on her coat, checking at the cash register.

"Watch the front!" she ordered into the kitchen.

"What about Slough Creek? You said, and there." He tried to catch her with his question.

"Oh," with a smile that made Buck's famous. "Nothing much.

I always seem to remember it, him."

"Him?" He put his beer down.

She was leaving. "Just some fella we met one day." She shrugged. "Can't even remember his name." Larry? Paul offered silently. She was leaving. He left it at that. I wonder.

"I'll be right back. Want me to bend your ear about it?"

"Sure." He wasn't so sure. Sure it's Larry. All the signs point to him. He wasn't much for karma and destiny and fate, terms that remained in the culture and conversations around him. But now he sat on a bar stool in Buck's, in Lair, Wisconsin and considered.

He was sure about leaving Mrs. Buck with an image of this fella she met one day.

He died. Oh, I'm so sorry. Paul heard the conversation, finished his beer, scanned the Coney Island wildlife and hit the road.

CHAPTER

The road went north past Madison, Wisconsin, towards Baraboo, Portage, across the Wisconsin river.

A sign for the Wisconsin Dells, a tourist brochure from a quick pit stop on the dashboard depicting the tender tourist trap.

The pit stop was to pee, the key ring to the Mobil rest room a plastic version of the state, as large as a county. Paul ticked off another slice of his country; crossing it was getting him to think of it as "my."

"Our" country worked too. Up ahead was our river, the great god almighty Mississippi.

Are all the dairy cows in the country living here in Wisconsin? A red pickup truck said "America's Dairyland" on its license plate. Yes they are, Paul.

Next check point would be Tomah, then Sparta, then La Crosse, Onalaska. Native names. Don't, don't. Don't even begin to think about it. Once upon .... now don't.

Portage, Wisconsin. Well-named. Across the Wisconsin river, a wide width of gray-brown water, worthy of the name river, worthy enough to flow into the Mississippi.

The trick was to keep an eye on the road and try and trace the river's altering course across the map. He did both.

A gray light now, a portion of blue, portions of clouds, overcast inching in around the edge of it all. He got a kick out of it all. Alone on the vast sea of America.

Just across.

Across what?

Once I'm across the Mississippi, I'm across.

He picked up speed. So did the setting sun, sending gray slants through the gathering clouds.

He knew the tides, the ebb and flow of the ocean. He rushed along on the tide, towards the Mississippi. Just across.

Rain on the windshield, thunder in the slate sky. He rolled down his denim sleeves, pushed aside and kicked aside the wrappers and the remains of the day's meals, rolled up the remainder of the window, hit the windshield wipers, adjusted the rear view mirror.

Hey, I got me a beard going. Who were those guys? Jim Bridger? John Colter? That made him smile. Mountain men. Mountain apprentice.

A heavy rain came. Nothing was wrong with this trip. The rain added to the new beard, the worn jeans, the comfort of going it alone, at 70 MPH.

A carton of warm orange juice, one of those plastic sandwiches from a plastic vending machine at a plastic truck stop. Made in America.

Sparta, America reflected its sign in the early evening.

Headlights came on, so did the lightning.

Wow! Wow! Something about Larry? Mountains in India, Tibet? Atop a mountain in India, Tibet? Was it a storm? Was it a sunrise? His bliss. So absolute he said. If it had lasted another moment I would have perished from it?

He rolled the window down, driver and passenger, and let the storm in. Yellowstone will be that? It will? Just across.

La Crosse, Wisconsin.

Lightning the only light. Pitchforks, barbed wire.

Frankensteins of it.

Hail in the rain, about a hundred yards of visibility. No sign of it visible. Paul squinted, leaned into the steering wheel, looking for a sign--a stack of rocks, a worn trail, a reflective sign that yelled, Mississippi River! "Youuhh!" he yelled, straining to find a turnout, a shoulder of space to approach the reason for the yelling.

There, emergency phone. Enough gravel, enough distance from the wakes of the eighteen-wheelers.

Now lean the car off as far as it will go. He maneuvered until he was slanted down to the right in the front seat.

Rain, period. He left the headlights on. They reached just far enough ahead to show him a low bridge railing. Got to be a river underneath it. You've got to get out of the car. Yeah, I've got to. Wonder why I've got to? He hesitated, turned everything off but the headlights, took a deep breath, got out.

The tractor-trailer trucks plowed past, Paul in the short grass, the ankle-high brush, up above the highway on level ground.

Soaked. So what.

A long, witch finger of a lightning bolt lit up some civilization away to his left. In the flash he could see where the knoll dropped off and the bridge began.

Wild. There was no more ground right now, just the wind wailing across an open expanse of water, choppy and dark, wide, no other shore in sight.

The sight of it stopped him in his tracks. He wiped the rain from his face. Great bodies of water weren't new to him, but one of the greatest bodies was.

He went down to it inching his way down to the first bridge piling, the bridge long across, low to the river, the river all over the place.

The bridge helped to shield him from some of the weather. He knelt to the dark rust of the river and stuck his hand in.

Paul? Is it baptism? Is it? Is it the Ganges? All right, Larry, here I am.

Tree limbs and other wooden scrabble rushed by in the flood of it. Riverboats, gunboats, barges, canoes, keelboats, and that one famous raft rushed by in his perception.

Thunder like gunboats. Damn, I'm soaked. Come on, you've got plenty of dry clothes. Take this easy.

He did. He found a twig and tossed it in. "All the way to New Orleans," he said.

All the way across Minnesota and North Dakota now. Wish it was just across the river. It ain't, Paul. Come on, let's get going. Let's get dry.

The car was nice and dry. He had to sit for a bit and take it all in, shake his head like, "whatta you know, how about that ... "

The engine, the lights, the directional, dry clothes. One semi, two semis, one cement truck. He got back on, got onto the bridge.

The thunder sounded far off now, behind him as he crossed over to the other side. It took a bit to get across, night shadow shapes of islands in the river, surrounded by the river.

The rain was where he'd been. Minnesota was now where he was going. He could turn off the windshield wipers.

The black edge of the storm, a sprinkling of stars.

"Wow!" A full moon, absolutely, totally. A total surprise. Big enough and clear enough as if the earth was its moon. It lit his way.

CHAPTER

What's left of my way west? Look at Dakota over there.

Badlands. That's the west. That's another farm, in the milky moon darkness. He settled into a couple of miles more of the good earth.

It lasted about a couple of miles, somewhere below Rochester.

"Shit." The flap, flap, flap and the slowing. A flat. "Shit." Lights up ahead. The car could crawl forward to them. Them was Purple Earth, Minnesota.

O.K. O.K., a break in the action.

The action in Purple Earth, pop. about 1,200, was the Viking truck stop, complete with an enormous standing, floodlit version of Eric the Red, complete with shield and battle ax and horned helmet.

Minnesota Vikings, football, was his immediate reference point. Must be. They must be nuts. Every tractor trailer in America must be here.

Like logs in a log jam, the trucks parked shoulder to shoulder, hub to hub, smoke stacks to smoke stacks, waiting for fuel, food, showers, all available from the sprawling glass and metal shed, complete with its own Viking on top.

Paul bumped in, the little tugboat that couldn't among the battle wagons, the cruise ships--two enormous double-decker tour buses, all windows, all red, all Mercedes.

A mechanic's bay was open, air wrenches like rivet guns, silver tools like a trophy case. He pulled in and shut down.

I'm on vacation, I'll let someone else do it. He needed to look around. He realized he needed to.

"Can you do a flat for me?" he asked the oil-soaked hands, the dragon tatoo, the coal miner's smile from the greasy face.

"Sure," eyes lighting up at the thought of what this was going to cost the latest road kill. That's what Paul thought.

"I'll leave it. I'll be back."

"Sure, sure."

Paul filled his need to look around. The two super red buses were unloading their freight out in front of an attached motel.

Ten thousand cameras on five thousand Germans filed out, one by one, stretching their arms, shaking their legs, speaking the German.

I wonder, Paul found himself wondering. He made a joke of Rod Serling's theme music and walked around to the front of one of the buses.

An acre of windshield, a driver in a mock gray Greyhound uniform enjoying a cigarette, leaning against the front bumper.

"Hey, how you doin'?" Paul asked.

The driver blew a cloud of smoke into the dark. "Pretty good, pretty good," pure Anglo American.

"Some rig you've got here." He felt he could say "rig" now.

He'd been on the road for a long two days now.

"The best there is. Count on them Germans."

Paul knew the answer, but he asked anyway. "Where are you heading?"

"Vegas, by way of Rushmore and Yellowstone."

"Yellowstone, huh?"

"Yeah. Sure beats Vegas and those four heads stuck into the Black Hills. If I had my way, I'd dump 'em all and go drive a bus in Yellowstone. But, three kids and a wife," and he shrugged his shoulders, tossed his cigarette. "Better check on my little Germans. All the way from New York with them. Good tippers, though."

Paul kept it to himself. I'm going to go and do what you just shrugged your shoulders about. "See ya, going to have a look around."

"Yeah, it's a big one, ain't it? Hey, want to see something? Get across to the other side of the freeway. I've been through here six or seven times. I still get a kick out of it."

"What?"

"You'll see. Take it easy."

"I will."

Wonder what he's talking about? Walking between the diesel skyscrapers, big cabs, enormous cargoes: two industrial turbines on a long flat bed, seven feet of frozen foods, enough wire fence for the King Ranch, enough furniture for four families in one family-size

Mayflower truck, then an empty section of the lot. The headlights, taillights of the freeway.

Wonder what he's talking about?

He got across to the green median without difficulty, sprinting between a break in the traffic.

Didn't look like anything was over there. A short road, a short exit down from the freeway, below a short hill. But there was some light against the clear, starry night.

Oh, well, I'm here. He ran across to there.

CHAPTER

At first he wasn't sure of what he saw. He stood on the down side of the short hill.

He was sure he saw a defunct gas station in the moonlight, rusted and ratty with weeds. Two empty lanes of blacktop, cracked and peeling, were on their very last chance.

That was out front. In back? He wasn't quite sure. There was a street light on over a tiny house with a neon light hanging like a professional's shingle. It said, VACANCY.

Vacancy for what? It isn't the Bates Motel is it? He decided to go down anyway.

The grass was still wet from the passing storm. He stamped his shoes dry on the cracked roadbed.

Now he could see two cars and a truck parked beside the tiny house. He could see, what? It looks like teepee poles above the little house. He walked over to the silent house.

There was a light on, soft yellow. A sign in the window said, OFFICE.

Office for what? a bright block of light next door around a bulging bush.

Paul stepped around the bush, and the bus driver was right.

An Indian camp, encampment, if Indians had truly become white men. It was a motel. Each cottage, cabin, room, was a cement teepee, complete with cement teepee poles protruding from the top, whitewashed and painted as if the walls were hides, the occupants adept at painting nature on the hides. A bright lamp lit each door, tent flap? A neon sign on a pole said, TEN SLEEP.

Glee, the shock of it a surprise party. He stood there and there was nothing, no sight, no sound.

Where did this place come from? The grounds were neat and orderly, the weeds and the grass cut back, the sidewalk among the tents level and clear.

Is it a Brigadoon? Whatever, if I can, I'm staying here tonight. I've got no choice. The sign said VACANCY.

"Hello?" as if no one could possibly be inside the tiny house.

"Hello?" and he pushed open the front door. It made a bell tinkle.

"I'll be right with you," came from a bird-like voice from somewhere inside.

Paul waited on a shelf of a porch, a desk closing off a box corner of it. A phone, a register book, books of matches, a sign on the wall with a warrior in full regalia, full pinto pony, "TEN SLEEP MOTEL." I wouldn't have missed this for the world. I hope this isn't Mrs. Bates coming.

She came from a side door behind the desk. She looked like she'd just been blown northeast from the dust bowl. Tiny and slender, raw as a piece of rawhide, every weather pattern in her face, her hair not quite white and not nearly near black.

"Good evening," she said sweetly, even white teeth, soft hazel eyes.

"Hi," Paul pulled from his glee. "Some place here."

She smiled. "Isn't it."

"Uh, you have a vacancy?"

"We do."

"Can I get in tonight?" sort of shy, boyish in her sweet old lady presence.

"I don't see why not," and she got a pen and a registration card, her hands like plowed earth.

"Got some folks staying tonight?" he asked.

"Yes. Sometimes a few. You can guess what Mr. Viking across the road did to us."

Paul didn't have to guess. He couldn't guess what TEN SLEEP was for. Why not TEEPEE or something normal like that.

"Uh, why Ten Sleep, the name?"

"Oh, ever been in Wyoming?"

"No." He added, "not yet."

"I went through once with my first husband. We stopped in a place called Ten Sleep. Just for a cold drink. It was so green, so lovely, after a lot of dry ground. It just stuck with me. When we bought this place I couldn't leave out Ten Sleep. Ten Sleep? Any idea?"

"No."

"Ten Sleep, a distance. Ten moons?"

"Oh, yes, I get it."

"So, that's it," bird-like.

"Nice." He finished the information on the card.

"I've got to run back and get my car. I'm over at the Viking.

A bus driver told me to come over and take a look."

"We get some of our business that way."

"I'll be back."

"Fine. You're in number six. The one with the grizzly bear on the side."

"Fine. I'll be right back."

CHAPTER

Right back with four cheese-burgers, two large french fries, and a barrel-size coke from the Viking's chicken-fried cafe. He was famished. He was American.

He had the key to number six, the key dangling from a metal feather.

A narrow sidewalk took him through the encampment, past the great elk, the noble bison, the eagle's flight, to number six. His teepee.

At least twenty, thirty feet in the air, as round around as two real teepees, extra large. A soft tan door where the tent flap would be. A grizzly bear, as gray and as brown as an ancient tree, and just as large, filled one wall. Around he went. A bobcat, yellow and tan, graced the back. A bend in a clear stream was the other side, all with a Navajo border painted, stitched all around.

Paul stood there with his twentieth century hard-tack. He studied the grizzly bear. Larry went there to him, the bear. Now me? He opened the hard wood flap and went in.

A knotty pine bed, a knotty pine dresser, a mirror, a phone, a closet, a TV, a slice of a bathroom, tan walls, the floor as red as Georgia clay, Charlie Russell prints on the walls, a make believe Navajo rug, and the same as a bedspread. "Holy shit," he said to the walls.

He laid the sacks of food on the bed. Showered, didn't shave.

He sat on the bed in his jeans, devouring the meal, looking up to look around at the place. Ten Sleep. I think I will. TV? The hell with it. From that he realized that he hadn't turned on the car radio or listened to a tape. Huh, he thought, and fell asleep.

No visions of bills to pay, parties to meet, appointments to appoint, am I right, am I wrong? Just visions of, of ...

The early morning woke him, and he remembered, instantly, not unhappy to be back alive in this world, just a bit disappointed that the dream visions of the night had to end.

A royal bear, a grizzly, wading through a shallow stream, stopping to peer up at him on a grassy knoll a few yards away. The threat, the danger, the exhilarating, Larry saying something from a distance.

What was he saying? Believe? Believe in this? This? Then a buffalo, a herd charging across a stretch of plain, Larry Darrell on horseback, bare back, scooping him up in a movieland stunt on the gallop up behind him, chasing after the herd.

A bridge across a full river. What river? The river rushed, clear and thick. The bear, the buffalo on the bridge--a dark metal bridge, and he woke up still feeling his feet on that bridge, that river, that bear, that grizzly bear.

He had to blink to make sure he was here in Purple Earth, in Ten Sleep #6.

Come on, let's go. Let's get going. Let's get there? Where? There.

"On your way?" Mrs. Ten Sleep asked.

"Yep."

"Sleep well?"

"Like a rock. Like a smooth stone in a clear stream."

"Oh?" Paul had the same word in his head.

"Where you headin'?" she asked.

He gave her a wide, wide smile. "Wyoming."

"That so? Where?"

"Yellowstone." She just nodded her head. Then she patted his hand. "Smooth stone in a clear stream, huh? You have a good trip."

"I will. See ya."

"Happy trails."

CHAPTER

The asphalt trail took him past Albert Lea through Minnesota's agricultural culture. Through a day blue and white and gold and green and the browns of the earth, coffee steaming on the dash.

He almost screeched to a halt. He could see why there was a town called Purple Earth. A field within a wire fence. A farm with silos like temple pillars. A tractor had turned the earth.

He had to stop and get out.

Dirt. The earth is brown, right? Versions of brown, right? Wrong, but so very right. He pulled onto the shoulder and got out.

He was right. It was black, almost purple. He went to the fence through the uncut brush and knelt down to it. Charcoal black, purple as a grape, the tractor's blade setting it up in lumps the size of dinner plates.

Purple Earth. He squeezed it between his fingers. Almost clay.

Brother. How many farms have I seen? Another one was orderly and well-used at the far edge of this black field.

What couldn't grow here? He stood up and turned back to where he'd come from. He tossed the round lump of moist earth like a pitcher flipping a ball. He squinted, from the sun, but also from trying to see across the distance. All the way back.

He put the earth in his left hand. The coin. That he got from his pocket. He flipped it. He raised its elevation. It went high, Alexander the Great tumbling in the Minnesota sky.

Paul caught it and squeezed it tight, feeling the earth and the coin.

Phew. He shook his head, knowingly. Something's up, bub.

Something if you told me a few weeks back, I'd been standing here in Minnesota admiring the ground. He flipped the dirt wad and turned to where he was going.

Dakota. Can't be ground like this there. So, let's go find out. He threw the dirt wad, a farmboy pitcher following through.

A name on the map--Rake, Iowa, just below him. Who lives in Rake? How did they get to Rake? How many live in Rake? What's the town they mentioned from Yellowstone? Gardiner, Montana? Montana. The word was round and full, saying it.

Indian spring. Not quite Indian, but still ... blooming along the wire fences. Yellows and whites. Paul didn't know their names. Flowers were O.K. with him.

Breakfast would be O.K. Up ahead in Fairmont, Minnesota? A Greyhound bus that said it was going to Los Angeles was all windows and wind. Everyone likes a bus. I'm no different.

There was little difference from farm to farm. Beautiful, rich. You could smell breakfast all around. Ham and eggs, rich coffee, buttered bread, orange juice, jelly, biscuits, waffles, pancakes, sausage. It was all growing in the fields nearby. Paul licked his lips, honked the horn for no particular reason, got it up to 70 M.P.H. for a particular reason.

CHAPTER

Daydreaming. He missed Fairmont. The dream was of buffalo, a buffalo herd. A dark bridge. A grizzly bear in the snow. He missed Fairmont.

He found Timber, Minnesota.

He found an old railroad car that was now a diner. He found it because it said, EAT over it in bold red letters.

He found a seat at the counter, the interior as if it was 1869 in the Timber Diner.

Portraits of bearded Americans. A portrait of U. S. Grant. A spittoon on a shelf. A long stretch of four different barbed wire on display along a board as gray as driftwood.

A menu on a piece of wood. A collection of arrowheads.

Photos of railroad trains under full steam. All of it against a wooden boxcar canvas.

The counter chairs were made of steel. Paul swiveled on his, make-believe kid in a make-believe soda shop.

All that breakfast that grew in Minnesota had been harvested.

It was all being served out through the stainless steel porthole between waitress and cook.

Paul waited and scratched his near beard. Two highway patrol cops, spectacular in their boots and saddles, took up a section of the counter.

What day is this, Paul? Thursday? Yeah, Thursday.

Maybe I'll get a paper. Maybe I won't.

Two telephone guys came in. Two guys with tape measures on their belts came in. Two guys in softened highway patrol uniforms came in. Smokey Bear hats, shoulder patches on their jackets, no guns. They sat two seats down from him.

Two seats the other way was the cash register, a framed photo of a young soldier in a camouflaged uniform propped against it.

"Serving" it said along the bottom of the photo.

Vietnam, Paul. I'd forgotten. Thanks for that. He looked away at a framed oil of a wolf on the run. He looked back at the young soldier's photo. He looked away at the two guys in the easy uniforms, Smokey hats on the counter.

"What can I get you?" got his attention to the young, maybe nineteen-year old waitress in the denim shirt open at the collar, a cigarette behind her ear, her ear attached to a pretty, sunburned face.

"Oh, breakfast please." Get my mind off that Vietnam photo, please. "Four scrambled eggs, home fries, orange juice, sausage, wheat toast, a side order of pancakes, and coffee?" The harvest was complete.

"You'll be able to handle all that?" from her freckled face.

"I think so."

"Growin' a beard?"

Ahh, flirting? Music to his ears.

"Tryin' to. Oh, uh, how come it's called Timber around here? I don't see any."

"Them, down there," and she nodded to the two easy uniforms.

"State Park. Used to be big timber around here. Wolves, too.

Farms," and she shrugged. "Still some land left, about ten miles from here. Couple of hundred acres of woods and a lake. Nice.

Park rangers."

"Thanks."

"Anything else?" lifting her eyebrows? Yeah, who's the kid in the photo? He didn't bother. "No, not right now," lifting his eyebrows.

Vietnam. Is that what was bothering Larry? Is that why? Part of the why? Part of why he's gone? He left Timber, Minnesota and day-dreamed on back to a beach on Long Island. He could see Larry splashing up out of the surf. He wasn't going to see that anymore. He came back to Timber, the weight and the aroma of his breakfast too easy to accept.

"Great, thanks."

"Enjoy it."

"I will." The two highway patrol got up and were menacing on their way out.

"So long, Cindy," they said.

"Bye," she answered.

"What brings you to Timber?" Cindy asked him.

"On my way to Yellowstone."

"Pick up, Cindy!" yelled from the kitchen.

"Yellowstone? Got any room?"

He was taken partially by surprise. "Not this trip."

"Too bad," and she went to work.

The breakfast made a man of him, its bulk testing his manhood.

The park rangers got theirs to go and got up to go.

Park rangers. Must be a good job. Paul followed them out.

He had to work hard at getting the pancakes down. The warm coffee softened the wad. He pushed away the empties and was taking-a-nap full. Like to take a nap with Cindy.

"So, you did it," clearing away his plates.

"I did." While she cleared and tallied up the delicious damage, he took a slip of paper from his wallet, a pencil from alongside the cash register. He wrote the name of his employer in Yellowstone.

"Here you go." She gave him the bill.

"Thanks. That was great." He took a toothpick from the dispenser.

"Here you go," his change. "I'll ride in the trunk?"

"Maybe next time. Here." He handed her the note. The mark of Zorro, with a Y, and he left.

CHAPTER

Snow. Snow? High up in Minnesota now, beyond Fergus Falls. Low, flat, gray clouds up along the horizon. Cold. You could hear timber wolves calling. You couldn't, but you could.

Paul rolled the window down, half way. These farms were near Canada. Wilderness? Up that way where the snow's coming from.

Fargo, North Dakota. There it was on the map, closer, much closer. Fargo. The word sounded like Tombstone, Dodge. Paul almost yelled yeehh-ha! Now, where to stop? In Fargo? No, push it on to Bismarck maybe? He'd circled a spot on the North Dakota-Montana border.

Theodore Roosevelt National Park. Like to get there in the daylight. See a park.

Checking the circle on the map, the next border caught his eye. The Red River was the rail fence. That particular song came to his mouth, instantly. He started whistling it. He started to notice that dairy cows were turning into beef cattle, steers, horses, rail fences, dry ground.

"Oh, remember the Red River Valley, and the girl I left, and " he didn't try the rest as the car crossed the narrow, clay red, brown gorge, ravine, gully, that snaked this stream to the Mississippi. Paul had been spoiled by the big river.

You could see an ancient American government building at the end of a green mall, a dome, and columns and bricks. Not hundreds of years, but back there to when there were marshals and sheriffs.

He was in Dakota. Badlands. He was thrilled.

An appealing public park beside the Red River said you could camp. He wanted to, he wanted to keep on. Daylight. Ride, cowboy, ride. The Missouri River is up ahead. Big water. Let's ride. His "yeehh-ha!" echoed in the car.

The dirty gold of the car matched the land it was passing through. Golden brown, with verdant splashes of green, grain silos alongside their railroad tracks taller, whiter against the vast, flat sky. Shapes along the horizon. Bluffs? Paul wondered, wonderful.

I wonder if it will keep on snowing. Cold enough, black curtain low enough on the horizon.

He got his wonder. The snow picked up, soft and thick, building up on the windshield, under the wipers. Then it was the sun pouring in through a door jamb in the clouds. Then snow, then the edge of two worlds. A great divide of all sunlight and a black and blue sky.

The dirty gold Chevy rushed into the light, two motorcycles and a freight train that stretched back to Chicago, back to a time of steam, raced on ahead of him.

CHAPTER

On ahead of him the Missouri River said two words: Lewis and Clark. Sacajawea. The way west.

Paul had been a boy. Cowboys and Indians up front--but off to the side, somewhat private, like a secret, like a magic, buckskin-buckskin men in their canoes. Always seemed to be setting off.

Lewis and Clark. Canoes on the Missouri. Lewis and Clark and Barnes, Paul.

Terri. He gave her a quick thought. She should have come along. Oh, well.

Oh, well felt good. Everything level, clear ahead, flat, raw, tilled, cracks and crevices of rocks, shapes of stone, shapes in mounds, driftwood dry barns, rust dead farm equipment. Wherever water touched the raw the wounds healed.

He guessed at Bismarck, North Dakota. Easy guess. German immigrants. He barely guessed at it, because across the Missouri from it was Mandan, sounding like Sacajawea's flag ship, something a French-Indian language had created, a real someplace to stop for the night.

Send the folks postcards from Mandan, North Dakota. Not exactly the Jersey shore. By the shores of Gitchy Goomy is more like it. Now where'd that come from? You could hear yourself laughing with yourself out here in the big Dakota space.

You could hear them coming. You could feel them going. Two fuel tankers, silver bullets, Montana plates, hurtled by. Closing in on it, Paul. Cattle truck, rattling, full of freight, left its odor going by. Breathe deep, Paul. Ahhhh.

Postcards. Yeah, some postcards. I wonder how my New York postcard, my New York license plate looks going through North Dakota.

Who hadn't seen Easy Rider? Who didn't imagine, make believe? Easily on through the alien territory he rode.

Oh, look, antelope. Antelope! He looked once, twice, three times, checking his rear view mirror, making sure nothing was about to crash into him.

The tan and rust orange brush grew into a long, low ridge.

Antelope standing stiff along it. Where are you, Paul? Those are antelope. I've never seen an antelope in the wild. The tough barbed wire fence. He pulled up to make it a little less wild, but there they were, African, Dakotan, dainty, tip-toeing along.

I wish I had a camera. I'm glad I don't have a camera. I'd rather remember it. He had a chance to. The antelope wandered away down the other side of the ridge--gone, vanished.

Did I really? Sure you did. Now for a nice group of pinto ponies, Sioux braves on board. He plucked at the barbed wire.

Probably not.

Barbed wire was the margin, the border, the thing that ties Medina to Crystal Springs, to Dawson, to Steele, to Driscoll, to late in the afternoon, to Bismarck and the Missouri.

CHAPTER

Bismarck, North Dakota. Who would have thunk it? Paul Barnes was a recent immigrant.

Bismarck. Compact, not huddled, gathered on the wide high plains, full green trees to make it a wet spot, church steeples to make it salvation, government domes to make it official, warehouse sheds to make it work, make it sprawl a bit, make it a sight for pinched eyes. Bright gray sun glaring on the good hard land.

Then it got real good. The sign said Missouri River Scenic overlook at 60 M.P.H. He had a good five minutes to worry if he was going to miss the turnoff to it. He used every minute of it.

Tourist.

I wish I had a postcard of this. I do? Well, a memento.

This was a memorable rest stop. Usually some square shape with bathrooms and a colorful wall map of "you are here." But this. This was a version of the Ten Sleep Motel. This square was a concrete teepee--a teepee without the painted skins; just the poles, joined in a circle. Just a parking lot and it, the tall, appropriate shelter.

Tourist season was still a few school months away. Paul had it to himself. About five hundred miles of view from this high point above the Missouri River.

Shit, I feel good. He walked to where blacktop met terra firma. The big river ran brown and gray and moving white, wide enough where some work would be required to cross it, some scrambling down to it, some canoes to go on it; somewhere it met the Mississippi and the Gulf. Paul tried to look up along it, along the cottonwoods to the Pacific. Shit, I feel good.

Mandan across the river looked like the cottonwoods could be palm trees, swaying on the high and dry. Buildings and boat docks, someone's horses enjoying life. Just add water, a river, and presto, civilization.

A little uncivilized. He couldn't help it. He put his hands to his mouth, megaphone. His sermon from a mount. "Larry!" He took his hands away from his mouth and spread his arms, embracing it all. "Larry!" sending it to all the rivers, to Larry.

Now that's what I call a rest stop. I better get going. But the sun was going down, behind Canada, dropping a country of yellows and oranges and golds and peaches and steel grays down across North America. The river changed to five different shades of river. The everlasting sky got itself some near northern lights.

Shit. I want to drive through this. On to Teddy Roosevelt Park.

On the Mandan side of the river the night showed its first purple, low and high in the sky. A star, two stars showed in what was left of the blue. The moon seemed small, lost in all the vastness. Paul rolled down the window and watched for stars.

They came out the way fireworks explode. A sky-burst of white star-bursts. Desert sky. Paul and his metal steed rode on to the next watering hole.

CHAPTER

No one lived out here. No front yards, backyards, garages, shopping centers, parking lots. There was New Salem and Glen Ullin and Taylor; just places people had settled, far from Arthur Levit.

Frontier? Our frontier president, Teddy Roosevelt. Paul could see the big face, the big teeth. Our rough rider. Up ahead now. About ten million galaxies overhead and about five thousand shadow shapes of badland bluffs and cliffs and level distances.

Paul drove head half out the window, counting the galaxies, straining to maybe hear a coyote preaching from one of the bluffs.

Dickinson, North Dakota made some electric stars. Great. A national park is next.

A circle on the map marked another park, a national monument.

Custer National Battlefield. I can stop there. Old yellow hair.

But first, old walk softly and carry a ... 1 think I'll just walk softly.

Chewing on some barroom beef sticks and cheese and crackers.

Soft-tack.

Deep dark in Belfield, North Dakota. Something in the air, something on the ground. The dull moon and the bright stars offered up a fifteen watt bulb. Lush? Maybe it was the map and the interior light: Little Missouri Natl. Grassland.

It felt like the grass was greener on this side of Dakota.

Soft green grass against the hard ground. The thought of it made him think of unrolled sleeping bags on top of it. Camp and sleep.

Medora. Nice word. National, park. Nicer words.

Dark, like it would never be sunlight again. Lit by the stars, a sign said Painted Canyon Visitor Center. Painted deserts, painted canyons. Who could resist? He didn't.

Cottonwood campground, with the sound of water nearby, the breeze in the cottonwoods, the night shapes--the brush, the high ground, the lumps and humps, the campfire grills, the wooden tables, the two tents, the pickup truck with a camper shell, the open spot, the engine off, the headlights out, the badlands as quiet as they were dark.

He worked quietly, flashlight, someone's cigarette making a red mark in another camp site.

His tent was a techno-leap from canvas cub scouts. Pliable ribs and pliable nylon. Presto, popo, shelter.

I'm forgetting to eat, as he unrolled the techno sleeping bag on the tent floor. Larry would appreciate this.

What have I got to eat? Some old orange juice, some crackers, cheese, and a salami stick. Yumm.

It was, sitting on the edge of the hardwood table, techno down vest keeping him warm, enough stars to match every wish ever made.

The flashlight illuminated the park's personal map, the course of the Little Missouri River. He could sense it right over his shoulder. Night vision of what was all around him.

Go see the river in the morning. Say goodnight. He rubbed at the coin in his pocket. He rubbed at himself. He felt like rubbing himself. It felt good.

It felt good, naked inside the sleeping bag. He felt for himself. He felt for the women images to make it fuller, better.

A waitress in Timber, Minnesota. A woman way back in Indiana? Feeling real good going away with it, smoothly, quickly, slowly, forcefully, gladly, quickly, quickly, quickly.

Ahhh, ahhh, ahhh. A level, low moan no one heard in the breeze in the trees.

His dreams were of buffalos and a bridge in flames.

CHAPTER

It wasn't flames, but inside the tent was almost white from the whole new sun. What in the hell is that bridge? was a split second of thought, the sun's glow and being awake in the outdoors of it too complete to worry about the second half of a strong dream.

Somebody was cooking bacon. From his tent it smelled of chuck wagons and cattle and rawhide, and maybe buffalo. He rolled out and remembered the make-believe women from the night. Fantastic.

Fantastic to be warm against the high plains morning.

Mr. & Mrs. Pickup with camper shell were the bacon, the smoke from their gas grill marking the encampment.

All that had been dark was now light. All that was black was tan and green and brown and crimson and ash and red and maroon and bluffs and cliffs and mounds and eroded shapes; a painted erosion.

Wow! Wow! Wow! as he turned a ceremonious circle. Wow! Wow, I'm hungry! Wow, I need to piss. The outhouse? Nah, do it in the wild. He remembered the river sound. He clomped on the frost, through the sage brush to it.

A covered wagon might ford it, but some of the horses might have to give up their lives to get across the Little Missouri's ample width, ample depth, and ample orneriness. The painted erosion waited on the other side.

Wow! Pissing in the sage brush felt good. Wow, I could use a shower! Wow, I'm hungry!

"Feel like some breakfast!" came the call from Mr. & Mrs., coffee cups steaming, bowls of hot cereal steaming, eggs and bacon sizzling.

The invite only meant him, the campground empty but for them.

"Me? Sure!" You bet I do, you great and wonderful people.

Something must have happened in the night. Paul said, "howdy," greeting the two gray heads of hair, the calm father and the motherly retiree faces, all in wool knit caps, down vests, jeans and cowboy boots, Oregon license plates.

"Howdy," back to him.

"Join us," the woman said. "Got in late last night?"

"I did. Thanks. Looks great."

"Coffee?" the man asked.

"Please," almost genuflecting to them.

"Here, have a seat," unfolding a lawn chair.

"Great, thanks. Beautiful morning."

"It surely is," she answered. "Surprised it didn't snow last night."

"Cold enough," Paul said.

"Want milk in your coffee?" the man asked.

"You bet. Uh, my name's Paul Barnes."

"I'm Muriel, and this is Harry."

"Howdy. You guys from Oregon?"

"Some of the time," Harry said. "Mostly where we feel like goin' now."

"Where are you from, Paul?" refilling his cup.

"New York."

"You've come far," from Harry, flipping the bacon, lifting the sunny side ups off the grill. "Two eggs, Paul?"

"Sure, sure. Got a way's to go yet."

"Where to?" Muriel asked.

"Yellowstone." As if he'd said Jesus, Christmas, grand-children. Muriel and Harry smiled at each other and nodded their approval, content to hear the word.

"Enjoy it," Harry said. That was all he said.

That was all Paul needed to hear because breakfast was served, on a tin plate. The bacon touched the eggs, the eggs touched the warm bread; the whole business touched him. He devoured it.

"What brings you to this park?" as he wiped the tin back to its pre-breakfast condition.

"Buffalo roundup," Harry told him.

Paul almost choked on the last of the wipe-up bread.

"Buffalo roundup? What buffalo roundup?"

"This time each year. That's why we're here. They thin out the herd here in the park. The Indians from the reservations come for the excess, the ones they cut out. Quite a sight."

"Indians? Buffalo? Here in the Dakotas, still?"

"Sure. Just follow us and we'll show you." Harry and Muriel were as proud as parents, telling him all about it.

He couldn't say, "holy shit," with mother Muriel standing there.

He could inside his car, pinned to their tailgate, being led to a buffalo herd. A herd. Not two of them in a zoo, their cloaks damp and matted. Harry had said, a herd.

It was all brand new to him. All of it was ancient, weathered, rolled and angled, slanted and cut, gouged and gullied, a pallet of pastels and hard grays, deep browns, thick greens, plateaus and pinnacles, meadows and ridge lines, hawks and more hawks, and the Little Missouri wearing its way along through it all.

Paul had substitute taught everything back home. Shop class to art class. Who's the artist, Paul? Come on, who painted these colors, these angles, these formations? With those colors and those shapes all around, he got it.

Cezanne. Of course. So much for Cezanne. He only painted it. It is far beyond.

Just beyond the Wind Canyon trail Harry and Muriel hit the brake lights. Buffalo, Paul, buffalo.

But Cezanne stuck for a moment more. The painter in France.

Paris in France. Larry in Paris, France. I wish you could see this with me, Larry. I bet you have though, somehow. I bet you have.

A ranger, famous hat in place, was directing traffic. Cars, tourists, visitors, parked on the road shoulder. Across the two lanes the wild west show had come to town. A circle of horse trailers, each of them hung with bridles and lariats. Two big stock trucks, red and white. Power pickups, four wheel drives.

Trim, tall horses with trim, tall riders, dressed for the occasion, if the occasion was 1870. Indians. 1970's Indians.

Yes, Paul, Indians--Plains Indians--raven hair straight down from under their stetsons or bareheaded with rope-coiled braids, beads and leather around their foreheads and sewn into their shirts, into their vests.

Two narrow, iron rail corrals. Not a hint of rain or snow or sleet. A few hints of clouds, the sun warm on everyone. Everyone standing in place.

"What do you think, Paul?" Harry leaning against the engine hood.

"It's something, Harry, really something. The Indians."

"They're Sioux." Harry might as well have said, "they're Gods."

"I see," is what Paul heard himself saying.

"Everyone looks ready," Muriel said.

"Ready?" Paul asked.

"They'll be coming," and Harry lit his pipe.

Paul looked to where what was coming might be coming. The green-brown grassland rose a bit from the road and lifted away, cut in two ways of greening grass by a brown on gray bluff.

The riders at the horse trailers saddled up. A ranger spoke into a walkie-talkie. Something was up. Something was coming.

Something came all right. Something absolutely suddenly. A tall rider and a running lead, a running herd of buffalo, split down the middle by the bluff. Something absolutely never seen before.

Paul's jaw dropped. The tamed wild west yelled and whooped and exploded in dust, lariats, buffalo, buffalo, buffalo, Charlie Russell and Frederick Remington without the paint and the canvas, without Charlie Russell and Frederick Remington.

Buffalo yelled at, coaxed at, shoved at, cornered, cut, horses taking orders, cowboys in all their glory; whoops and hollers, turmoil, metal gates banging shut, tailgates banging down, dust settling, yelling.

Yaahh? was all he could think. Where in the hell did all this come from? The buffalo were barging on the corral, dust and horns and hooves and bulldozer brown heads.

How many? Hundreds, thousands. Paul counted each one as a dozen.

A dozen things were happening, a dozen voices yelling, coaxing, shoving, stampeding the big browns up a ramp and into the big red and white trucks.

Absolutely suddenly. "Ayehh!" Paul whooped.

"You said it, Paul!" Harry yelled at him, tapping out his pipe, the three of them watching the riders chasing some of the buffalo back over the hillside, and then just dust.

"We're off to another spot, Paul, if you're interested?" Muriel asked. "Golden eagles." The big diesels hauling the animals blew their diesel horns-ships under way. Paul felt the same way.

"Golden eagles?" He almost... "No, I better get going. I have to get going."

Harry smiled.

"Yellowstone, huh?"

"Yep." Yep felt like the surprise of "howdy." Paul smiled.

"Have a safe trip." Muriel placed a kiss on his cheek.

"Thanks. And thanks for this."

"Our pleasure, Paul. Good luck." Harry and Muriel both shook hands, firmly, warmly.

Paul watched them go in his side mirror, the heavy warm stink of the buffalo in the slow moving trucks ahead of him taking him out of Theodore Roosevelt National Park. The park map said Medora--to Yellowstone--465 miles.

A cup of coffee, a two pound cinnamon roll, a counter, just donuts, just five swivel seats, park pennants, stuffed buffalo dolls.

He got the front seat adjusted just right, the coffee cup balanced, stuck between windshield and dash. 460 miles.

A few clouds, small in the enormous sky. A color blue. What color blue? You never saw a sky so blue. So blue you could cut it with a knife. That's how blue.

Paul, that's a rodeo cowboy going by. A blue and white pickup and shell, Montana plates, horse trailer, straw stetson behind the wheel, red bandana around his neck, horse tail flying out from the speeding trailer, a championship buckle in painted gold on the side of the horse trailer, some name, some title painted under the buckle. WHOOSH! and it was all gone.

Hope he's a bronc rider. I always liked the bronc riders.

Way out west back in Madison Square Garden. Roy Rogers and Trigger, bull riders, bronc busters.

I like that Montana license plate. Mountain range on it.

Here came another one for his inspection. Another one.

Hey, I must be in Montana. A sign in the shape of the state said welcome to the word mountain in Spanish.

Mountains any minute now, Paul. Another few minutes and it was Dakota without the Cezanne. It looked like Dakota without for a long way. Bare, not a Rocky Mountain in sight.

Look at the map, jerk. What did you think? That, white, on the front seat, not a splash of the color green until somewhere near Billings. He noticed Glendive. Check traffic, check map, check traffic, notice a blue name alongside a flexing blue river.

Notice the thin, delicate name--Yellowstone. Yellowstone River.

"Yahoo!" He would have waved his Stetson if he'd had one.

Do I stop? Do I? The answer came from long ago. Every boy ago. General George Armstrong Custer. Yellow hair. Last stands in the woods down your block. Below, Hardin, Montana. Custer Battlefield. Now, decide right now. Of course you stop.

But first visions first. The Yellowstone River.

There it is, the highway west, the highway for the rest of it.

Dry ground, oasis river, wide enough for steamboats, and keel boats, narrow enough to get a wooden bridge across it.

He wanted to drive the car into its historic current.

Sacajawea? He wanted to drive a canoe forward through its white and brown current, May rains and melting snow swelling it, stretching it, filling it.

Instead, he drove as fast as he could. Left at Glendive, Montana, drive as fast as you can, beaver pelts in the trunk, floating along with the make-believe barges he put in the Yellowstone's current.

Miles and miles of Route 94 to Billings and then down left to Hardin. The Yellowstone was a trickle in an ocean of bare browns, raw tans, groves of green.

70 M.P.H., checking, checking for state troopers, Texas Rangers, vigilantes, war parties. No smoke signals on the horizon.

75 M.P.H.

Running the rapids past Miles City, miles of wide open, patchy spaces. Crow Indian Reservation a patch out there on the map.

A dot on the map, a bump in the road, a blink, a 60 M.P.H. turnoff down to Cottonwood, Montana, population 172, industry-ranching, farming. Housing--wood frames and red bricks, rusting farm equipment in the back, near the sheet metal shed, horses in the yards, dogs on porches. Fuel--three red pumps under a sheet metal awning, a pickup in the mechanic's bay, a general store across a wooden porch. Food--"microwave in use" the sign in the beer-plastered window announced. The car made a little dust in the gravel driveway.

A curing shed of beef jerky and beer and peanut bags, sandwiches, sausages, pickles soaking, rotating, roasting hot dogs.

A slapping screen door brought a curving piece of beef jerky, a walking piece of dried rawhide to the front counter. He looked like a coyote without the hair. "Howdy," nice as you please.

"Get some gas?" in awe. Here was his first Montanan.

"Fill 'er?" like Gary Cooper coyote.

Do I dare? "Yep." He dared. "Where's the mountains?"

"Out a ways," with a nod of his coyote face.

Orange juice, microwaved sausage and muffin. Big bag of salted almonds, quart of milk. He could hear the gas pumps chiming the gallons.

Hawkin 50. The name plate under the big buffalo gun hanging on the wall beneath the buffalo head. His grandfather could have used it. Or him? "That er'll be eight dollers," the grandson said.

"And all this." Paul indicated his supplies. "Should get me to Custer Battlefield."

"Headed that way?" Coyote hands on the register.

"Yep," almost biting his tongue.

"New York, huh?"

"You can tell?"

"I kin tell."

"I guess so," coyote man.

"Yep, ole Custer got his pretty down there on the Big Horn."

"Pretty," wasn't what he had expected. Great expectations? A fella named Larry Darrell? He pass through here awhile back? . . . Not that I recollect.

Paul played with the conversation as he gathered the change.

"Your gun?" nodding to the Hawkin.

"Yep. You say howdy to ole yella hair for me."

"Yella hair? Oh, Custer. I'll do that."

"Saw his kind in Korea." Paul felt a land mine. "Well, thanks. Take care."

"Yep, you bet." A black dog left off chasing his car.

Cottonwood took its name from the plush cottonwoods, drinking from the flexing, ever moving Yellowstone.

CHAPTER

Purple clouds moving across, moving in--ghost riders in the sky, stampeding, lightning sparking from their hooves.

Hail and rain and snow and sleet blasting the windshield, Billings, Montana somewhere under all those elements. Oil tanks, industrial oil tanks close by. Must be the edge of town. Junk yards right at the edge of the road.

Keep an eye peeled, buddy. 1-90 south to Hardin.

The storm blew east, silver light beyond its western edge.

Trucks throwing up rain water. Hold tight to the wheel. There it is, 1-90. 7th Cavalry, Sitting Bull. Eyes peeled. Directional signal, exit, boots and saddles.

Crow Indian Reservation off on the map. Reservation meant the same thing on Long Island. Concentration, and not a camp.

Something other than Theodore Roosevelt National Park began to begin inside him. Outside the windshield wipers cleared the hail pellets. Something not so clear inside him. Someplace called Hardin, Montana went by. He was headed to a place where things had come to a head, to an end, tragic. But he kept at the 70 M.P.H., rubbing the Alexander coin in his pocket, settling the something tragic going on inside him.

Going on, a sign said, Custer National Battlefield. A gulp in his throat for some reason. War was the reason. The one still in progress, and Larry's war--the one that was to end all of them?

"I've heard them say that about that war." Larry, almost with a smirk.

Maybe I should just keep on? But coming in, the Little Big Horn came into view, full and firm, narrow, bent and rounded, curled and twisted, taking its sweet, sweet time between the cottonwoods, through the lush grasses. It was absolutely tranquil.

He felt better. Better stop. All this way the green of it was most inviting. You couldn't hear cavalry bugles.

Early season silence as he drove in. Have I ever been on a battlefield before? Gettysburg? No. Yorktown? No.

No battle for a parking space. No one around. No one. Paul got out and closed the door, quietly.

You could hear the wind in the silence, see it moving the tall, dry grass, ghosts in their sheets, their uniforms, their headdresses. He walked to the crown of the hill. A pure white cemetery, level cut green grass. A national cemetery the park map told him.

Down there, on the meandering river, the tribes were encamped, now, if you looked long and soft enough.

Spooked was what he was. How many arrows in the chest did I take as a kid? How many times did I ride to the rescue? Too many? Too many graves.

He turned from it and headed for Custer Hill, where the real arrows and the real chests, and the real carbines.

A stone obelisk marking the spot, naming the names. This sucks, Paul realized. Killing ground. The wind blew, the grass swayed.

The ground. Where they fell, where the natives fell.

Where the natives stalled the manifest of destiny. Paul felt Sitting Bull, felt for him. Better than Erroll Flynn and all that.

All that was left on the grassy rise were the stone white soldiers, the headstones gathered in the wild grass.

I shouldn't have come here. How have I come to be here? Just drive a car and come here. He lowered his head and barely shook it from side to side.

Come on, get out of here. Out there. Out there across the wide open spaces. The wide open spaces were all butterscotch and gold from the afternoon sun. A light mist of rain began to fall on this place.

I'm glad Larry's not buried in the ground. Better to be on the wind, in the mountains.

He waved to the ranger in the entrance station and pointed himself towards the Bighorn Mountains.

What battlefield? What ghosts? His first western mountains cured him of that. 10,162 ft. of them cured a lot, snow in between the pine trees, sharp, short peaks, sharp, short extensions of the yellow ridge lines under the gun metal clouds.

Clear as a bell. High up in the belfry. The way west from Greybull to Cody to, yes, Yellowstone.

Mountains. There they were behind him, in the rear view, on the windshield, reflected along the back window. I've arrived.

Route 14, foothills and ridge lines working their way up on each horizon, flat out between, front and back. Flat out to Cody, Wyoming.

Buffalo Bill Cody. Every motel, every bar, every gas station, every single motel tried to attach itself to the great white hunter. Every motel in America was here on the flats. A sprawl of them, a boomtown of them. Sore eyes from them.

Buffalo Bill Museum. Red lights, neon lights, gave him time to think about it. A giant plastic buffalo let him forget about it. It was now under a hundred miles to his destination. Another time Buffalo Bill.

Another red light, two dozen more motels. Elbow room, shoulder room, a tunnel blasted through the yellow rock, a wide, flat reservoir, peaks up ahead, road construction equipment ahead.

Elbow room, shoulder room.

Shoshone River. Cottonwoods like a Cottonwood National Park.

Nothing but a river, pure and simple, complex as creation, creating a tall brown canyon, canyon walls, chimney shapes, smoke signal platforms, pinnacles and posts, dark shade across the narrow road, cold, shades of mounted warriors on the wind-worn ridge lines.

Holy shit. This is some piece of road. And it went on that way--a canyon, a lost land, sheltered and secret, with landmarks of life in small cabins, canoes leaning against a log wall, red metal mail flags at attention, all as scrubbed clean as the green forest attached to the canyon.

I gotta stop. A trash can and a picnic table, tires on gravel, the Shoshone National Forest.

He dumped all the cross country wrappers, all the bags, all the bottles and all the cups. The river close by sounded like the wind; the fudge-brown cliffs were silent; the tall, thick pine forest was stoic.

This is the forest primeval, almost, he joked to no one but himself. A place called Wapiti just ahead, and then the end of the journey.

Now it begins, Paul. What? A big chunk of a lot I think.

Wapiti waited for the dudes and the tourists. Gas and food and horses and a log lodge, and "Gateway to Yellowstone." I'll take the gate if you don't mind.

The canyon walls opened up to taller, higher, grayer peaks, thinner trees, more meadow between road and river, rail fences, park entrance two miles.

A hawk circled, a raven complained, a stomach tightened, a face smiled, a foot let up on the gas. Yellowstone National Park.

The brown and yellow sign said it all.

CHAPTER

Saturday, May 10,1972, about 5:30 p.m., elevation, way-up and rising. Paul made a note of it, staring back down the way he'd come. Where did all the elevation come from? I felt it? Sea level had been his life. Hawks weren't sea gulls. Snow caps weren't white caps. He rubbed his hands together--a feast awaits.

Wait until tomorrow to go in? It will be dark, soon, up here nearer to the sun? The still warm light in the sky, in purple streaks, in an orange on a rouge, said there was still time.

Mountain standards of time. Let's go in.

In was almost open, a ranger with a red beard closing shop, closing the entrance slots, a sort of Alpine chalet meets Howard Johnson toll gate. "This is grizzly country," a sign announced.

That one and only bear sprang from the sign. Good. That's what I've come for.

He flipped his coin high in the air. It came down cold and heavy, solid, secure. He got back in the car and finished this part of the journey.

"Hiya," he said to the ranger, all in green, all alone but for Paul.

"Howdy. How are you?"

I'm here. It's me, Paul Barnes. Don't you recognize me? "I'm fine, real fine. I've just arrived."

"Arrived?" from a weather-worn, wind-burned face.

"Here. I'm going to work here," from his window.

"Welcome then. What sort of work?"

"Buses."

"Oh, yeah. Tour buses."

"Yep."

"Well, welcome to the club. Where are you headed now?"

"To, uh, Gardiner."

"Well, you still have a ways to go."

"Really?"

"Never been in before?"

"Never."

"Here's a map for you. You have some employment verification? So you don't have to pay," with a smile.

Paul loved him. Not him, but him in that hat, that green uniform. It felt like a lifeguard's uniform; nature boy, comfortably, naturally correct.

Ranger Marshall, from his name tag, unfolded a map. Paul produced his letter of acceptance from the Yellowstone Park Co.

A snow plow, as angry and as ugly as a rhino, a Yellowstone rhino, charged down the road, pounding into a left hand turn and into the pine trees.

"Great," with a nod at Paul's letter. "You're here, and here's Gardiner."

It was a cross country trip, across a small country. "Geez, how big is this place?"

"Two and a half million acres," with pride, with pleasure.

"You've got about eighty miles of it to go. And go slow. There's snow up ahead. The snow plows were working today.

"You got lucky. Usually not open this early. Take it easy up over Sylvan Pass. The rest of the way will be smooth." He pointed to a spot. "This Dunraven Pass here at Canyon is closed. You'll see the sign for the way around. It'll be a beautiful trip this time of day."

"When does it get dark?"

"You'll have plenty of light over the pass."

Snow plows in May? wasn't asked.

"Oh ," the ranger folding the map for him. "Keep an eye out for a sign that says Lake Butte. On your right just before the lake, coming down off the pass. Stop there." Not a suggestion, something obvious.

"Lake Butte. Will do."

"Well, take er easy. Have a good time. I think you will all right. " He left Paul there and walked towards the dark pine forest.

Will I see any bears? was too much a tourist. Two and a half million acres. Geez.

CHAPTER

From up where he was he could measure what he saw in yards, in an acre, in a gap in the pines. A green meadow, a narrow space between the gnarled, vertical mountain pass.

Snow, in plowed wedges, each the height of the engine hood, on each side of him. All alone, with a scaly, shattered shingles rock face, two narrow lanes of no traffic, and a scarred wooden guard rail to keep you from falling into the pewter creek in the kelly green meadow below.

Eagle Peak, 11,358 ft. His map on his lap. Out to the south from his exact location. Its locality put him up in that neighborhood.

A wind came down a funnel, shaking the car. The ice still alive in the shade on the road would be turning black.

"Mountain man!" he yelled out the window, holding on to the steering wheel for dearest life.

Fog, mist, sunlight, sunset, all of them stuffed into a rock frame in a gap where the pines didn't dare. He slowed, stopped in a shale turnout.

The wind rose and fell. All around was shattered rock, granite gray, battered, suspended stacks, ready to slide further on down from the wall to wall heights. Absolute wilderness except for the gouged-out road, and the metal platform with what appeared to be a gun emplacement. Really? he thought.

What the hell? The wilderness of it, the slant wall of it, the snow of it. Avalanches? They must shoot them.

Not a soul but his. This ain't no interstate, no park I've ever known. He knew hurricanes. He felt one up here.

He was worried the car wouldn't start. It did, and he crept away from this wind gap.

The gaps in the pines opened up--bodies of water. Soft parts of the body. Small, oval lakes, gray driftwood pines dead at the water's edge, snow and ice getting ready to give back the whole lake.

The road curved down, pot holes to make Manhattan blush. A long, enormous sky to make everywhere blush. The first few stars.

A gigantic lake.

What! And then the pines concealed the what! Didn't I just see a gigantic lake? A squat, little brown and yellow sign--Lake Butte. Got to be a lake out there. He went to have a look, up a gravel road, more fire break than road.

A platform without pines. The beginning of time. He rolled to a stop, breathless, speechless, undressed, naked to a sight he'd never seen.

A lake. No, more than a lake. Paul was of the Catskills, the Adirondacks, where lakes could be had in a hike, in your sights.

This lake, gray, thick as iron, was a vision. It would take an expedition to make your way around it. It, of what he could see of it.

A forest, thick as animal fur, blanketed its shoreline, its surrounding ridge lines, right up into the surrounding mountain snow lines.

I am blessed, was the best he could do. It was the best anyone could do.

A "You are here" sign told him what to see. In the pink-shot, rouge-rubbed sunset sky, far off in the distance, he could barely, just barely, make out the tops of the Teton Mountains. The sky over the lake was a sunset prism of colossal colors. "Fuck ... " It, all of it was a turning point in his, in a life. He knew it. Not a boat, not a house, not a bait dock, not a shop in sight.

Wilderness? Wildness anyway.

He read the stars. The additional ones told him darkness was coming. I better get going. The floating ice on the lake, the blue ice rim along its shoreline held him tight, there.

Come on, bub. You've got a ways to go. The car engine sounded like a jet engine in the sanctuary silence. He rolled down the window and let the lake spill into the car. He let it spill into him. A flat, wide open spot along its shoreline. Mary's Bay.

A sand, not a sandy beach, the wind coming up, the lake becoming a lesser ocean, waves coming ashore, splashing against the ice, the driftwood trees and the gravel sand.

Paul knelt to it and drank of it. A baptism.

"A toast. I'm here. I'm here, Larry," quietly, so only Larry would hear. He took a palm of water and let it run out of his hand, down his shirt collar, ice-cold along his chest, his stomach, his groin.

"Ahhh, brrr," shaking himself.

Cold, night coming, darkness closing around like an extra blanket, a warm coat. Paul zipped up his jacket and turned on the car heater. "Ahhh, warm." His headlights lit the place without street lights.

Headlights lit a buffalo, smack dab in the middle of the road, the road being a bridge across the neck of water where a lake became a river, the Yellowstone River.

Paul couldn't believe his eyes. But his eyes convinced him that a stout, very stout, grandfatherly buffalo was taking its time crossing the bridge, the bridge like a jumbo size dug-out canoe chopped across the water.

Like Little John and Robin Hood on the log, Paul waited, the buffalo being Little John.

What a fuckin' incredible situation. The big brown robe got scent of his machine and got out of there, back across the bridge at a heavy trot, long goatee swaying.

This is an amazing fucking place, already.

Man, I need some sleep, some gathering up of this. He moved along under the sandy grains of the stars.

Shapes. Dark shapes. Was that a moose? I thought that was an elk running from the headlights.

The dark screen of pine trees ended. A valley lit by the moon and the stars. A mountain peak lit by the snow. He groped into a turnout wide enough for a circle of wagons.

An owl made like a bat. You could hear its wings for miles, miles across this silence, across this land before the telling of time, without humans, without him.

The placid river, the Yellowstone, was as calm as a silver bracelet. "I'm in love," Paul whispered. The shadow shape rolls and hills around him heard him.

Come on lover boy. Let's get going. You've got a lifetime here. He heard the thought lifetime.

The thin pines grew back, steam smoking in among them. What? Boiling steam alongside the road. What? Some buildings in a cleared spot. A road junction, Canyon Junction. What canyon? Lifetime, Paul. He turned left and sped through about twelve miles of pure pines, and then a fog of steam at the next junction. A forest fire? Better call someone? There wasn't someone for miles, and no one appeared to be running to the rescue. The headlights beamed, Norris Geyser Basin.

Must be geysers. What? Thirty miles to Gardiner. Adam and Eve eat your hearts out.

Meadows and marsh out there in the dark. Sharp curves, rough spots in the road, elk, yeah, elk all over the place, stocking feet of snow at the base of the narrow pines, narrow road, always some flow of water nearby, a flat expanse, mountains for its horizon.

Paul slowed down across the expanse. He envied no man, no woman. I love it, he told it.

It closed into a golden wall, a gorge. Two narrow lanes hung from the golden wall, twisting and turning, dropping down off the golden wall, then steam like the earth was boiling. Turning a sharp corner and then a yellow and white sight, unseen by man, by this man. A mushroom mount of angel food cake, smoking, steaming, pulsating.

He watched it go by the way he sometimes watched an ocean wave rolling in, beginning to end. "Yellowstone." Buildings, a wooden hotel, heavy store headquarters, flag pole, sidewalks, civilization, Gardiner 5 miles.

He dropped down to Gardiner, down from Mammoth Hot Springs.

"Mammoth is right." A river made the road bend to its form. A fairly wide open space, a midget chalet entrance station, then candied neon lights out in the big dark. Carnival colors in all the natural. Gypsy camp at the edge of the natural. Gardiner, Montana. The end. The beginning.

CHAPTER

Gardiner, Montana, scattered above the Yellowstone River. A high steel bridge separated the separate scatterings of low, even buildings, motels, short streets and gas pumps. All of it was secluded in a sort of mining town rawness and ski resort softness.

The softest bed there ever was. The Wilson Motel, with the Yellowstone for its backyard. Paul emptied his pockets on the dresser. The big coin rolled to a stop among the nickels and quarters.

Tomorrow I'll try and find out about him. Tomorrow I'll start a new job. Some worry in his gut. Will I be all right? What will be expected of me? Etc., etc., etc. He could hear the Yellowstone. He undressed and got into bed. Smooth water swept over him.

A burning bridge, a fire. God damn it! The phone in the room rang. Wake up! He did. Shit. "Yes, yes," he mumbled into the phone. 6:30 a.m., mountain time.

Mountain time came in the open door. Pure oxygen, pure blue sky, and what looked like antelope in the meadow across the road, sunlight burning the cover from a peak buried in snow.

Antelope? as he dressed. Must be, they sure ain't deer.

Food. Tons of it, he joked. He didn't have to go far. The Town Cafe, like a prop for a Wyatt Earp episode, under a wooden porch, behind knotty pine posts.

"I'll have three scrambled eggs, potatoes, sausage, juice, wheat toast, three pancakes, coffee, please," speaking as an expert.

"Comin' raat up," the young woman with the Alabama drawl drawled.

Mr. Nothin' Fancy was the decorator. Chairs and booths and tables, orange; a short counter, orange, racks of antlers, buffalo skulls, two guys at the counter who invented the roll-your-own technique of pulling the pouch string tight with yer teeth.

Working range hands, their jeans and denim shirts not exactly clean and not exactly filthy. Their red bandannas were tied neatly, dashingly around their hefty, sun-burned necks, their stetsons still on, all their sweat, and all the weather still there around the hat band. Tooled leather belts, boot heels made for stirrups, eating as big a dose as the one Paul had ordered.

His dose came and he dove in, green uniform customers, in those round hats, taking a seat nearby. Nearby two French-speaking visitors toiled with the American menu.

The two range hands finished up and made like historic artifacts across the dining room.

Paul finished up and made like a keep-your-mouth-shut-ears and-eyes-open-day-one-rookie on a full belly.

CHAPTER

Yellowstone Park Co. Personnel. A wooden sign outside an airplane hanger-size warehouse of soft tan, almost adobe, two timeless buffalo pulling at the new grass in the meadow across the road, a stagecoach going by.

A stagecoach? Paul asked himself. A long yellow flatbed truck, but a stagecoach just the same, locked in place atop the flatbed, Wells Fargo wheels and all. He pinched his full belly to make sure he was dreaming with his eyes open. He went into the warehouse.

He had a nose for it. The nose registered the fragrance.

Young, single women. Many of them. Many of them in the partitioned, divided room. Arriving, working, scurrying, reporting, being. Paul Barnes breathed deep. This is fuckin' paradise.

One of the fragrant workers came up to him. She came up to his chest, curly brown hair, freckles, a sort of farmer's daughter about her face. A strong, tight body in jeans and a blue sweater.

Her makeup, like most of them in here, was what she'd been born with. It was more than enough.

"Hi," she said, openly, enthusiastically.

"Hiya."

"Reporting for work?"

"Yes."

"I'm Karen."

"I'm Paul Barnes."

"Well, hello," not shy, not a step back.

"Hi. I'm glad to be here."

"We're glad to have you," not hiding sizing him up and down.

This place is fuckin' paradise. "What's your job here?"

"Personnel. I check you in."

"Great. Shall we?"

"We shall." He followed her past a bench, fragrant as a bunch of flowers.

He smiled at each young lady. Everyone smiled back, one young lady with Miami Univ. on her chest, another with New York Yankees on her ball cap, another with the complexion and braids of a native.

He followed Karen into a small office.

"We've been expecting you," she told him.

"Thanks. It was quite a trip across."

"You drove from where?"

"New York."

"The Big Apple, huh?" He liked the way she said it--with awe and awareness.

"Not quite. Long Island."

"Oh. You must be tired from it," as she handed across the forms to be signed.

"Well, kind of."

"I've got just the thing."

"Oh?" liking the way she said that.

"Hot pot."

"Hot pot?"

"You are from New York," laughing a little.

He laughed a little. "Huh?"

"You'll see. You soak in a hot spring. You might need it," folding some forms. "You get the tour bus drivers. Crazy bunch."

"Yeah? I'm nervous all right."

"O.K. Here's the last form. We'll take an I.D. picture later. I guess you're staying up in the bunkhouse. Up in Mammoth. Know where that is?"

"I passed through last night."

"Like it?"

"Loved it," not joking.

"Well, I'd like to talk some more but there's other folks out there. Why don't you come by the K-Bar around eight tonight? You can't miss it. Just around the corner. Gardiner isn't exactly New York."

"Good."

"Any questions?"

Only one. "Uh, did you know a fella named Larry Darrell?"

"Sure," right away, right to a delicious smile.

"I knew him."

"Where?" surprise in her "where?"

"Back on Long Island."

"Really? He was," and she hesitated, twirling her pencil.

"He was different. Lovely. I didn't know him well, but I knew him."

"He was, Karen. So, I'll see you later?"

That was enough for now.

"You will. You can tell me more about him."

"I will."

I don't. I do believe this place. An elk herd, at least twenty females, were feeding on the fresh-salad lawn outside the bunkhouse.

The two story bunkhouse. Railroad workers, the steam type, would be right at home in its wooden frame and wooden halls. There was the young Jack London stepping out of the communal shower.

Almost.

Jack Cummings was Paul's roomie. From Montana, born and raised and fished and hiked, and worked in Yellowstone for eight years, and single, and a Frederick Remington model at age twenty five, black hair, blue eyes, cowboy squints.

I gotta start writing some of this stuff down he told himself as he loaded himself into the car to head to town.

Day one was done. Meeting the executives. About as comfortable a bunch as a worn shirt, or patched jeans. He let his jaw relax--new job. He relaxed among the worn shirts and crisp jeans. Everything was going to be all right. He was going to Old Faithful to lead a group of twenty veteran and rookie drivers.

Tour buses. His roommate Jack would be among them. Jack knew the ropes. He undid a few of Paul's knots for him.

I gotta get me a journal. I'm an American with some artistic inklings, ain't I? I'm on an adventure, ain't I? I know people will love to read it someday. Won't they? "Ha!" He punctuated, and headed into town.

"Oh, man! Oh, man!" There was a bull elk with a rack of horn worthy of a winter tree.

And this is only day one, Paul. Not a street light, not a burger bun, not a gasoline price.

Like a piece of tumbleweed with neon lights--little town below, the mountain world all around it.

The K-Bar, right? If you blinked you'd still see it. There was a lot of the little town around the big, yellow and brown K above what looked like the last place Bill Hickok was ever seen alive, on this side of the Yellowstone.

A cowboy bar, Paul? Parking next to a leather goods shop, an outlet for outfitting modern mountain men.

Cowboy bars. The stuff of legends. Not the most savory ones, but he noticed some of the young women from the morning heading into the K-Bar, Pendleton shirts, Indian jewelry. Cowgirls too, Paul. Got to look for Karen. He pushed on a door Bill Cody might have pushed on.

This wasn't any Buffalo Bill Cody blocking the doorway. Looks more like the deerslayer crossed with one of Quantrill's raiders.

He was a head taller than Paul, in a worn out, brown, range hand duster. A long, clean ponytail, held in place by a leather knot, fell from under a worn out John Deere cap. Moccasins on his feet, the first pair of Levis, almost white, on his legs, and three days of beard on his thin, lean face.

"Excuse me," Paul offered up. The deerslayer-raider didn't move, so Paul inched, touched his way around him.

"Easy on me co-ed," deerslayer-raider said.

"Fuck you," was right on Paul's east coast lips, but this was virgin territory, a virgin bar, and this guy looked like he had the goods. Paul stared at him, made a mark next to him. Who in the fuck? And speaking of fuck, he laughed to himself. Look at it all.

Sixteen women for a few men. One small pool table. One T.V. above the bar, one jukebox, one pizza oven, several tables, plenty of beer advertisements, one large, scenic lake covering a wall, pitchers of beer on each table among the women.

Where's that woman Karen? There she is, waving from a back table, with enthusiasm. Deerslayer behind him was laughing about something. Paul did some pick-up sticks moves through the pool cues and the knees hanging from the bar stools, from the row of guys who could have passed for a group photo at the driving of the golden spike.

"Hiya, New York," was Karen's greeting. In a black turtle neck, black slacks, and a flash of Arizona jewelry, she sat with two other women, a guy and a pitcher of beer.

"Hiya."

"Glad you could come," Karen told him.

"Me too," beaming. First things first. "Who's that creep at the door?"

"That? That's Gary Delling, poacher," with an emphasis on "poacher" from the guy at the table. "Hi, I'm Terry," he said, reaching across to shake Paul's hand.

"Poacher?" shock in his question. He disliked him twice as much.

"Always somebody around here," Karen said. "He does do his share I guess. Always trying to get him, ain't you Terry?"

"He poaches from the park?" amazement in Paul's amazement.

"Yep. Terry's a ranger."

Paul nearly fell at his feet. Blond and scrubbed. "That's what he does, poach." The ranger took a sip of beer.

"That and a million other odd jobs," the woman with the short brown hair and the manly face added. "Got any odd jobs? He's some character."

The Gary Delling character turned for the door and left.

Creep. Paul made a mental note.

"How about a beer?" closed the notebook.

Paul went one hundred and eighty degrees from it, from Gary Delling. He mentioned Larry Darrell.

"He lived in a little trailer out towards Yankee Jim Canyon." Terry's wife, Carolyn, blond, scrubbed. "You'll see it when you go out that way. I knew him a bit. We all did," nodding at everyone at the table. "He was a gentleman. Lots of the gentle." Each one of them at the table nodded in agreement, Paul included.

"Yes," Paul finally said, head spinning, head settling into the idea that Larry existed here, among these strangers. But now, now they weren't. "I used to see him in the summers, in the evening. Gentle. The whole scene. On the beach where I used to work."

"Small world, Paul," Terry said. You and him ... to here."

"We were all sad, about his death." Karen spoke for all of them. "Sad may not be the right word. Sorry may be better."

"That's why I'm here. I came to find him again." Paul poured ranger Terry a beer. "Where are you from, Terry?" pouring out the last of the beer, the bar beginning to go home to those homes gathered under a chunk of the Rocky Mountains.

"Michigan. Familiar with the Upper Peninsula?"

"No."

"Still pretty wild. High above the auto factories. It's still O.K. there." All of them left "but here" unsaid.

Joan, with the hard face and the gleaming white teeth got up to go first. "I can introduce you to someone who knew Larry here.

Spent more time with him than anyone."

"Could you?" leaning towards her.

"Sure. Mary Cole. Studies the grizzly bears." There it was, for the first time, on location. Grizzly bear.

It sent a shock wave up Paul's spine.

"That would be great," masking the shock wave of wonder at the fact that man-eaters were present, nearby. He felt a warm hand on a warm part of his thigh. Not a shock wave.

Karen smiled a delicious smile--the kind most men want to see after a few beers in a warm bar beside a warm woman.

"I'm taking Paul hot-potting," she announced to everyone, only the five of them left in the bar now.

"Lucky boy," Carolyn laughed.

He thought he was going to be.

CHAPTER

The Gardner River, squeezed narrow by the rocks and the road, poured down white through the rocks. Two buck deer in the headlights of Karen's pickup. They danced away on ballet toes.

Overhead the stars left little room for black in the mountain night.

"You won't need a bathing suit," Karen told him. "Natural will do." She made a quick left after a very short bridge over the Gardner. A sign just barely in the headlights--Continental Divide.

She parked in a chopped-out parking area on the Continental Divide. One other car, 11:00 p.m.

A moon, white as a star, within touching distance, the Gardner River within kneeling down and drinking from it distance. The distance across the swift running water was two leaps by a deer.

Karen and Paul followed a path as hard as concrete.

"Just up here a bit." She came back to him and held his hand, kissed him confidently, slowly, fully, damply.

An Adam and an Eve, he was thinking. A Paul and a Karen anyway.

"Come on, I want some more of you." He quickly followed, wondering what in the hell, what in the heaven was up ahead.

Steam up ahead pouring up from the river? They stood above the river, warm steam warm on the face.

"Go on, take your clothes off," laughing. She was already to her panties.

The air full of steam from the hot water current, pouring into the Gardner. They stood on the hard rock shelf above the pools of warm water, naked now. Two voices from the pools below.

"This way," and she took him by the hand, warm, cold on the skin, cold on bare feet, cloud shadows rushing in overhead. She took him down a cut in the rocks.

Hot water, white as rapids in the dark, rushed into the river from out of the rock face. Pools of warm river water against the rocks.

Paul's professional toes never hesitated. The river was crystal cold, Karen in it up to her small, firm breasts. She went quickly to one of the hot currents.

The shock of the cold water on him was an ocean in May.

Powerful. He rubbed his face in it and went to her.

"Ahhh," went out into the silence. The hot water was perfect, as natural as creation, relaxation, the water pouring over them, mixing with the river, cold on their feet, on their thighs, steam billowing around their heads.

"Hot potting," Karen announced.

"I like it, I like it," and felt something anyone would like.

"Ohhh." She leaned into him, rubbing him, floating on him.

The clouds covered the moon and the stars. It began to snow, lightly, thick enough to catch on your tongue, in your eyelashes.

She licked his tongue, his ears, his eyelashes, his neck. His knee floated between her thighs, floated out, floated in, the river racing by, full to the brim.

"It's snowing," Paul whispered in her ear from the end of his tongue.

"Ummm," and she lifted up to standing in a shallow pool of water, tall enough when Paul stood up to have him right up at her warm, cold backside, a backside as plump, as firm as a new pillow.

She bent, she spread, she welcomed. He erected, he probed, he found, he pushed.

"Uhhh," among the snow flakes. She pulled, he pushed, she pulled, he pushed, the water splashing from the push, the pull, the push, the pull, the pulse, the pulse, the "uhhhing," and the "ahhhing." They heard themselves.

They dressed themselves.

"Great stuff," Karen told him.

"I'll say. We'll have to try it again," buckling his belt.

"Maybe. My fiancee comes into town tomorrow." A green light went off in Paul's head. Sex was one thing, getting involved was another thing altogether. He suddenly liked the word fiancee. Karen could dig it, then get on about her business. So could he. Too many opportunities await to rush into any limitations.

"Oh?" he answered her.

"He's a bus driver. You won't have him at Old Faithful. So, maybe ... " with a kiss "... we can get together again sometime."

"Sure, sure," with another fifty "sures" left unsaid.

"The snow is beautiful," on their way back.

"July and winter," she said.

"What? What's that?"

"The seasons up here. Snow. Any time, any day. Want the weather to change? Wait fifteen minutes."

"Winter must be powerful up here."

"You'll probably find out."

"Think so?"

"You're hooked. You've got ranger written all over you."

"Think so?"

She stopped at the truck, the river showing some white water in the dark. "Sure," she said. "Here too," taking him by what they'd shared.

"Maybe so, maybe so," purring, kissing her hair.

The obvious question as they started back to town. "Ever see a grizzly bear?"

"Sure. A few times. I've worked here for six years. Used to see a lot more. But they finally wised up and got them back into the back country where they belong. Roadside bears, too. Black bears all over the place.

"But those days are over. You'll see bears, but back where they belong. You'll hear a million versions of the bear stories. Lots of science and lots of studies. The bears are fine. Could be finer, but getting better.

"You'll hear all the numbers. They're out there ... " and she didn't finish, glaring high beams in the windshield from a Willis Jeep, station wagon version, splattered with mud, grinding a gear up the hill. Then it was by them.

"Your friend," Karen said.

"Who?"

"Gary Delling. Your poacher."

"Asshole," like he'd known all along.

"Maybe next time," with a laugh.

"What? Oh," realizing with a laugh.

"You know," patting his knee.

He blushed in the dark, laughed as they passed the tour buses, parked in a lot outside of town.

"You drive tomorrow?" Karen asked.

"Yeah. Looking forward to it."

"Watch those gears."

"O.K. See you later?" outside the K-Bar.

"Probably, Mr. bus driver, dispatcher," winking in the interior light. A coyote, out there in the dark, in the park, celebrated the night.

CHAPTER

Mr. bus driver. Open road, a smooth, strong, MCI diesel stuck to a road between Montana on the left and right, the Yellowstone alongside, and nothin' but blacktop.

Paul was getting it. A few days, a few pounds of hamburger ground out from the double clutching.

He got the rear duals of the brown and yellow tour bus on the white lines and hauled it, coming back out of the Paradise Valley where it was snow caps and green grass jackets, uninhabited but for the few who had lived and gone to heaven, Paradise.

Now past the long, low brow of the buffalo jump above the river. If there were still natives it would still be in use.

Now through the native shapes that the winds of time had fathered.

Now Yankee Jim Canyon, where the Yellowstone tumbled and grumbled a bit, the road curved to follow its flow, then past the Devil's Slide, a long, smooth deep scoop of pastel earth from out of a hillside like ice cream from a serving spoon.

Paul felt the power of a straight away to Corwin springs.

"Pullover for a bit, Paul." Don. Retired Greyhound father figure, fatherly plump, fatherly gray, bolo tie on blue shirt with dark slacks, father figure to the rookie drivers.

"Sure," and he showed him what he'd learned, doubling it down in gear, just touching the touch brakes to slide into the pullout.

"Just wanted to check our friends down there," Don said, the big engine humming.

Down there was a straight stretch of the river, as smooth, as brown as high water can be. Down there across the river there was agriculture and fences, cattle, horses, irrigation, brown cliffs, buildings, tin roofs, tin siding, mobile home units, tractors, water towers, gravel roads, high fences, people. There were diesel spills into the Yellowstone, there were attempts to tap into the geo-thermal world beneath the ecosystem; there were fences interfering with the antelopes' migration from in and out of the park; there were weapons, bomb shelters, doomsday, revelations, speaking in tongues, upsetting the balance of nature's way; there were too many on too little. Religion, obsession, possession.

There was a name for them--the Church of the Triumph and the Universe.

Paul got an ear full. The talk of the town, especially when the town was the size of Gardiner, about the same size of this bunch out here.

"I hear they have armed patrols at night now," Don said softly, hurt in his softly. His tenth year in Yellowstone. Hurt.

"Freaks," was Paul's contribution, not hurt, pissed off. Get out! Get lost! "The last thing I thought I'd ever see out here." Don had the passenger door open.

"The Feds wouldn't buy the land?" Paul had a bit of information.

Don wasn't listening, he was watching the four wheel Broncos coming and going. Paul knew all about mega-man Malcolm Jobes by now, selling off the acres to the California guru, gurette come lately, Elizabeth the Prophet, and her followers. Followers with check books. Elizabeth the Profit.

"Bomb shelters." Don left it at that.

"Better get back ... some classes to finish."

Paul hid his sigh. Classes. The when's, where's and why's of Yellowstone Park. How can you expect a man to concentrate when an elk is wandering past the window; when you think you've spotted an osprey? So he didn't, concentrate, concentrating instead on why the sky was so absolutely, positively blue.

He was concentrating now on that black iron bridge across the Yellowstone. A one lane bridge. Access for Elizabeth and her brood. Concentrating on his burning bridge dream. Breaking concentration to shift to a fabulous white cloud formation he imagined into an Indian hunting party.

"Mary, the grizzly bear lady will talk this afternoon," Don reminded him.

Paul snapped to it. "She will?"

The black iron bridge shrank into the distance.

CHAPTER

Paul's ancient coin went well in her hard worked hand. Mary the grizzly lady. Her image, her handle. Mary Gregor, her name.

"Larry's?" she asked, holding the coin. White, even teeth, short black hair, a narrow, little two room house up on a hill above Gardiner. Simple and efficient. Simple and efficient, genuine, her face. Green eyes, in her young 40's face. She was wind-burnt and brown.

"See up there, on Electric Peak?"

Paul looked out across Gardiner, across the Yellowstone River, up into the gray clouds anchored to Electric's broad peak.

"She took his ashes up there." Mary placed the coin on the porch railing. "She" was Sophia.

"You knew her?" Mary asked him.

"No. Just for a few moments really."

"But you knew him."

"Oh, yes," then silence as they both watched the gathering storm gather atop Electric Peak.

All the information he'd been getting for the past week was nothing to this. How many miles around Yellowstone? How much of this and that, how many when's and where's, and what of it all he was thinking now.

This has no history, no photo copy, no photograph. How many bears? He'd forgotten the number. He'd been told. "They're out there was the way Larry counted them," Mary had told him. That's the way I'll count now.

Now the rising storm was worthy of any ocean, black as coal, cold, with the sun a glaring white within it.

"So, you're off to Old Faithful tomorrow?"

"Yes," he answered, taking up the coin.

"Where we found him is nearby. Ask about Mound Geyser. By Ojo Caliente spring. Someone will know."

"Would you like to show me?"

"No. You should go to it yourself. You knew him. You'll see this place of his. He found Yellowstone complete there."

"A heart attack?"

"If you like," refilling his coffee cup.

"Did you see him before? Before he died?"

"Yes. As often as I could. A letter came, from Chicago."

"Did you see it?"

"Yes."

"From Isabelle. Poor thing. Her grandson was killed in Vietnam."

"Oh. Isabelle. I think she was someone from Larry's time in Paris."

"Someone important to him."

"I think so."

"He went off alone after that. More alone that is." Paul made a smile, familiar with his friend.

"What did he make of that bunch out there?" meaning them, the religious cult.

"He'd say, poor souls, and lower his head."

"Assholes is more like it."

"I agree. But we all can't be Larry."

"Unfortunately."

"Yes, you did know him."

"He's why I'm here." He measured the gathering storm. You could measure it with the lower end of a thermometer.

"Now that I'm here... "

"Settling in?"

"Yes, I am."

"Be sure to go out to the Lamar Valley. A place of Larry's."

"Lamar Valley? I will. Uh, I don't think I've asked you how you met Larry."

"In the Lamar Valley, on a trail," and she didn't offer any more. Paul didn't pry.

The storm announced with thunder. Like everything that had made the earth. Rain and wind and snow and hail and thunder and lightning and cold. It sent them inside.

CHAPTER

Grizzly bears--the motif of the two rooms, and the kitchenette hanging from a wall.

One motif kept Paul's eye. Where grizz had been. A color shot of the shore ring around an ample little lake. Like a roto-tiller had paid a visit. A roto-tiller had. Grizzly claws and grizzly snout--rooting around, leaving its mark, its size, its persistence, its precision.

Those scars, behind her ear, on her neck, on her forearm. A deep crescent scar and two crooked scars. Mary's scars. They made Paul shiver.

"More coffee?" she asked. "With a bit of Jack Daniel's in it?"

"Sure," most assuredly.

The storm was one of those "if you don't like the weather, wait fifteen minutes." Light began to show in the small room. A glow from the Jack Daniel's began to glow.

"I filled out a ranger application today," Paul announced.

"Already?" smiling. "People usually wait a few weeks."

"That popular, huh?"

"You tell me," sipping from the glow.

"That popular." He thought it would be all right. He raised his glass. "To Larry?"

"To Larry," almost a whisper.

"I'm getting to like Jack Daniel's more and more."

"Goes good with the bar life."

"It does," and they both knew what was being left out. "It sure does." Just sipping, looking around her home. Powerful binoculars, field pack, a microscope, plastic bags, full of hair? The national bear with a fresh salmon from a fresh waterfall on one wall, the mother bear, as gray and as silver as Larry's coin, with her cubs, with a geyser going off beside a river, on another wall. A small desk, with small yellow tags wrapped in a rubber band, took up most of the space in one corner. A tall tripod, and a hand-held radio, re-charging itself, stood in a corner. There were bear claws, like deep sea fishing lures, on the low table where he set his coffee down. The tiny bedroom door was closed. Two trumpeter swans, like intercontinental doves, flew across a poster across the door.

He flew out the window with them. He came back.

"Anybody from that clan out there come into town?"

"I doubt it. Not to the bars. No welcome mat is out for them."

"If you can't worship this out here, what can there be to worship?"

"Ignorance, greed, loneliness, desperation. Black magic? She's got them fixed on I'm not sure what. The armageddon is coming? We shall survive? Weapons," and a shrug of the shoulders.

"Speaking of weapons. Poaching. Do the bears get it?"

"Sure. Everything does. The wild west, Paul. Rough, tough business. The winter brings it out in spades.

"The rangers get after it, the poaching, but two and a half million acres of park remember. A few small states to cover. Maybe you'll find out."

"Yeah, maybe. I've got a nice wad of Veterans preference points going for me."

"Then you'll do it." He shrugged. A brand new day outside. The storm stampeded away, leaving clouds of white, sky of silver gray.

"Thanks for the Jack," he told her. "I better get going. Still a few things to throw in a bag." They shook hands, equally.

"Let me know how you're doing. When I'm out your way I'll stop by," holding onto his hand.

"Mound Geyser, right?"

"Right."

CHAPTER

Geysers. Hundreds, thousands, millions of them. Hundreds anyway. Norris Geyser Basin--on his way to Old Faithful. The earth being made, boiled up, boiled over, spewing its guts, its fire, its steam.

Two weeks of Gardiner was the bar tour, the local points of interest, the women being made, boiled up, boiling, venting.

Roni, Pittsbsurgh. The woman who couldn't say "yes, that's enough." Black Canyon's high desert walls ricocheted their giggling, their "yessing." Caroline. Maybe nineteen, maybe Los Angeles? A hiking machine, a soft machine, a room of her own, a mountain moon out her window, full, the lightest of yellows, above the gray cliff face known as Everts.

Yeah, smile you lucky son of a bitch. The Norris geysers blew up around him, from the moon scape, the earth scape all around him.

He smiled his luck, his wonder at this other new park, the boiling mud, the boiling steam boiling in between the pine trees.

The park took him past Gibbon Meadows, golden and green, empty, yet full to its brim--its brim, a rim of lodgepole ridge lines.

Two elk with two new Bambis. If I keep stopping, I'll never get there.

There became the Gibbon River, narrow, pliable, the road like rocks across it, shaped to it, then the river plunging off Gibbon Falls, tall enough to qualify, small enough to make it as a cascade falls.

He rode it to Firehole Canyon Drive, an osprey taking him into the heavy shade from the hard scrabble canyon walls, the Firehole River in shallow rapids, going to the Madison, the Madison to the Missouri, to the Mississippi, to the Gulf. He knew that now. He felt a part of that now.

He knew there'd be chipmunks here, here where the thermal warmed Firehole fell off a picture-perfect lava flow.

Paul fed the fifteen hundred chipmunks, gray ravens and ground squirrels that scampered up the rocks for his pre-packed peanuts.

Only he was there, to hear the sound of the falls.

Light traffic on the winter worn road that took its turns from the swollen, about waist-deep Firehole.

Bronze buffalo calves in the mother, sister, brother, father, of all meadows. A road ran into it--Fountain Flats Drive. It rang a bell. That Mound Geyser Mary told me about is back there? I'll go back there and see about Larry. Not now.

Now I just need to stop and peer at this buffalo herd out on the flats. Mothers, fathers, brothers, sisters, and the cousins of the small bronze ones lying on the ground, their mothers licking them alive.

Now remember Paul, they are bison, North American bison. A fact in all the fantasy, in all the fact.

Now there was bubbling mud and a Calliope geyser; and then a rushing into the Firehole, the river clearer than glass. "Whew!" was the best he could do.

"Holy shit!" was the very best he could do. Look at this. A swooping highway interchange took him off the main road and threw him at the Old Faithful Inn.

If Nordic gods had an Olympus, this would be their lodge, or his thoughts to that effect. Bavaria, homestead, skiing frontier, saw mill, Tolkien, Teutonic.

Paul Barnes was in luck. It went off as he was sliding to a stop. The geyser blew skyward, lifting itself up; up in a thick column of water and steam from a mound of gray coral, just a stone's throw, a car door open in the parking lot from the Inn.

Up it climbed, against the 8,000 feet of blue sky background.

"Old Faithful," he uttered.

114

CHAPTER

Journal entry #1--1ast week of May, 1972.

Of course, the geyser, Old Faithful. Anytime, day or night, always there. Beautiful, then it's boring, then it's magical, then it's normal, then it's a privilege.

Tourists beginning. Turkeys they are. Already interfering with my play time. And what play time. The buses leave for the day and I'm free to play basketball--in the gym here. Go swimming, go hiking.

Yesterday into Sentinel Meadows with Mr. Montana, Jack Cummings. I'll try to write it. A place lost in time. About a twenty-minute hike from the road. Smoking geyser mounds, extinct geyser mounds, sandhill cranes like some kind of condor. Grass so green it would burn Walt Whitman's eyes. Hey, not bad writing.

There were four bull bison out there like they'd never smelled a human.

Swamped with information but I'm diluting it, siphoning it all through the incredible physical power of this place. I'll take the physical fantasy over all the facts.

Ice still floating on Shoshone Lake. Three, four miles into it. Lewis & Clark eat your hearts out. A moose as black as coal, bizarre as some prehistoric camel.

I don't belong to it yet, but I'm settling in. Here in my one room cabin. Cafeteria food is garbage--but who cares?

Ginny coming tonight. Going hot-potting nearby. Beers and laying in a soothing pool far from the madding crowds and the nosey rangers.

Ginny, interesting. Amherst, Massachusetts. Lives near Emily Dickinson. One of the great cast of bus drivers. Who seem to be accepting me. The veterans that is. The seasonal college types, like Ginny, are fine. But the big boys, the truck drivers, the range hands-- from Seattle to Ogden, they're coming around. They have a life here. Good money, a place to live, a place to play.

I'm their boss, their babe in the woods. Boy, I am Tomorrow, yeah, tomorrow I go to this Mound Geyser--where Larry . . .

Man, oh, man. What a trip so far . . .

CHAPTER

10:30 a.m., Mountain Standard Time. Standard morning. By 9:00 the high, wooden lobby of the Old Faithful Inn was full, emptying, full, emptying--breakfast for the French, the Germans, the Japanese, the Sun City retirees, their diesel buses waiting for them, waiting to wait on them.

Paul sat in a broad-shouldered leather chair beneath the feudal, fortress-tower fireplace, relaxed, as usual, checking down the who's, what's, where's and what times of today's schedule. His schedule read Mound Geyser--as soon as.

From a window, from a doorway, from the balcony, from under the knotty pine of the front porch. It, the geyser going off. He stood on the front walkway, under the pine awning, watching it again, focusing out the benches, the buildings, the people, watching it only for its pure white entertainment.

The tour buses blew their diesel and pulled away, full up.

Paul checked with the tour desk, the young ladies answering every question asked of them, from what time is dinner in the rustic-raw dining room alongside them, to what time is the next eruption, to who were the original authors of the Constitution? Paul gave them his time frame and where-abouts, and hit the road.

The road through the high plain plateau was beginning to sprout RV's, Americans. His little green company truck was just that, in behind a few of the RV dreadnoughts.

Florida retiree tactics by the RV skippers. Break whenever, back up whenever, never signal, never-never land. Paul couldn't blame them. Look around: where the earth bubbled up all around them, the lodgepole pines staffed with elk, the geyser basins impossible to pass, whipping an unannounced turn into a steaming turnout.

Paul kept on, repeating the reasons why all this was here.

Who told me this? Let's see; Lewis & Clark didn't come this way.

Neither did Brigham Young. No gold here. No beaver pelts here? No military exploration? Civil War? No one believed the tales the

116

mountain men told of it. I think that's it. The world's first National Park. U.S. Grant, 1872. The Hayden party, first reconnaissance of Yellowstone. What year? Prior to 1872 was his reference point. He stopped the check list at when the U. S. Cavalry ran the park. His turnout--Fountain Flats Drive.

It took him away from the main road, a side road with elk on one side, bison on the other, and the bones of those who didn't make it through the winter, still showing some meat, their skulls flashing their bleached white teeth.

The flat, little Firehole River curved out from the pines and lolled through a meadow. He drove through the pines and met the river at Ojo Caliente spring, one of the 10,000 versions on the thermal theme-- boiling water, boiling steam.

A few yards of iron bridge took him across the river, swift, swiftly running under the bridge.

Good directions from Jack Cummings. The worn out ground on the left, turn out.

The trail was a groove in the ground. Fishing the Firehole.

Not all that far in were his instructions. Just bear to the right along the river. You'll see it.

He pried the big coin out of his Levis. He squeezed it for good fortune.

Grizz. Always. He'd been in-park long enough now. Be wary, always.

The trail was marked with bones, marked with two thermal pools, green and aqua-marine. Animal tracks in the mud, the river as pure as day one of Genesis. A meadow, a coyote prancing across it, two bison having at their feed.

Listen for the water cascading, were part of his instructions.

He heard it. That's all he could hear.

He went left to the sound, and it boiled up at his feet. A geyser, a thermal pool, about the size of two hot tubs. A hole in the gray, brain coral rock was bubbling like water in a saucepan.

Big bubbles of it. Boiling hot from the earth's guts.

What a fuckin' scene, he fuckined to no one but himself.

Nothing but flat, open ground across, way across the river to a few geysers playing like a calliope. A pure white cascade, about the height of a kitchen table fell at his feet.

The Mound Geyser bubbled up, rising up, up a few feet, pouring itself down a channel of rainbow algae, emptying into a deep pool of the river. A high mound of a dripping, oozing thermal feature across the river dripped rainbow blood. An ant-hill-like vent blew a jet of hot water and steam, down stream, almost in the river. A trout rose from the pool, fishing for flies.

Larry's last day, last place.

Paul cried. He kept it from weeping, realizing he'd come to a place that was Larry's, his--his and mine now.

He sat down and let the cascade serenade him. A hallowed place.

He kept himself from saying anything silly. He knows.

He laid his head on the warm earth and dozed off. Maybe they should have left his bones here. Finding him must have been sad.

But no violence, no ache, no crying out. Fine. He fell asleep.

CHAPTER

The geyser smelled like sulphur, but he could smell salt water, ocean salt, a long stretch of white sand, Larry standing there, staring out to sea.

I've found my home, Larry. Home. His dream gave Terri back home a thought. I wonder how .

He started to wake up. Two women's voices. All back home was forgotten as soon as he turned to look.

Like the most beautiful tomboy he'd ever seen. He couldn't take his eyes off her. He didn't want to take his eyes off her.

The two of them stood up behind the geyser. He was just below them, sitting up now. Nobody noticed him.

She had hair the color of cornstalks in the fall, rubbed with the chestnuts of the fall. It fell straight, straight below her ears, held back in place by a light green barrette, like a fence for it above her brow. A tan of milk chocolate. Khaki shorts, light hiking boots, serious gray socks, legs made for a man, a woman, tall, not slender, not heavy, not fat, not hard, not soft; enough of each, enough of her in her white T-shirt to remind you about women.

Her face. Thick brown eyelashes, heavy lips and a healthy nose, smooth cheeks, smooth, Mediterranean eyes. Strong, smooth, female.

"I found my wife, Larry," he joked in a whisper.

She laughed out loud at what her companion had just said. Her companion was just another woman.

He said, "howdy."

"Oh, company," she said, not quite surprised.

Paul could see the simple gold earring pierced in each ear.

He could see her immaculate teeth. I love you. I want to feel those soft mounds, that rear end, that womanly outline behind your zipper. I want to be with you, always, here in Yellowstone.

I'm in love with you. "Uh, beautiful spot, isn't it?" throwing out a line, holding on to it.

"One of the best," she said, holding his look, measuring him, smiling at him, sending something to him.

She likes me, I can see that. She'll come to love me. I hope that.

"Are you visitors, employees?" he asked.

"Employees," her short, curly haired companion answered.

"I'm not interfering with your privacy am I?"

"Certainly not," the most beautiful tomboy answered. "We're not on your toes, are we?"

"No." Should I tell her? Of course. I'm in love with her.

"A good friend of mine passed away here."

"Here?"

"Yes. I came out to, well, hang around him."

"Oh, I'm sorry," husky and soft together in her voice. "Heart attack or something? How old was your friend?"

"No, no, it's not a sad story at all."

"Oh? Why don't we sit by the river?" Why doesn't your friend make herself scarce? "Sure. I've seen quite a bit of the park already, but this spot. Something ... "

They sat on the alkali ground, the white cascade at their feet, Paul, the woman, the friend.

"What's your work here?" she asked, no noticeable national accent in her fine, fresh voice.

"I'm the bus dispatcher at Old Faithful."

"Oh, by the way, I'm Rachel, Rachel Cramer."

"Hi. I'm Paul Barnes."

"I'm Cindy." Who cares? "Hiya."

"Well, the big boss," and Rachel laughed.

"Yeah. You can see what a tyrant I am. What about you?" interest pouring out of his question. Tell me everything, everything.

"I work at the raft trip company in Gardiner." Great. I love you twice as much.

"Tell me about your friend." She got comfortable on the ground.

CHAPTER

"He sounds like someone I'd like to have known. I must have missed him between seasons."

"Funny. I feel that everyone does know him."

"Hmmm."

It was big, talking with her. He was careful.

"How are things in the rafting business?"

"Right now not so good."

"Oh."

"That religious gang out on the Yellowstone." Paul sat up straight. "What?" Venom.

"They dumped a truck full of fertilizer off the road into the river. The truck's still there, and we're waiting for the chemicals to wash themselves out.

"A major pain now that the season is starting. Major pain that they are."

He squeezed out a response. "Damn them." This is my place now. This is going to be my woman. "I've been here a few weeks and I've had enough of them already."

"Get used to them. They're planted out there, with enough lawyers to keep the state of Montana and the Federales at bay."

"Maybe not, maybe not," more a statement than a hope.

Rachel's girlfriend had wandered away up river. To dwell on the church of the absurd was not to dwell on a day, a setting, a woman, that were all changing, fixing his world.

"You live in Gardiner," he asked her.

"Out of town a bit, in a small trailer above the river. Come for a visit sometime."

"I'd like to."

"You're from back east?" lying flat on her back, soaking in the sun, a woman at her leisure. Paul made love to her.

"Where are you from?"

"Here and there. Seattle mostly. Service brat."

"How did you wind up here?"

"Oh, some guy."

Paul's fixed world collapsed. "He with the raft company too?"

"No, he's in Europe with someone." That "someone" sounded like another woman to him. His world got re-organized.

Her friend wandered back, irritation showing, telling. "Want to start down to the lake?"

"Sure," Rachel answered, considerate. She stood up and brushed herself off. She towered over him.

"It was good meeting you, Paul. Call me? My number is available on info."

"I will," leaving out "I will, I will, I will."

"Yellowstone Raft Company, in Gardiner."

"It was a pleasure meeting you. I'll look forward to seeing you again," standing up.

"Me, too. I was glad to hear about your friend. He found a wonderful spot to leave from."

"Thanks. Have a good trip down to the lake."

"We will. You'll have to come to Lake Butte for a sunset sometime."

"Anytime."

"Bye."

"Bye." I love you.

Mound Geyser went off in celebration.

CHAPTER

Dear diary. He got a kick out of that, this journal entry.

Another week gone by. I met her, I spoke with her on the phone. She's almost 60 miles from here. I'll see her soon. Soon, soon, soon. Rachel. He wrote it again. Rachel.

I could spend a lifetime here and not touch it all. A long day hike into the Bechler region--to the edge of it. Water, water, everywhere. Cascades and streams and tributaries and waterfalls.

Southwest section. Wild, with few visitors this early in the high water, the moist marsh water. Can feel the hair on my neck standing up. Grizzly bears. Maybe not, maybe never, but ...

A quick run up to Craig Pass. Just before the top, a miniature lake beside the road, under the road, large, round lily pads that will show a large yellow bloom--so I'm told. I believe everything I'm being told. On a clear day up here you can see the tops of the Tetons. I'm on top of the world. I've got a tour guide, the best. Jack Cummings--Mr. Montana I call him. Yes, he can spin yarns. With a little extra sauce I think. I'm his sidekick.

Rachel, Rachel.

All is smooth. I think I really work for the bus drivers.

Fine with me. Gives me more time to shoot hoops.

Old Faithful geyser is like a good neighbor now. Glad to have it next door. Sort of oblivious to it now.

Sitting on my stoop, having a few beers. What to do tonight? Someone suggests we drive out to see the new bison calves. Just your average Thursday evening.

Rachel, Rachel. Got to stop that. So many ladies here. And she's far away. Damn. She's right here in my face. He didn't write what he was seeing, feeling, tasting.

Rachel. He closed the journal.

"Hey, Paul!" someone yelled. "Let's get a beer at the Bear Pit."

"Sure." He was.

CHAPTER

White chemical fertilizer--round, white clumps of it on the Yellowstone. A flash like a lightning bolt. A stampede of red-eyed bison. A coyote tearing at a carcass. The sound of thunder, like an explosion.

The thunder scared him awake, snap, upright, sweat on the bed sheet. Early morning, frost on the early June windows.

The phone rang, shortening his, "god damn, what was all that? One minute I'm with Rachel, and the next I'm in Dante's inferno." The phone rang.

"Yes, what?"

"Is this Paul Barnes?" It sounded very official. "Yes?"

"This is Donna Hearns, from park headquarters."

Uh-oh. What have they caught me at? "Yes, hello."

"I'm calling about your application for a ranger position." He sat straight up, having had enough jobs to know what it meant when they called and said that.

"Yes?"

"Well, we've reviewed it, and we'd like to offer you a position."

"You bet," holding on to the edge of the bed.

"One thing," from the voice on the phone.

One thing nothin'.

"We'd want you to start next week."

"Next week's fine, fine."

"Good news, huh?"

"You could say that."

"Well then. Come up to Mammoth on the fifteenth and report to the Mammoth district office. You'll have to do at least forty hours of training. Your military police time seems to fill in most of the training needs."

"Ha. I knew that junk would payoff someday."

"No you didn't."

"Ha. You're right."

"I see you work for the concessionaire."

"I do."

"Any problem leaving them?"

"No."

"Good. We'll see you then. Congratulations."

"Thanks, thanks."

If he'd owned pistols, he would have fired them in the air, or ridden his horse down main street, or had a shot of whiskey, or kissed a pretty girl.

Instead, he held his coin. He held it against his forehead.

"Yes, yes."

"Hey, Jack! I'm a ranger!" he yelled across to the other cabin.

Jack was doing his best Gary Cooper, sipping his coffee from a tin cup, saying good morning and good bye to a young lady.

"Well, ranger. The boss here's going to be a ranger," giving the red head with the German accent a kiss on the cheek.

"Hey, well, where'd the ranger business come from?" extending his hand, wanting about as much to do with official uniform business as a range-hand riding fence.

"As soon as I arrived, I did an application," warm from the words.

"Where?" tossing out the bottom of the coffee.

"Mammoth?"

"Well, so much for the bus life."

"Yeah," pride in the smile.

"I'll buy ya a beer in Gardiner some night."

"Great."

"Wanna walk over and get some breakfast?"

"Nah. Want to walk around a bit, enjoy it."

The bit he walked was out to the geyser. Frost on the ground.

Frost, close to snow and ice. The tourists were still at breakfast. Old Faithful was just steam, but down the wooden walkway, down in the valley of the geysers, Castle geyser, like a crusader parapet, and Bee Hive geyser, like its name, were exploding, firing into the frosty air.

He walked. He took a deep breath of it all. A golden marmot chased its mate under the boardwalk. An elk dripped Firehole river water from its soft mouth. A bison made a fur boulder in a warm green spot among four firing thermals.

Good news here was even better, nearly perfect.

Paul felt that--nearly perfect.

CHAPTER

A slice of a moon came up. In its half-blue light, Mammoth Hot Springs, the boiling, seeping terrace mound of it was a piece of lunar landscape.

The lights from the squat wooden hotel, and the stacked stone government buildings on the mown lawns below were a peaceful settlement.

Paul was up on top of the terrace, scanning all that he now possessed. All the government forms were filled out. All his measurements were off to Colorado for his uniforms. A day of one hundred introductions, evaluations and instructions was done.

I've got it wired he assured himself. I've won the lottery.

Tonight I can enjoy Rachel. Easy, bub. You can enjoy meeting her, dinner with her, in her place. What a place this is, checking his watch. Time.

Wait a minute, wait here a minute. Out there, out there in the distance, shadow shapes of forests and hillsides--another park, another Yellowstone. He noticed.

I haven't been out there. Douglas fir, Alpine, high places, valleys, separate. Tower and Lamar. Good. I'll go there soon.

A woman. What valleys, what high places? His headlights found elk, campground fires, steam, rivers, the light of Gardiner. It was good to be back home. I've been gone a long time. He laughed at his veteran of a few weeks.

He crossed the Yellowstone and followed the only road, past the minor league rodeo grounds, past the log Forest Service office, past four lazy dogs, and out of town into the absolute silence.

The sound of gravel under the tires. Down off the road to a single wide, half trailer, half bunkhouse, half metal, half wood, all the way to a twenty foot drop to the river, the trailer above the Yellowstone, riveted, chained, nailed, weathered in place, a small empty corral empty in the moonlight.

You could tell out here, in the mountains--the way other people have lawns and shrubs and lawn mowers. Kayaks or canoes, skis, snow machines, horses or snow shoes. Leaning against something, standing in a quarter of an acre, hanging from a shed.

Rachel had a kayak, a covered snow machine, a yellow, four wheel drive Subaru station wagon.

Her lights were on, the only ones for a few hundred yards.

Smoke from a metal chimney stack. Paul knocked on the metal door.

"Well, howdy, ranger," with an emphasis on the "howdy."

Red was his blush. "So, you know," shy against her, against her being back lit by the wood burning in the tiny fire place.

"Of course, come in, come in. Everybody knows. War drums, smoke signals around here, Paul. News goes quickly. Everybody has their ear to the park service."

She took him into a compact living room, warm, soft, brown, crowded, comfortable. A frayed, third-hand Navajo rug on the floor. A short, brown leather couch, a frontier rocking chair, a wicker chair, a coffee table like a slab from a saloon's bar, and the walls covered in elk and big horn sheep and lakes.

The place invited you to hunker down. He hunkered down on the couch. Rachel went to the phone booth kitchen.

"Mannn," so she couldn't hear it. She wore a white muslin dress with bare neck and bare arms. This wasn't bare weather. The bare was covered a bit by a washed out, red long john shirt, gone almost to pink, the three front buttons open, her neck, her shoulder blade showing. Moccasins and gray wool socks, turquoise on her wrist, on her ears.

"Mannn … " He could hear the river below. Wonders never ceased around here.

"Nice place, Rachel."

"It is. Take a look at the bedroom. Great view from there."

I bet there is. "O.K." First, a narrow storage area. Her own REI outlet. The bedroom was all bed, tall enough to stand up in, a shallow closet, a night stand of raw wood, a window about the size of the whole wall. Lay in the bed with a quilt of pastures and grasslands and you'd have Electric Peak, a shining river, and the earth of Montana for a night light.

"Not a bad view," he shouted back to her.

"Right! I saw it, rented it. Food's ready!"

"What's on the menu?" taking a yard sale seat at a yard sale table. "Steak and salad. Like rice in the rest of the world."

"Well, thanks a lot. A treat."

"Have to stay in good with the rangers." He blushed.

"Really, Paul. It's good for you. Have an idea where you'll be?" sitting with the rest of the meal. "Oh, want a beer?"

"Sure."

"So, here's to your quick promotion." She raised her beer bottle.

"Hear, hear," he saluted. "I think I'll be here at Mammoth for a bit, then Tower they say."

"Good out there, Paul. Away. Far enough. Close enough to back here."

"So I hear."

They heard it together, stopping the meal for a moment. Deep, slow, from a distance. A siren.

"What's that?" Paul asked.

"Them."

He knew. "Out there. The cult heads?"

"Yes. I've learned about it from here. She's here. Elizabeth, the Prophet. Comes in from California. A call to prayers."

He almost shuddered at the thought. The thought of it out there from where he sat.

Rachel shrugged. "The neighborhood's falling apart. How's the food?"

"Free, fixed by someone else. Great."

They laughed at that. The siren moaned to an end.

"Want another beer?"

"You bet. How'd you like living in Bozeman?"

"Fine. Plenty of winter. Plenty of quiet. Plenty to do. My first Montana winter."

"You came from where, Seattle?"

"Yes," at the refrigerator. "Spent a few years around the country with my pal Charley. Then a stop in Seattle. We both worked for a sports equipment company. Then to Yellowstone, then to Bozeman to work at Bridger Bowl, a ski slope. Then I got dropped on my head by my pal Charley," quickly, indifferently, slowly, cruelly.

Does this guy still exist? How, where, when, what if?

Rachel came back and sat down. No what if's about it. He's not here, I am, Paul thought.

"Do you handle a raft on the float trips?"

"Not yet. I handle some of the business end. Reservations, office business, hauling the rafts to the river, hauling the tourists. The float guide will come. Not exactly the wild Colorado out there."

Out there was eternal silence. Geez, I'd love to stay with her tonight. His beer had two sips left.

"I'll come visit you at Tower," she said.

He forgot about tonight, and saw the future.

"You work tomorrow?"

"Yes. Business begins to begin. Mr. & Mrs. American are on their way."

"God bless 'em. Here's to the visiting public. Long may they give us jobs."

"Love 'em, hate 'em." She hoisted her coffee cup.

Quiet. Continue, end the evening, relax, love, quiet.

"And you come to us by way of New York?" she asked, relaxed.

"Uh-huh."

"Sounds like it," with a laugh.

"As they would say in New York, no shit."

That laugh left the night half full.

"What time is it?" He made the make-believe motions of looking for a clock, not so relaxed.

"Uh, almost one."

"Well, I'll leave you to it. Thanks for dinner. I owe you one, once I'm living in something more than a sardine can."

"Got you in the quonset squats behind the bus garage?"

"Yep."

"Roommate?"

"Nope."

"Something, anyway."

"Anyway." He got up. "Thanks, Rachel. It's a pleasure spending time with you."

"Me, too, Paul. Glad we could do it."

"I'll talk to you later," at the door.

"Please."

It went smooth. He went forward to where her skin, her smell, her flesh, were very near. Nearer, with a hand on her waist. She stood up taller and stepped into him. Her cheek, her neck, her lips, her arm over his shoulder.

The lights went out in Georgia, in Montana. All the lights in the world, like the world turning down its oil lamps, saying good night, go to bed, content with life, content with events, with a kiss.

"Good night."

"Good night."

The cold air rushed into the hollow man.

"Ahhh!" He sucked it in. He savored it, flavored it, fondled it, felt it, ate it, pulsed it, licked it, kissed it.

He thought he heard a gun shot. You could have heard one from another state. He heard a crack, an echo, and no more.

"Cowboys." I wonder where that cowboy of her's is? Far, far away, Paul. Gone.

His was the only movement on the road.

It was the talk of the pistol range, the pistol range a few miles down the Yellowstone.

Drive out under the stone stack of the Teddy Roosevelt Arch, then down the hard-tack of Stephens Creek Road, eventually to Stephens Creek ranch--where this part of the park kept its horses and its gear: light green bear traps, like miniature submarines, snow machines, horse trailers, hay bails, rail fences, parked and stacked around the stately, solitary ranch house.

Fifty yards square of brush and elk thistle had been scraped away. A few cardboard cut-outs to shoot at. Semi-professional.

Eight rookie rangers and two veterans, five higher-ups.

"Somebody shootin' down at hell's half acre last night." Dave Hess. Could roll his own by the time he was three. Droppin' snuff since four. Chief district ranger. Park ranger from the earth's first parks. Raw as a tire tread, gray as a ship's captain, a smokey bear hat bleached almost white, bent enough to make Gabby Hayes proud; green khaki trousers, long sleeve uniform shirt, with a black turtle neck, scuffed brown Wellingtons, a pistol hung on his belt, Billy Bonnie style.

Paul was impressed. Not by the pistol range, or the short tour of how to use your weapon. I'm not going to use a gun in here--couldn't be. Carry it on you, or in the briefcase. Will do- briefcase.

Dave Hess got his attention. The boss of course, but also a livin', breathin' American hero. He held center circle, the other higher-ups rather tame, rather officious, rather dark hair and trim features up next to the dust cloud of Dave Hess.

"The crazies were chasin' somebody off." Everyone paid attention to him. Most everyone laughed in agreement.

Standing around, coffee from a kitchen urn in the back of a pickup. Time to talk before the drills. Clouds filled the sky, rushed out, rushed back in.

"I understand they're well along on their fall-out shelters." Michael Lander, chief law enforcement ranger. Short and fidgety, serious, neat black moustache. He shook his head in disgust.

"One of their doctrines?" senior seasonal ranger Ken Hiller.

Thin and sad-eyed, pale for all the out in it. "They will emerge after the holocaust, the nuclear war."

Dave Hess spit on the ground. No major leaguer could compete.

"Whatever. They did some shootin' out there."

"Heard somebody might be trying to poach on elk inside their property."

"How'd an elk get beyond their fence?"

"That fence keeps 'em cut off pretty good." Around the rangers went.

"Used to be they wasn't out there." Dave Hess had spoken. He tossed his coffee and gave the circle to Hayes Nelson, a linebacker, a headquarters ranger; a weapons instructor. Paul listened up. Period.

Paul wore brand new. Dave Hess's uniform the day it was born.

Paul, a rookie among these park service veterans of Alaska, Virginia battlefields, Texas hill country, Laramie, Wyoming.

"Why would anyone want to poach an elk?" came out of Paul's mouth.

"Cuz they cut its head off and eat its meat." exclamation point, stream of tobacco spit, Dave Hess.

"Let's get goin'."

Goin' was running back and forth, forwards and back, making believe you had some real interest in this annoying, basic training.

Two shotgun blasts for each of them and they were hot, tired, dusty, qualified, complete.

"Pick up them cartridge shells and that's done. Yaa'll did good enough," and his high mountain eminence, Dave Hess, mounted a horse and rode away.

Paul was impressed.

CHAPTER

He was nervous as hell. He was comfortable as hell, checking himself out in the door length mirror. He gave the brim of his stiff new smokey hat a stiff snap with his finger, Fred Astaire style.

Class A's. The jacket, with the national patch on the shoulder, everything straight out of the box. Straight out of some make believe. "I'm a ranger in Yellowstone National Park," he told the mirror. He beamed, he shook his head in beautiful disbelief.

Nervous because he was off for a day with Rachel.

"Hi, Rachel."

"Paul? Hi."

"Bothering you?"

"No. Just sent a load of Floridians down river. What's up?"

"Well, it seems I'm required to take a tour of the park. See what the other ranger stations are like. Have to go to Canyon and Lake. Uh, want to join me?"

"When?"

"Today?" Please, please, please.

"What time?"

It's yes, yes, yes. "Around one?"

"I think that will work."

"Great."

"How about if I meet you at the K Bar?"

"Fine."

"See you then."

"Great."

He replayed the phone call as he undid his class A's. Green tie, long gray sleeves, polished boots, pure black belt, creased trousers, the hat.

I need a drink. One hour and a half to Rachel. Watch your top knot, Paul. Huh? Wonder where that came from? He got into the classic denim shirt and jeans.

He took the long way to the bar, the long way being one block of Front St., Front St. like one block of a studio front for a frontier town.

Next to the drugstore, an empty store front, busy inside with the bare basics: a cash register, a counter top, an advertisement on the wall, a Colorado river trip on another wall.

A handsome woman was at the cash register, a brand new ranger taking a peek at her as he rolled by the two big gray rubber rafts parked on trailers in the street.

He parked between an old school bus, with a new life as a shake shingle Hatfield homestead on wheels, complete with a crooked black chimney, and a mud splattered pickup, complete with the requisite lazy black dog flat in the flatbed.

Dogs and children welcome in the K Bar. Paul welcomed himself with an Olympia and took a seat at the bar.

A pat on the back from a resident bus driver, hello from a happy co-ed, congratulations from a park maintenance worker, an overall scan of the establishment. A supposed poacher down at the end of the bar, ratty ball cap, ratty beard, a bandaged hand, downing a beer.

Paul noticed. He's dog meat, and yet. And yet, Paul? Where'd that come from? Somebody out there being shot at by the cult heads? Is that where it comes from? Some demented respect? Some grudging admiration? Maybe he was shooting back? What's that bandage? What are you thinking about? Poaching an elk? They ran into each other's scan. An instant, a notice, a taking note, a hand on Paul's shoulder--a warm hand. A "howdy, ranger," from a soft voice. He tried not to spin the barstool into the floor.

"Hiya, Rachel. Good to see ya." He wanted to kiss her hand, a hand holding a bright postcard.

"Writing postcards?"

"No, getting one." She showed it like it was a bug she'd caught. "From Europe, Paris," with a frown, a face, a shoving of it in her back pocket. "Stopped at the post office on the way over."

"Paris?"

"Not much compared with our day today."

"Madam tour guide?"

"Sure. Show the rookie the ropes."

"Want a drink?"

"Not right now. Let's get a six pack and go? Lunch on the road at Canyon perhaps?"

"Perhaps is good."

"Hiya, Rachel." One of the rafters. A skier, a rock climber, a kayaker, a thirty inch waist, a shock of blond hair, a face. Get lost, Paul thought, almost out loud.

"Hi, Terry." Goodbye Terry. "Shall we?"

"We shall."

"One minute." A mental note of him, down at the end of the bar.

"What is it?" Rachel asked.

"Business." One minute. "Enough. Pleasure?"

"Pleasure."

CHAPTER

Across a high bridge, above a narrow curve in the Gardner River far below, Mammoth Hot Springs in the back window, another slab of the two and a half million acres about to be revealed.

"Let's stop at Undine Falls first? Just up ahead."

"Sure." Sure, anything for you Rachel. Anything for you with the yellow bandana around your neck, the green turtle neck, the Navajo brooch, the tan down vest on your lap, those legs in those khaki trousers, those toes in those serious running shoes.

"I'll show you a good view of Mammoth, too."

Up through the rocks and trees, boulders and Ponderosa pines, Aspens, watch for falling rocks, forgetting the lodgepole pine, finally.

Paul turned off to the left and parked with two other cars.

"Madam tour guide?" he offered.

"Follow me," and she patted his hand. Blood, the boiling hot spring of it. He took a deeper breath and followed her.

A double falls, tall, well below towering, tame, trim between the trees, enough sound from its falling water. Paul wanted to play Niagara Falls with Rachel.

She took in a big whiff of it. "Ahhh. No cash register, no tourists, no nothing but everything."

"Beautiful word, Undine."

"Mythological."

Like you, woman. They heard children coming.

"This way, ranger."

He followed the bare outline of her underwear against her slacks.

Steep piece of ground. She hoisted him up and they got themselves up higher above the road, higher above the tops of the pines. "Look," Rachel proclaimed.

Look was real good. Back from where they'd come. A distant mound, steaming, yellow and tan, banana and brown, protruding from the hillside, unlike all else around it. A thermal feature, featured.

"Well named, Mammoth," he said from leaning against a rock.

Like I hope I can be if we ever make love.

"Unique view of it. Always, Paul. Imagine the first white eyes?"

"Being here, I don't have to imagine it."

"One spot can hold you all day."

"Always," he answered.

She turned to him and smiled, deeply. "Yes." He could hear an acceptance, a pleasantness, a delightfulness, an indirect sense of himself in that.

"Much more out there, Paul."

"Take me to it, Rachel. Take me to it."

"I will," kissing him on the cheek.

He blushed for two miles, making himself notice the deep shade, the perfect shape of the picnic spot camped next to Lava Creek, a bull elk scrapping at the velvet on its early antlers, four brown bison, the unopposed view across the verdant meadows, the shallow ponds, the ridgelines, the mountain climbs that marked each distance.

"Like it?" Rachel asked.

"Love it," without turning to face her.

CHAPTER

"Stop here," she told him.

Here was a turnout with enough elevation to put them well above the rolling grass meadows. High enough where you could take in a wrap around of mountains in Montana, mountains within the park, rugged, empty mountains, within reach, miles and miles away.

"Christ."

"Right."

Their's were the only voices. Rachel handed him a beer.

"Let's build a house and live here."

"I'll drink to that," was her answer.

Paul coughed, coughed. "Still getting used to the altitude."

"And the clean air?"

"A bit I think. That pure oxygen."

The pure oxygen scattered her hair. He held his breath.

"Thanks," and he stepped to her. A kiss on her cheek.

"Uhmm. You're welcome. But you ain't seen nothin' yet."

"Oh, I don't know," looking her in the eye as much as he could from glancing away. She closed her eyes in meek recognition and took a sip of beer.

What needed to happen had. "Let's go?"

"Let's."

Beer cans between their legs, rain-made lakes beside the road, a black moose dipping her snout into the rain-made reeds, a flock of coots flocking across the crystal water, quaking Aspens, black shade from the Douglas firs, walled in by rising walls of vegetable and mineral, always an animal.

"Another turnout up ahead, Paul. Slow down a bit."

"How come you know so much?"

She tilted her head, little-girl like. "I'm a woman of the world," batting her untouched eyelashes.

A roadside line of lodgepole pines. "Here, in here." The pines opened up. All this world did. He was a boy again, up in one of those New England tourist towers to see three states.

This wasn't any state. This was nature, as pure as he'd ever seen it. A road was right behind them, but this.

As the eagle flies, all of it went out to the edge of it all.

Raw rock, soft grass, narrow gorge, high rolling hills, jagged, wild, white mountains an eagle's flight away to the northeast. A blue bird, more turquoise than blue, joined them on a tree branch.

"A mountain bluebird," Rachel told him.

Paul followed it away, crouching down, taking it all in, taking it out of his back pocket.

"That your worry stone?" she asked.

He held the coin to show her.

"My," and she crouched next to him--like they were together with something newly unearthed, some secret, something uncovered.

"Paul. This is something ancient. What is it?"

"It was Larry's. I wish he was here, with us." Us sounded mighty good to him.

"I think he is, Paul." She stroked his hair. "From this I can feel it. He belongs to many times?"

They knew this was a good moment. Still crouching, they met and split their lips, wet, something newly discovered.

"Now I'm glad he isn't here."

"A voyeur?"

"Ha."

"Let's voyeur some more park?"

"I could kiss you."

Their laughter sounded great.

CHAPTER

Quiet here at the road junction, Tower junction. A road led away to the left.

"Lamar Valley out there, Paul," from the front seat.

He got out and stood under the fort-like flag pole, Old Glory flying over the corrals, the log house, the bunk house, the trailer, the creek, the kiosk office, the Tower ranger station.

He walked across the main road and stared, gazed out between, beyond the cut in the flat hills, beyond the six bison.

"See something?" coming up next to him.

"Huh?" not turning away.

"What's out there?"

"I don't know, something." His "something" didn't mean elk or bear or coyote. Rachel heard that.

"We'll go out there on the way back?"

"I think so." He turned to her. "Will we have the time?"

"We'll make time." A sigh. "Nice here isn't it?"

He turned to look. "It is. Just enough civilization. Minus that gas station of course. I met the lead ranger here at the pistol range. Nice fella. One place I won't have to pay my respects."

"Want to pay some respects to Roosevelt Lodge?"

"Sure," but he stayed put, scraping the roadside gravel with the toe of his shoe, returning to the unseen Lamar Valley. Rachel could see the pinch in his brow.

"Ready?" she asked.

"Ready," with a short, deep breath.

A short trip to Roosevelt Lodge, under the ranch brand, fence post entrance, up the gravel road through the rough and ready wooden cabins, past the fly-fishing main lodge, the tethered horses, the stage coaches, the chuck wagons, the early settlement of it.

"Not exactly Old Faithful Inn," Rachel said, the car starting to climb up from the junction to Tower Falls.

"Just right," he answered. "Food, clothing and shelter, and Yellowstone."

CHAPTER

"Here's how it got its name. Yellowstone," Rachel announced.

Yellow stone like no formation of stone he'd ever seen. A fence post of a canyon wall of it, sliced away in some seismic rearrangement, sliced in wedged sections like fence posts.

Couldn't stop, too narrow, a cliff dwelling swell of a hard scrapple, soft yellow canyon wall to the right, the deep cut down to the Yellowstone river on the left.

"We can pull out up ahead," she told him. "Tourist-ville."

"Tower Fall?"

"Good guess."

"It sticks out on the map."

They crossed some big running water beneath them, around them. A suddenly large parking lot took them in. Gifts suddenly appeared. Film, toilets, T-shirts, tourists international.

"Want to hike a bit, down the blacktop?"

"Sure, sure. Tower Fall?"

"Tower Fall."

They could hear it over the small crowd, the Japanese, the German, the Dutch, the "hey, honey, don't forget the camera!" There wasn't a crowd allowed beyond the log rail fence. Here was where a canyon began, where the woods grew down to the intermittent thermal steam, down to the shallow rushing Yellowstone.

"Tower Fall. Dignified," Paul said of the tall, narrow, precise turret, running full, falling in a tight cascade.

"It's just like Disneyland," Rachel joked.

"Say again?"

"A tourist buzz word, buzz phrase. Unfortunately the plastic is the reality, the reality the imitation."

"I see. How unusual for the tourist set."

"Yes. Pump an ecosystem dry, build an amusement park. Reality."

They both shut up from that and watched a two-foot-tall raven swoop down onto the rail fence. A beggars banquet.

"Seen enough?" Rachel asked.

"It keeps its dignity."

"Yes."

Backing out of the parking space you had to watch out--people on vacation, self-immunized to the paying attention of their real lives out there where the dignified falls didn't.

Rachel and Paul on their way again.

Herds of mustangs, ponies, cloud shapes, grazed in the sky as they began to climb.

Climbing, just below the sharp curve to begin Dunraven Pass over Mt. Washburn. High up, about 8,900 ft. up, with a rolling, rising, unending view of a northwest American green Yellowstone.

A green no house had ever sat on. Brown forests where no roads ever brought trucks. A lush land unto itself, unto Rachel and Paul leaning against the hood of the car, Rachel sort of leaning against him so he'd know it. He knew it.

He did like a child. He laid his head against her shoulder.

"It's not like Disneyland, Finland, Greenland, New England, or any land," with a sighing.

"It's got you, Paul," kissing the top of his head. He felt it in the bottoms of his feet.

"It and other things," he said to her softly.

She knew. She didn't answer.

The wind came up and reminded them of the elevation, the tastes of winter always on the wind.

"It's all so lush," Paul said.

"You'll see real lush in a bit."

"Oh?"

She turned full to him and leaned herself up against him.

"Will it be better than this?" he laughed.

"You decide," kissing his neck.

I've decided, I've decided.

She drove and they curved up, a road hanging from a mountain, the mountain in June spring--wild flowers.

"Wild flowers," Rachel announced.

"Wild flowers," Paul responded. "Holy shit!" was the rest of his response.

Blankets, carpets, shawls, veils, acres of them, pallets of them, pink and blue, yellow and red, tall and short, in among the trees, all over the open ground and grass.

"Not your average garden, Paul."

"I'll say. Can we pull out?"

Her answer would have to wait. A double-wide house on wheels blocked the view ahead. The flowers grew on either side of them.

"There, there," Paul pleaded. "Enough room?" Up against a scarred log guard rail.

"Enough, enough," tilting the car into a slight dip with a slight drop of only a few hundred feet into the pine forest.

"Go ahead," Rachel told him. "I'll man the flashers. Run across."

"You bet." He slammed the door, checked for oncoming traffic, got a brake-burning tour bus, waited, got across, jumped a shadow cooled mound of snow, jumped body first into a field of them, ankle deep in mountain spring, on his back in the rainbow camouflage.

He sat up, childish. "Come on, come on!"

"The car!" she yelled back across.

"The hell with the car!"

Flashers on, she sprinted across. Childish. She landed right on top of him, bodies in the bouquet.

If the earth moved it did to embrace them. He embraced her.

Her leg found a place between his. They both felt those full warm places. They both felt full warm tongues and lips.

"Help me, help me, I'm living," he whispered to her.

"Help you out of your jeans you mean."

"Uh, uh-huh. Uh, yes, yes, a million times yes."

She helped him with her lips, her leg.

"A thousand times not the best spot for this," at his ear.

"Got ya?" sitting up slowly, her leg, her meat still on his thigh.

"Well, well, ranger," smoothing back her cropped hair.

A family in a station wagon stopped just below them, all the heads inside curious at why a car was stopped here.

"That's our cue, Rachel."

"Got ya. Come on." She pulled him up. He needed her help.

He needed a beer. He got one from the back seat. It went down like the first one of a hot summer day.

There were patches of snow, Dunraven Pass, the summit, always flirting, mating with winter.

"God," that tastes good," side by side with Rachel, beside a wind-gnarled pine, a vista across the silent plateau. A canyon's upper walls somehow dropped away from the nordic forest.

"Makes me hungry," she said of her beer.

"Me too," and he left the male remarks unsaid.

"We can get a bite down at Canyon Village. Howard Johnson's."

"Howard Johnson's?"

"You'll see."

"Let's see this for a bit more."

"No rush, no rush."

A coyote hunted a rodent on the hillside. A hawk had the same idea, low in the gray blue sky.

"There's a fire lookout up there, Paul. Up on Washburn. A house of a sort. Good duty if you can get it."

"Yeah? Not a bad view."

"No, not bad."

They thought they saw a moose among the trees.

"There, there!"

"Where, where?"

"There, in there."

"I can't tell, I can't tell."

"It was there. I think!"

"Let's eat."

"Let's eat."

"What time is it?" he asked her, the car bracketed, narrow between the lodgepole pines.

"Three?"

Only three? Seems like we've been gone forever. He looked over at the other part of we. Intent on the road, a woman, soft of skin, sensuous of face, equal up on her pedestal.

She spoke. "Canyon Junction." A four-way stop out in the clearing. Paul began to remember.

"I've been here. When I first came in."

Rachel waited at the stop sign for six motorcycles, gleaming like new kitchens, new plumbing, matching mini-trailers behind, radios in their helmets, retirement checks in mom and pop's matching pockets.

"So, you've seen this?"

"Only in the dark."

Left turn into Canyon Village.

"Going to visit the ranger here?"

"Yep."

"O.K. You do your respects and I'll get some sandwiches? Then the canyon." She emphasized "the."

"You bet. You were right." He surveyed the settlement in the trees. It only took one scan of the snap-'em-together, throw-'em up ticky-tack to get the Howard Johnson's effect.

"Let's get out of here quick."

"We will. Meet you back here?"

"Right."

The ranger station was a make-believe chalet.

"Just like Disneyland," they said laughing.

"Soo, how was it?" Rachel asked.

"O.K. You know. I'm the rookie on the block. Half-hearted interest in me. But good, faces with names. Interesting to hear the radio traffic. Anyway, so much for business."

"We'll eat by the canyon wall?"

"We'll eat by the canyon wall."

Like a pale-face European coming out of the woods, out from Europe and into a clearing where this new continent stood full in his face. Something enormous as they curved into a parking lot up near the clouds. Something shining yellow and silver white, golden. Something plummeting, something sheer; the edge of it, the colossal hint of it.

A log railing, a foot path to a captain's turret rock, yellow and silver.

It opened up, plunged down, stretched out. A canyon, narrow.

An eagle could cross it the way a man crosses a room. Not a state's worth, a four corners' worth. A single colossal gash of golden yellow, crimson stained, a white-green river, the Yellowstone, carving away far below.

Paul felt it in his knees, in the hair on his arms, on the goose bumps. Rachel stepped back a step from him when they reached the rail guard above, in the middle of it all. All was a waterfall from mythology, mythological gardens, from fact, from cooled lava flows.

It flowed, it fell like a standing river, far down the canyon from them; near enough to see all its centerpiece, all its aquamarine and foam white descent.

It's religious. Paul spoke to it. He spoke to the great yellow father, mother, sister, brother.

He wanted to kneel down. He did in his heart, in his spirit.

"Oh, god, Rachel. No ..." he added. "This is god. This is."

The sun lit it. A ray of sun that carved a canyon. Same god.

Paul took it in down river. A painted desert, in the middle of everywhere. He took it in up river to the solid waterfall, solid as faith.

"Look, Paul," she practically whispered. "An osprey."

Black and white it owned the canyon. His mouth didn't drop open. His soul opened up, filled itself on rhyme and reason.

Larry, the reason for being here. The reason there was life.

He only felt for the coin. It was there, he was here. The cycle of things.

"I'll never leave here, Rachel. I'm home."

"Home is where the heart is."

"It's here."

"Come on," softly, "here come the hordes."

A Japanese bus tour, in suits and ties, like they were being punished, closed in, en masse.

"Want to see the waterfall?"

"I do." He pried himself away from it, forty, fifty, foreign and domestic cameras clicking.

They both knew the tour bus driver. "Hey, Terry," to the curly-haired diesel wrangler, having a cigarette on the front bumper.

"How goes it?" he asked. Rachel answered for Paul.

"How's tips?"

"Tips are good. The Japanese are not the French." Paul was already in the car, unable to participate in your average conversation right now.

"Speechless?" she asked him.

"No. This may be the most important day of my life."

Her calm nod of agreement told him he wasn't overstepping their knowledge of each other.

The diesel bus roared into action. They went quietly.

CHAPTER

The sound of it was the song of the sirens. The sight of it was right at your feet, within arm's length, the spray on your jacket, in your hair.

The rock that made the river fall was lava black. The lava flow that had cooled an eternity ago made an upper falls, around a bend, around a gorge in the river. The river turned again and fell into the canyon.

Paul listened, heard creation. He watched: thunderous cubic slabs of the Yellowstone, constantly. He saw the power, the frailty--of himself. He felt the strength of his new connections.

Rachel was arm in arm with him. "I love it here. The song of it."

In full chorus it plummeted, unaware of them and their day.

"We forgot to eat our lunch," above the song of it.

"Hungry?" she asked.

Yes, let's find a warm room, you warm, wonderful woman.

"Famished."

"Come on, we'll have a picnic."

"A spot you know?"

"Of course."

They raced to the car, Adam and Eve's children.

They stopped to let a full grown bison robe, a full grown male, cross the road. His horn could puncture their radiator. He climbed an embankment and galloped into the trees, then into a flat meadow.

"Up there, Paul. Used to be a grand hotel. A mile around it they say. Wooden, like you'd see in the Canadian Rockies."

"Where'd it go?"

"Suspicious stuff. Charley read up on it." There was that name again.

She didn't seem to notice.

"Maybe it was burned down by someone. An economic decision? Concessionaire business? Anyway it burned and the world got Canyon Village."

He was paying some attention. To his left the Yellowstone was beginning to unfold, straighten out, take over the scene.

"The river looks beautiful."

"Yes. Calm here. Let's stop before we go in to Hayden Valley."

"Food?"

"Food. Here, just up on your left."

He spotted the picnic table and pulled in, far enough away from the road so the flat, wide river was the only means of transportation.

Never ending. An osprey appeared from the magic and began to fish. An osprey fished by diving into the flat, wide river for trout.

Rachel and Paul sipped a beer, ate a sandwich, sat on the picnic table and watched what few humans get to see.

"Seems like I've been here forever, Rachel."

"A lot to absorb."

"You bet. From buses, to rangers, to poachers, to religious freaks," to loving you. Maybe the osprey heard the last part.

"You'll get them all, Paul. More of them. More of this. Which is the reality, right?"

"The poaching and the cult are reality."

"Not this?"

"This? I'm not sure yet. I'm getting there though. Religion?"

"Not like the folks out of Gardiner?"

"Never."

He let himself go to the worship of things, of day to day living. The osprey made him forget. The osprey would eat, a healthy trout in its talons, climbing away with it.

Rachel? will you marry me, right here, right now?

"A friend calls it Yellowstone's Olduvai Gorge: the birth place. That's next," was her answer to his silent proposal.

"Let's," was his.

The Hayden Valley. The turnout was a biblical site, sight.

"I came through here in the dark. Literally," he was quick to add.

Here there was a moose down below on the Yellowstone. Swans.

Bison. Elk. Geese. Honey-brown hills to Irish-green pastures to green forests to mountain boundaries too good not to be true.

"Hayden Valley. The Olduvai Gorge."

Paul was reading the interpretive sign. Grizzly bears. "If I see a bear it will be."

"Best place. Out across the river, up in the tree line."

"Perfect, perfection."

Perfection reigned in the five o'clock sun, barely a hint of the late sunset to come.

"Man alive," he gushed, taking it all in; all the creeks, all the ponds, all the rolling distance back to Mt. Washburn, sharp against the perfect blue.

"Wait until you see the pelicans, Paul."

"Pelicans? Where, here?"

"Up the road a piece." She laughed at the hickism.

"Sure enough, Rachel."

The swans below on the river began to begin flight, building steam just above the surface of the lazy river, gaining elevation, air, rising into it like they were the flags of this perfection.

"Swans mate for life," she said.

Why don't we? silently.

Silently, they moved on.

The earth wasn't silent. It boiled, it burned, it threw up volcanoes of mud, scalding water, boiling steam, for some reason, here, all of a sudden.

They kept on, a destination ahead, some passing interest, some passing awe in the common character of Yellowstone.

"Let's give it a look up here."

"Grizzly bears?" he asked her.

"Next best thing. Pelicans."

"Almost."

He pulled into a turnout large enough for an English Land Rover covered in Alaskan mud, Alaskan plates, and a Corvette with a sail-white convertible top.

The Yellowstone bent and straightened out, closer to itself, its source now.

They walked a trail sunk a good foot into the ground.

"Oh, yes, we've got them," Rachel purred.

"Where?"

"There. See, by the bend. See."

Sure as hell. "I thought they were stones." Sure as hell. Rocky Mountain snow pelicans from the Paul Barnes book of bird watching. As sure as Florida had Pelicans.

One of them floated away from the pack, unmistakable snout, unmistakable heavy set drift across the water.

"I'll be a son of a bitch." He gaped as one of them showed the length of its wingspan as it made like a torpedo dive bomber off the deck of a carrier, slowly, heavily sweeping into the air. A pelican.

"Now I've seen it all."

The Corvette couple, in natty matching leather jackets, shook their heads in belief as they passed back up the trail.

"Bloody beautiful." The Alaskan-Australian bush couple agreed.

"Bloody right," Paul told Rachel. "I knew I'd see pelicans in the mountains."

"Doesn't everyone?"

"No. Thank goodness."

Rachel got like everything around them--all natural and soft.

"Thank you, Paul," and a natural soft kiss.

"Bloody good, Rachel."

They followed after the Land Rover. To the lake.

CHAPTER

The lakes from his youth. You could skip stones across them, swim out to the raft, see the rocks below the surface.

The pines stopped growing and there was Yellowstone Lake. The sun went behind a ridgeline of clouds and the surface of it was gray, maybe like a part, a healthy part of the North Sea.

The sun hiked back out and you got most of the lake. Most counties would fit its size, circumference. Another park unto its own self. On a map it was a mark. On the earth it covered a portion of the surface.

"I'm always shocked when I see it again."

Paul knew what she meant. He knew from the twilight darkness when he first came in.

In the full light it was a shock. That first white man laying eyes shock.

"I took a drink from it on my way in. Sort of a baptism."

There were two bison feeding on the grass behind the hotel as they curved into the complex. They stopped to consider two of the earliest Americans in relation to an American hotel, long and colonial, as yellow as the stone, its broad back to them, its colonade front porch facing up to the lake.

"Couldn't exactly dip someone in here for a baptism," Rachel told him. "Alpine lakes are meant for being on top of."

They swung around past the log ranger station, its front yard an enormous mountain lake, a hard silver in the strong sun.

"Just up by those benches," were her directions.

Four gulls jumped away as they pulled in, the window bays of the Georgian hotel above them, the choppy surface of the lake, island dots floating on the surface, before them.

"A caldera," was Rachel's comment.

The distant mountains ringing the lake made it the mouth of an ancient, ancient volcano.

"Good use for an extinct volcano."

"But is it?" she asked. "The magma is just below us, pushing up, ready to make a new park."

"Any day now?"

"Not today," and she patted his thigh. "Come on, you have rangers to visit. I'll stop in at the gas station. A girlfriend works there."

"This her view?"

"Yep. Has an apartment above the pumps. This is front and center."

"O.K. I'll meet you at the pumps?"

"10-4, ranger."

A day cruiser, reminiscent of presidential yachts, of presidents before the great war, cut a white path across the lake.

The lake turned a green, a slate, a pewter, a black. It made small white waves against the shoreline. He could feel the ocean of it. A star appeared in the hint of night.

Rachel appeared at the pumps. Paul saw her from that starry kind of distance. She waved, he hurried, she met him at the car.

"So, what do you think of the lake rangers?" from behind the wheel.

"They mentioned Lamar Valley. Even with this out here. You could hear the reverence in their voices. You could make a good career here."

"Definitely. Martha, my friend at the gas station would never budge. I'll show you her apartment later?"

He thought he heard a lot in that invitation.

"One more stop first?"

"Lake Butte?"

"You know?"

"I know, I know."

CHAPTER

He knew there'd been a bridge during his first contact.

Wasn't there a bison on it? Now it was still nearly daylight enough to see the industrial log across the namesake river, the namesake becoming a river again from the lip of the lake.

"The Yellowstone." Rachel had her window down, breathing of it. "Fishing Bridge. Walk across?"

"Sure."

Fathers holding their sons and daughters, their daughters and sons above the tree trunk railings, pointing to the water. Cars in the middle, people on the sides, Yellowstone Lake wide open, feeding the river.

Trout. The setting sun sent silver light into the water.

Cutthroat trout. All the ones you'd never hook, never land.

"Are you a fisherman, Paul?"

"No, ants in my pants."

"Have you seen the fly fishing set yet?"

"I don't think so."

The river didn't make a sound as it slid by underneath. You could hear the work of pelican wings in the quiet.

"I wonder what you'd make of them, the fly fishers."

"What about you?"

"I enjoy the sight of them. They fit, somehow. I'm not a great fan of hooking fish but they fit in the rivers. Oh, they used to be able to fish here, the visitors."

"Here? Really? Talk about fish in a barrel."

"Imagine a shoulder to shoulder line of avid American tourists, with hooks and lines."

"Great! Great! Frightening, but great."

"It can get a little frightening across river there. The Fishing Bridge cabins. Grizz makes other grizz over there. For a few millenium. Now there's a residential area. Not exactly Yogi and Booboo."

"Yogi and Booboo. I'd forgotten them. The bear, Rachel. Always present."

"When he or she tears into a tourist it sure is."

156

They followed a ten-year-old with a bear riding a bicycle on his T-shirt.

They got the car and crossed the Yellowstone and followed the swoop of the lake.

"Mary's Bay." A stretch of raw shoreline, driftwood timbers, short white-cap waves on a black and stony beach. French fur trappers in canoes, or nobody at all would be fine.

Two coyotes fed on a bison carcass, across the road in the undulating meadow.

"Dear diary," Paul joked. "Freaked out of my friggin' head."

"You ain't seen nothin' yet, cowboy."

That sounded like a lot of Yellowstone, and a lot of other stuff.

The road took them up on a palisade above the steel blue lake.

A rock island, a stalagmite rose out of the water. The road rose in an alpine curve above the alpine ocean.

CHAPTER

Two pin-points of light, green and white, made their way across the darkening lake, making their way back to safe harbor.

Paul and Rachel had front row seats for the darkening. Lake Butte, under the northern sky, the Wyoming aurora.

Bands of shimmering orange, coils of light yellow, banners of red rouge began to shimmer, coil, unfurl across the endless sky.

"All the way round, Paul. The road follows the lake to West Thumb. You can see otters." She had one foot up on the sign indicating the points of interest, near and far, far away.

The sun blew up the sky. An explosion of gold and blonde.

The sky filled with ancient visions. Paul was alive under it, ancient in it, positive in it. He came next to her and put his arms around her waist from behind her.

"Look," she whispered, falling back against him. "See? You can see the Tetons."

A pink floodlight backlit them, enough of the signature peaks in another park.

"I see them," closing his arms, his lips on her neck.

"You do?" knowing that mattered less than this.

"Uh-huh," at her earlobe, her ear, his hands under her shirt, along the softness, along the warmth of her stomach, his fingertips warmer, down her belt near to all of her. Warm flesh. Warm steam of the geysers. Warm waters, lava-warmed earth.

A streak of purple whipped across the sky. A curtain of black began its descent, wine-purple against edges of pink and maroon, silver shafts in there with it all.

Paul's hands were a man's. Rachel was a woman. He came to some of that, his tongue on her ear, hard against her backside, his hand on what all around them wasn't. The sumptuous heft of her, there under her shirt. He had to bite her, a bit.

"Ahhh, shit, Paul. You're just what the shaman ordered."

He heard some kind of cure, some healing, healed in that. He kept on, gone over to where all the rivers met, all the trees grew, all the

158

bison wandered. His hand under her from behind, fingers on her front, herself, her mount, her fount.

She turned around to his hands. The sky, the rivers, the forests. You could hold them. Paul did, his knee between her, pushing, lifting, gently, his hands on the warm bones of her spine, his lips, his mouth a lake with no bottom.

"Ummm."

He heard her "ummm."

"Let's go back," breath in his ear.

His hands came out from under her shirt, off her slacks.

"No, no, Paul." She ran her tongue along his neck. "Just back to the lake. I have a key, for us."

"For us?" his nose and lips in her hair.

"Yes," and she lifted her head away. "We can stay here tonight. There's a couple of toothbrushes."

"I'd love to," was enough said.

She took him by the hand. She took him by the thigh, beside him as they came down off the butte, the heel of her hand just there where he felt his imagination, his reality.

"In the morning, I'll tell you a great Yellowstone Lake ice story."

"Yes, in the morning."

They drove along under the first stars. The first of millions.

CHAPTER

"Who's apartment?"

"Martha's," pulling back the front curtains to give them the lake in star light, flat and black, empty. "She runs the gas station underneath."

Just under them, four pumps, couple of hundred logs to build the office and the work bays, the upstairs apartment worthy of some skier's alpine retreat. Heavy logs, heavy furniture, heavy bed.

Heavy they felt, beside the window, wrapped in each other.

She gave him the first of the real heaviness. A hand on his waist, a slight nudge to the side. Her hand across his zipper, down his zipper, up his zipper, tongue included.

Both of them as silent as the place outside. Words of love.

A sigh, a moan, a grunt.

What was amazing was he could believe it. He did.

Rachel worked his belt buckle, slowly, teaching him something about being a man.

A woman's hand felt at the place where his spine met his butt, his butt met his legs, his legs met his thighs, his loins.

Rachel brought both hands to his side and shoved everything down. His belt buckle hit the floor, everything exposed.

"Ahhh," she told him with her hand.

"Ohhh," almost with tears in his ohhh.

She made what was ridged harder. She made what was bulge purple, what was hanging hang heavier.

She made his skin move. He felt her lips on his knee. He dared to look. Down on her knees, untying his shoes. "Kick off your pants," was her magic spell. He kicked them aside.

She kissed what was hanging heavy and came up to his mouth.

Each other, self, in the taste.

"My turn?" he asked, pleaded, choking on it. Her teeth on his neck, the pad of her hand rubbing him against himself was answer enough.

He lifted her shirt, her T-shirt. Opening a window on the first spring day. The wind in the willows. The bare feet in the grass. The man's mouth on the woman's form. The forms fit in his mouth, against his tongue. She chewed at his hair.

That sound. Like the breaking of twigs, kindling, opening a lock, a gift package. Her zipper coming down. Anticipation, like waiting for creation.

He felt the first of her panties. Cashmere, Arabian silk, the veils of Kashmere. Paul knew the place, but this was brand new.

He placed his fingers on the tight line of elastic. Her slacks dropped by their own weight.

He heard her hiss with delight and awkwardly pry off her shoes with each foot.

Now it was all white cloth, just white cloth, the heft between her thighs hefty to the touch, the cheek, the lips, the tongue, the lick, the thirsty man finally at the well.

He played with the elastic, pulled it, released it, felt her filling up its slick backside. He couldn't wait any longer. Down.

Down, with a scent of all living things, all the moss of northern forests, all the tilled ground of fertile plains. Down.

Fresh water onto dry ground. Rewards, solutions, freedom, fresh air, warm breezes, earthy odors.

She was nude but for the light band of cloth at her ankles.

He helped her out of them, dangling them on himself. Himself loved the feel of them. He loved the smell of them against his face. He dropped them aside.

He was where he wanted to be--on his knees to her, her hair, that hair, her softness, her moist, her legs apart, his fingers beginning, his tongue waiting.

They paced it together. A finger, a motion, more finger, more motion, more finger, more motion, more finger, more finger, more finger.

"Ahhhh."

"Ahhh," sliding out the more finger, more finger, more finger.

"Ohh. Eat me, Paul, eat me?"

He did.

CHAPTER

Heaven and earth. It was never better than this, because it never was this. Her black-brown hair on his forehead. Now she was turning herself, all over his lips, his face, wiping it all against the back of her hip. Now she was lowering herself. The inside of her mouth on the outside of him.

They fed. The hardwood floor felt cool, fire and ice. He felt his own lava.

They fed. Paul yelled, Rachel savored. Rachel ate full of it, some on her cheeks, on the tip of her nose, the roof of her mouth, the walls of her cheeks, the cup of her tongue, the licking of it from his stomach.

Speechless. There was no speech for this. "Rachel, Rachel," was what he finally said.

He heard her laugh with satisfaction, like she'd done something she didn't think she was capable of.

She got up on her knees and faced him, massaged him, massaged him, massaged him until she got him there, the length she wanted him. "Come on you, fella," by the hand, by the massage.

The bed was a cloud floating on another cloud. He floated around behind her. She floated to a kneeling formation. He floated forward into her.

The crisp sheet was fitted at the four corners. It kept its form as they tried to work it free, freely having at each other.

Freely grunting, freely grunting, sweating, osprey free, wild, flower free, free, free, free .

Paul dropped away, hollow as a log, content as a well fed animal--a wild animal.

The other animal rolled next to him. "Feel all right?"

"Like I'm dead. No strains, no pains." He gave it a chance.

"Love."

"Ummhhh," and she snuggled next to him.

He wanted her to say the word, the word love. I love you, Paul. But all of her in the log-poster bed was all he would ask for.

CHAPTER

The morning, the light, butterscotch and gray. The woman coming awake, the man awake with the realization in the daylight.

"Good morning, Rachel."

"Morning, fella," rolling over on her back, sheets and blanket covering them.

"Feel good?" she asked.

"Like I've never felt. Say "me too," Rachel, say it.

"Good," was as good as it got.

"Hungry?"

"Famished."

The kiss tasted of morning, waking up, last night.

"Want to hear my ice story first?"

"Sure." He got snuggled in next to her.

"Once upon a time in the deep winter," laughing. "Anyway, the winter here freezes the lake several feet deep."

"Yes."

"Well, in the land of winter, spring was finally coming. A couple of guys I know decided to camp out on the lake. When it begins to break free of winter. Can you picture them out there on the ice pack?"

"I can picture anything here."

"They heard the ice breaking up under them."

"Grinding and cracking?"

"Not quite. That's the story of it. A siren's song one of them called it. The moving ice sent up a song, a moan.

"They knew it was time to get off the ice, but it called to them. I guess I'm quoting. They had to pry themselves away from it, afraid to stay, afraid to go."

"Ulysses comes to Yellowstone."

"Yes, the song of the siren. I love to tell it, hear it. I wish I could have been there to hear it." She rubbed his back.

"Well, what do you think? Some story?"

"I wish I could have been there. Like mythology." But the reality shut him up, his face on her chest.

"Where's the apartment owner?" he finally asked.

"Hiking the Thorofare. Across the back of the park is Martha's description. As raw and as untouched as you can get here, Paul. Deep into the guts of it. Four days worth."

"So, we can stay here for four days?" tickling her.

"Wouldn't that be nice. But don't you have a ranger career to start? And I've got tourists to keep from falling out of the raft."

"Too bad."

"Breakfast?"

"Breakfast?"

CHAPTER

He wanted a breakfast of bacon and eggs, slab of ham, mound of potatoes, thick coffee. Something to fill his feeling, his hunger.

But the tour groups, complaining in German, Dutch, Japanese, French and Israeli dominated the hotel dining rooms.

So, bananas, a tall glass of juice, a bay window seat, a deep cushioned chair, the lake. Not bad, not bad.

A small blue and white cruiser was making its way across the empty expanse, its wake white on the green-gray. The English couple next to them had binoculars trained on it. "Care for a look?" the husband asked.

"Sure." Paul focused them. Two guys drinking coffee, fishing rods, against the bulkhead, canoe in tow, 'Mr. Natural' painted on the cruiser's stern.

"Marvelous sight, isn't it?"

"It is." Rachel took a turn.

"I bet they're headed for the south arm. No power boats allowed."

Take the canoe in," scanning the lake with the glasses.

 "Henry, time for our bus."

"Very well. Like to be with those fellows."

"Yes, dear."

Rachel and Paul had a short laugh at their expense.

"I guess we better get our bus going, Rachel."

'Mr. Natural' was a dot out on the lake. A ranger was giving directions on the steps of the back entrance.

"Got your uniform ready?" Rachel asked him.

"You bet."

"Good luck." She leaned over to kiss him.

I won't need it, I've got you. I do, don't I? "Thanks. For everything."

"You're welcome for everything."

"Didn't you mention something about the Lamar Valley on the way back?"

She touched his cheek. "You'll find it on your own. We better zoom back to Gardiner."

"Zoom, zoom."

They had plenty of company on the zoom home. The world was coming home, home to Yellowstone.

PASSAGE

CHAPTER

Pride. Not the fleshy, cosmetic version--the kind that goes right to the bone. Paul Barnes, from top to toe. Brown on gray and green, and that famous, flat hat. Long sleeves, gray shirt and a green tie, creased trousers, blood-brown Wellingtons with a dull shine. That hat. Pride, right through.

A gold park service symbol tie-tack held it in place. A pine cone with branches belt was tight around his waist. His gold badge was clipped to his chest. He whistled that whistle that good looking women know so well.

He got it as soon as he stepped outside, briefcase with all the forms and one revolver, one holster.

"Morning, ranger," two tourists told him, their "ranger" like "good morning, father" to a priest.

They fell in step with him, 49'ers T-shirt, Yosemite Valley sweat shirt.

"Our son wants to be a ranger," from the wife, from a feeling of the job being a vocation.

"He's eighteen now and starting to look around," the 49'er father said.

Geez, this feels good, Paul was thinking. Geez, I wish they'd leave me alone. "Well, I wish him well. I hope he makes it," spoken as a true veteran of about ten minutes on the job.

He was at his car, they were at their camper van, a 49'ers logo fit for a B52 on its side.

"Football fans?" Paul asked.

"Can you tell?" the wife laughed.

"Well, go 49'ers. And I hope your son makes it."

"His name's Roy. He lives in Santa Cruz . . . "and he kept talking to Paul through his car window. And he kept talking as Paul pulled away. He saw them waving to him. He felt their respect.

He went through his schedule. Two days here at Mammoth, then out to Tower to settle in out there. Dinner tonight with Rachel, at the religious cult's restaurant at Corwin Springs. When in Rome she says.

And while we're in Rome she says, I'll show you where your suspect poacher lives. Fine, fine and fine.

He was waved through the employees gate, slowly up the hill to Mammoth behind two bike riders, wind burned, sun burned, road burned, lean and tough, the distance they'd come all over them, all over the packs attached to every non-moving part of their bikes.

Paul gave them all the credit they deserved with a wave and pulled around them.

A lone elk was surrounded, every state in the union, every camera make in the world. One of the tales he'd heard was that the elk actually posed for the visitors. He smiled at that the way you'd smile at Paul Bunyan--sure.

Another of the tales he'd heard was a tourist kid killed by a deer. Feeding it potato chips. No more chips, deer doesn't understand, sticks an antler in the kid. He checked in the rear- view mirror to see what sort of distance the folks were keeping from the elk. His job now.

His job was beginning its day. A horse-trailer hooked to a pale-green park service truck, two horses standing quietly, long combed tails hanging over the rear doors, pulled up the hill followed by a bear trap, a long length of corrugated pipe welded into a better mouse trap, being pulled by a pickup.

Paul couldn't see if the trap had an occupant. On up the hill, the flag flying above the green traffic median, two female elk feeding on the green of it. A parking space in front of the post office, two stone bears like two library lions on the front steps, a pale-green station wagon patrol car parked in behind the fortress bricks of the ranger station, museum, visitor center.

He didn't feel a rookie. I can eat all this up. No sweat.

He got his gear from the back seat. No sweat. He put on the hat.

Pride, right through.

168

CHAPTER

As he had hoped, as he had expected. The day, the shift, the park, the increasing visitor population. Schools were closing for the season around America.

All American ranger. That's how he was treated. Giving someone directions up on Swan Lake Flat, the sun, then the clouds, then the hard blue off and on against Bunsen Peak, or doing the patient duty of correcting an auto accident, a mobile home into a guard rail, the owner-under-qualified-operator apologetic, respectful--"yes, ranger, sorry ranger. Listen, could you maybe stand in a photograph with me and the wife?" Paul Barnes, ranger, would be in a slide-show on a wall in Missouri some evening.

There was a lone moose in the aspens that needed protection.

The folks wanted to pet her. Here was a prehistoric creature, capable of killing a horse. Paul's warnings were heeded, the folks back tracking, cameras exploding.

The park spoke through the patrol car's radio: weather reports, fire reports from the mountain lookouts, bear sightings, a voice from the back country, deep in it, correcting some camping permits, campgrounds full, road conditions, snow conditions, even for June. Someone calling for a tow truck, a check on a license plate, another voice from another part of the park. A voice Paul was now part of. He could feel the hat, feel what it did to people.

"700 Alpha, this is one eleven Barnes."

"Go ahead, one eleven Barnes," the friendly, grandmotherly voice answered. Irma, Com Center Command.

"Just need a traffic accident report," parked up on the upper terrace drive, above Mammoth, above the warm steam from the mother of the earth.

He got his number and got out for a bit, hand-set radio on his belt.

A mother used him to frighten her disobedient children. "See, the ranger can hear you yelling." The kids kept yelling.

The adults though. Friendly, like he was the town marshall.

And the question, ever the question: "Where are the bears?" with surprise, or hurt, or annoyance, or downright pissed-off. I didn't drag this bunch two thousand miles not to see a bear.

Paul had to explain it to all their feelings. He was a park ranger, born in the limbs of a tree, learned to crawl in lush meadows, grew to the stature of ranger through truth, justice and the American way. His word was gospel to most of them. They came round to his idea that bears couldn't live on cookies, and the visitor couldn't live off their government settlements if a bear decided to rip apart one of your third graders.

And of course, there was paperwork. It was work, but this office crossed the Yellowstone, followed the Gardner, stopped at Indian Creek campground; quiet among the pines where he could catch up.

Back at Mammoth Hotel the folks were licking ice cream cones, two employees were tossing a frisbee on the green lawn while some tour luggage was being unloaded. Paul was two floors up in the hotel, rounding out his shift by giving oxygen to a senior visitor high in the mountains for the first time. Paul and the senior wife walked him down to the lobby and set him down in a bison-size leather chair.

Their genuine thanks made a good day better. Life was good, absolutely, positively. And I get to add Rachel to it tonight.

CHAPTER

She was burned brown by the sun. Roasted, brown as coffee, with cream.

"Looks like you've been on the river," stepping into her warm room, her warm arms. Black slacks, a pure white long sleeve turtleneck, a thin, raw, black necklace against the white.

"Out of the office today, doing some rowing, some steering," warm against his ear, his neck. "Hawaians," getting a down vest from the chair. "Have you heard about them?"

"Not sure, what?"

"Kind of indifferent to all this around them. They come from paradise. Let's go on vacation if we must. Perfect crowd for me.

Laid way back while I took them down river."

"Solo?"

"Not quite. One of our veterans with me. But never mind that. What about you?" a white smile across her brown face.

"Come on, I'll tell you on the way."

"Remember to bring your bathing suit?"

"Yep."

Chico Hot Springs was in the plan. Soak in the public, the local historical pool, pools.

"I'll be right with you," he told her, and went to the closet size bathroom. A postcard with the New York skyline on the toilet lid couldn't be missed, especially by a native.

He reached to flip it and read it. Never mind.

Rachel waited in the evening cold. The moon made a crescent over Montana.

"Ahhoouu," he wailed, quietly.

"Coyote man. It must have been a good day as a ranger."

"Piece of cake, piece of cake. Having your cake and eating it too."

"Speaking of eating." She slid closer to him on the front seat.

The closer they got to it the more it seemed to permeate the air. The Church. A sense of an evil, like a curse on a tomb, in a jungle. The natural order upset. A presence you could sense, and see. An uneasiness down there across the Yellowstone, lights shining, not a twinkle of a motel light, not a glow from a bar room, not a puff of firewood smoke. Industrial energy. Bad intentions in, on the Holy Land.

They both felt it.

"Still want to rub elbows with them?"

"Rub my fist in their face," with a laugh, with a "sure, sure."

Rachel made an eerie sound effect from a B Sci Fi. They laughed. A coyote wailed out loud.

CHAPTER

There was still plenty of light to see the lights across the river.

"Huh," Paul uttered. They were standing in the parking area, in front of the long, wide, rambling, wood frame Country Kitchen. Its wide, rambling porch was pure Americana.

"Huh what?" Rachel asked him.

"Oh, just that bridge. I see something like it in a dream I have. Haven't had it for a bit, but."

The black metal bridge stood out across a river with no other bridges.

"A dream?"

"I'll tell you about it tonight?" he asked her, begged her, close to her.

"That'll work," and they climbed the wooden steps into the Americana.

"Like Mormon missionaries," Rachel whispered to him out the side of her mouth as they stood waiting for the gingham hostess.

Paul didn't meet too many Mormon missionaries in the suburbs.

But he could guess. White, white to the bone, bland in the bone, bland in the face, in the frame, in the eyes--in the eyes of the convinced, confused, oppressed, possessed.

"So, you have to run under their guns each raft trip."

They sat at the Norman Rockwell table. Red and white table cloth, heavy chairs off America's porch. The gingham hostess went to get two cokes. No alcoholic beverages.

"Literally under their guns," Rachel answered him. "I hear Elizabeth the Prophet's husband is in Missoula, answering to a weapons charge, the Prophet herself back in Malibu with the IRS."

"And these are the people who are going to surface after the nuclear wipe out?"

"Pleasant thought."

The prophet's people were working the sparse crowd. The women had their hair pulled back. The young men had hair like TV news people. They looked healthy--awfully healthy, like no hang-over had ever hurt them, no child had ever called from jail. Maybe that's what was over there across the river. None of that, an attempt at none of that, a facade of all that.

"What's got you deep thinking, ranger?"

"Invasion of the Body Snatchers. The good people," with a nod at the surrounding barn dance ambiance.

"Careful they don't get you."

"Careful I don't get them," tension in the jaw.

"I think you're outgunned."

"I'll get my poacher friend."

"That might do it."

"Ready to order?" the waitress with the pulled back hair asked them.

CHAPTER

The rainbow trout, the rice, the corn, the two cups of coffee didn't feel like much, stretching his arms in the parking lot.

During the meal he felt they were watching him, without shifting their eyes. He sure was watching them, catching a glimpse into the kitchen, following a waitress back to her station, trying to get an answer to just who packs up their life to come and praise some snake oilers, and fuck with Yellowstone? He felt the empty lump of it in his stomach.

"I could see you really enjoyed it," Rachel said to him.

"Look at Electric Peak," he answered.

The end of the day was now down behind the enormous hunk of the mountain that could be seen from where they stood. Silver light, spotlight, sharp focus, night coming up in purples behind them.

"It's dessert, Paul."

He snapped open the car door. "Let's go see this poacher."

"Guilty until proven innocent?" getting in on her side.

Some big machine was making some big machine noise across the river.

They didn't need the headlights yet.

"See that side road?" Rachel directed.

The main road ran towards Yankee Jim Canyon, to a narrow curve with a few pines beneath a shake shingle ledge, to a gravel road up to a green grass hill, a log house with a view, a blunt side road below the house to a cut in the hillside. A small log cabin with wooden posts to hold a roof over a porch sat in the cut.

They were stopped on the gravel road, a wire fence running down to the cabin, a TV antenna on its wooden roof. Paul reached back for a pair of binoculars.

"That's his place," Rachel said.

He gave it a look. What did I expect? A cave, empty beer cans, skinned hides? There were a few hides, hung neatly on the front wall.

"Coyote hides," he said to Rachel.

"You get bounty for them around here."

A few leg traps dangled from a post. A wooden rocking chair on the porch, a conga drum, some sort of dinner bell that looked like a shell casing. Not a twig, a rock, a stone out of place.

No one home. Paul tried to focus on a look inside. A stone fire place, the corner of a table, a corner of what looked like a flag with a red star.

He tried to put Gary Delling, shaggy and workin' on your car oily here in this order. Unusual was the best he could come up with.

"That's enough. I feel like a peeping Tom."

"Maybe he's peeping back at you right now?"

Paul looked around. He didn't see any vehicle. Maybe.

Maybe? He felt a thing like the thing he felt when he'd looked out towards the Lamar Valley. Something definite.

His veil was lifted by the Paradise Valley, night down in it, the sky just about black, headlights tracing the Yellowstone, the weight of it all like goose down when it snows, like rivers when it's summer. They turned at Pray and crossed the river.

CHAPTER

Emigrant Peak was a massive shadow, present, there in the dark. A narrow road was cut in the hills, the heights that made mountains. Then there was a white, wood frame hotel, and a white fence as bright as lights in the dark.

"Chico Hot Springs," with a pride, a pleasure, a pleasantness in her voice. "Not exactly raw, but that's what's so nice about it."

They parked and she walked him around the family farm house hotel wing, the attached bar wing and her "come on .. . " up the ramp past the arcade videos into the pool, steam rising in the iced mountain air, a few heads of hair and faces in the steam.

"I like it, I like it."

"Boys room there."

"Meet you at the pool."

It sounded remarkable to him, here in Montana. My Montana? he dared to dream.

He didn't waste a minute. His toe told him the water was bath tub warm. Cold air, warm water. "Ahhhh," diving in, surfacing.

A surface of overhead crowded stars, hillside shapes.

The shape of her, in her full piece, full grip suit, pubic mound and breasts prominant, thighs dominant. Paul went under, made a shout under water, came up, Rachel's head beside him.

"This will make you forget your troubles," running a hand back across her wet hair.

"What troubles?" kissing the wet lips, getting a wet one back.

"Ready for the royal treatment?"

"Here?" feeling her through his suit, under water.

"Don't you wish. No, over here in pool number two." She waded away.

He watched her slip over a low wall and into a square pool, steam off a male body sitting on the edge.

"Come on," her face over the edge back at him.

His hand went in first. Hot. Not warm. Almost so you couldn't get in hot. Almost. He slipped over the edge and felt the spa of it, the massage of it, the sapping of it.

Heads in the cold air, bodies in the tub.

"Rachel, Rachel, Rachel," came out of him, warm and well soaked.

"It gets better."

"How?"

She stroked across the three yards of the width and sprang out. Dripping water she opened a sliding window in the wall. A face, some words, two ice cold Rainier beers.

Paul sat on the steps into the pool, half-in half-out, awaiting his grapes, his beer.

"Where does the water come from?" the iced beer to his forehead, to his throat.

"From heaven. Up in the hills somewhere. Or from a boiler room?"

"Who cares, right?"

"Very right," half way in beside him.

She patted him on what she could pat of his thigh.

"Well, here's to Lamar," an iced can toast.

"Lamar?"

"I think you're going to wind up there. Something you about it."

"The land that time forgot?"

"And it forgot hamburgers, televisions, tourists, religious cults, the race us humans run. You'll have all the girls after you too."

"Oh?"

"You're own house. A house in the middle of everywhere, and that hat."

"There's only one girl I want," as serious, as positive, as heartfelt, as quiet, as close to her as he could get it all.

Rachel stayed close. "What, no girl back home? No one you left behind?"

"No."

"Now don't say no. Everyone's got someone, had someone."

I don't want to tell her about another woman, any other woman.

"There was. Terri."

"Terri. So?"

"Not all that much. Larry Darrell died out here. I had to come. She wanted me to stay. I couldn't," and it was as simple as that. He shrugged to define how simple it was, how it really was now.

"You know, I haven't thought about her until now."

"And?"

"She's not you. She's not here," with another shrug.

"Are you so sure?"

"Sure. Is there something you need to know?"

"No," with a quick kiss on his cheek.

"So, Rachel. What about you? Wasn't there a Charley? Aren't there about forty raft rowers chasing you? Some guy's skeleton in your closet?"

"Not exactly a skeleton. Alive and well in New York right now. Charley, I did tell you?"

"Yes, you did," strong and somber.

She heard both of them. "Oh, Paul. He's just somebody that dropped me on my head. A long time ago now. Gone and forgotten."

He remembered the postcards. "Have the bumps healed?" He stroked her hair. He meant it.

"Yes, doctor. All healed now. All nearly drunk on one beer."

"It's the water. Makes you weak."

She dived in the hot pool. He dived after her, weak.

Strong. I've got to be strong around her. She's coming over to me. She is.

CHAPTER

Journal entry. He felt strong in his uniform, on a meal break in his no-food-in-the-refrigerator, one narrow closet for his clothes, two tiny rooms for his shelter.

He could still feel her, fresh from Chico Hot springs, on all fours, then underneath him, then on her front porch in the chill morning all around him. He wrote of that in his journal.

He wrote out a time of this day, a time of this night on a note pad. A report for later.

Earlier he'd made an arrest. He still felt the ease, the strength of it. Some drunken kid, far from home, far into co-ed tequila, taking it out on some warehouse windows.

Sorry, sorry, but I've got to lock you up. The skinny blond kid didn't quite get it. Paul was the law, but a law with one of those national hats, so young sonny went quietly, terribly sorry, terribly disappointed when Paul closed him into the hard, narrow cell in the official lockup among Mammoth's government buildings.

Not a totally unpleasant surprise to Paul. I am sort of the law after all, and boys will be boys and he also knew by now that the whole business was played out over the eight p.m. park radio.

Points, reputation, professional points among the rest of the rangers.

He finished the bites of a burger, replaced his hat, closed his notes, stuck the dish and the glass in the sink, took his talisman coin from his watch pocket and snapped its edge against the wooden cutting board to hear its fullness, completeness, hardness, strength.

Four more hours and you'll be done here. On to Tower ranger station.

He opened the journal and wrote Lamar Valley in it, closed it and went back to work.

CHAPTER

Just up the hill from Gardiner, just up past Boiling River, the sky was on fire.

It took a few seconds to register on his on duty-brain. It wasn't scenery, the sky was on fire--fire.

He came over the last roll in the road and there it was, a campsite in the Mammoth campground on fire, burning royally, colorfully, fully, completely, dangerously, emergency.

He gunned it and got there, alerting the communications center, the fire truck.

The adrenalin felt good, competent, under control because the campers weren't as he curved into, between the campsites, each site yelling, pointing a different direction, the fire full among them, full into two trees.

He hit his lights and hit the brakes. Right away he knew-prepare, amateurs, accident, family-size tent burned to its aluminum frame, all their gear on fire.

The father was fighting fire with frantic behavior.

"Christ! Christ!" he yelled at Paul. "My kid! My kid!"

"Back there, ranger! Back there!" another camper yelled.

"The pump fountain!"

He held the steering wheel steady, backing up the thirty yards.

"Oh, my baby, my baby!" a woman, a mother cried, her infant in her arms, under the cold water, the infant's shoulder, arm, half her face burned, peeled of its skin, crying, screaming.

Paul made instant sense, order of it. "Get in the car! Get in the car!" mother in a bathrobe, infant naked in her arms.

"My baby, my baby girl," not as loud in the back seat.

Paul got to the father. "I'm taking them to the clinic!" out the window. The father seemed to understand, holding two young children.

"Hurry, ranger," he said.

Paul did, telling the comm center, and the park the predicament he was extricating these people from. "There'll be someone waiting at the clinic ..." the radio told him.

They passed the fire trucks on the way down. Low crying and whimpering from the back seat.

"Take it easy, take it easy, we're almost there," as easy as he could say it. He turned off the flashing lights and turned into the one level, hard-rock medical clinic. Everyone was waiting.

The doctor and the nurse took the baby. Paul took the mother's arm and took her in. He sat her down. The doctor reassured her, went to ease the baby's pain.

Paul eased away from them, out into the fresh air and took a major dose of it.

The boss, Dave Hess, a spit stream of tobacco juice onto the back lawn. "Tough stuff. Poor little kid. Propane, right?"

"Definitely."

"Good you got there so quick."

Paul heard congratulations and envy. Action was action in the mostly inactive ranger world.

An ambulance backed in.

"What'll they do, take her to Lake hospital?" Paul asked.

"Right now. Let me go in and check up. You need to?"

"No. I'll let her mom take care. I'll go down and let the dad know. Let me calm down a bit."

"Good goin', Barnes, uh, Paul. And now ya'll get Tower ranger station."

"Yeah." He was going to say something about being a ranger out in Lamar Valley, but now wasn't the time or place.

He sat in the patrol car, in the campground, noting the time and place in his official notes, the baby's family slow-motioning themselves into their van, starting on Paul's directions to Lake hospital.

He completed his shift in silence, silently saying so long to Mammoth Hot Springs, the Mammoth hot springs terraces sending up columns of smoke signals.

Good signs. He signed off with the comm center.

CHAPTER

Goodbye to Mammoth and Gardiner. Only about twenty miles away at Tower, but the park changed so much in so few miles.

He went to the K-Bar first.

Pool balls clicking, good crowd crowding together, laughing, bragging, eating, drinking, enjoying.

Karen threw her arms around him. "Hiya, handsome. Where's your girlfriend?" without being nasty.

"Rachel?" Away in Bozeman for a few days."

"Oh."

"Where's your fiance?"

"Away in Jackson for a few days."

"Oh?" and they both laughed, knowing a secret, a secret wet on their tongues.

"I've come to say so long," with an embarrassed laugh, different now because of Rachel. Different because he normally would have jumped at the chance, jumped on the chance.

"So long? Where are you going?"

"Tower."

"Lucky you."

"That's what everyone says."

"Buy you a beer?"

"Please."

She made them a place at a table with a crew of bus drivers and wranglers, guys you'd find standing behind the fold-out kitchen of a chuck wagon.

The beer-guzzle talk was of the park. Paul hung on every word, his words given a certain extra weight because now he was government.

They joked him up about speeding in their buses, catching their illegal fish, hiking their illegal trails, finding their mythical grizzly bears, but all in all, all of them felt a pride in him, for him.

"Thanks, I gotta go."

"What's your rush?" hand on his knee from Karen.

"I want to see if Mary Gregor is home."

"She's always home," from a bus driver.

O.K. That's one reason why I want to see her. That solitary, satisfied feeling I got from Larry. It's around her.

"See you at Tower," from two dirt-stained wranglers.

"Come back in and let me buy you a beer," from an Ohioan bus driver.

"See you all," from Paul.

He made his way through the co-eds out into the big Montana night.

He took the road up to Mary's. All her lights were still on.

He knocked and Mary was glad to see him. "Well, hello, Paul. Please, come in." Mary had company. "Paul, this is Jason." She paused. "He's from our church out on the river."

"Oh?" meaning oh, yeah? Paul gave him an oh, yeah once over.

Young, maybe twenty-one, short blond hair, trim, sun-burned face, freckles.

"He's left them."

"Oh?" still not sure, still on guard against them.

"Please, have a seat," Mary removing a stack of topographic maps from the hardwood chair, removing a compass, binoculars and a canteen from the arm.

"No thanks, Mary," eyeing Jason, eyeing Mary. "I've just come to let you know that I'm moving out to Tower."

"Off to Lamar?"

"Uh, no."

"Close, Tower," with a knowing smile.

He stopped eyeing Mary. "Maybe."

"I'll come out and visit you."

"Sure. I didn't mean so long."

She followed him to the door. He heard Jason say, "good night."

"Good night," out into the open air.

"He's fine, Paul. Trying to find a way out. He's a surfer from south California."

That meant beach, ocean. Paul relaxed.

"The perfect place. You'll see."

184

"Maybe we can hide him out in Lamar."

"I'll see you soon?"

"Soon. Oh, I thought it might excite you to know that I followed a grizzly in the Canyon area a few days ago." She followed him to his car. "I've been telling Jason about Larry."

He smiled. "Thanks."

He drove home, making believe that he could follow a grizzly bear.

CHAPTER

"You follow Specimen Ridge out to Slough Creek." They were up on the Mt. Washburn road, on the Tower side, the Tower sub-district side.

His new boss, Dave Ellison, big, round, and pink with a Yosemite-Sam moustache, was giving him the overlook of the Tower patrol district.

Vast, as Dave Ellison ran an arm out to encompass the hefty rise of ground, green grass and thin forests that made Specimen Ridge, the ridge under a fleet of clouds under full white sail.

"We go out just beyond Slough Creek, then Lamar begins, the northeast sub-district."

"I see, I see." He did, sheriff of all he surveyed, enchanted, in love with it. He heard Dave Ellison say something to him.

"I heard your fire on the radio. Good work. Did you hear about the other fire?"

Enchanted, Paul heard himself say, "other fire? What other fire?"

"Out at the religious ranch."

He listened up. "No."

"Stack of hay bales. About three in the morning."

"Really?"

"Now get this. Somebody said it might have been started by a flaming arrow."

"Really?" absolutely amazed, up here, where you could climb on board one of those cloud ships, talking about hearing a tale of flaming arrows.

"Is it true?"

Dave Ellison shrugged his droopy shoulders. "Could be. Anything's possible. Somebody says they saw something."

"Far out, as they say." Did I see a quiver of arrows hanging on what's his name's porch?

"Another friend of the prophet's I see."

Paul hesitated, new on the job, new to this boss. "I guess so."

"No explanation required. Did you meet everybody this morning?"

"I did." He ran the three other rangers quickly through another screening. Dan. A wide open face, wide open smile, a handshake worthy of a man, a friend. Ed. School teacher, out on a summer lark with his sail boat and his whole family. Looked like the local hardware owner. Bill. A Mormon from Utah. Empty, flat, white in the face. A shop-teacher type with a chip on his shoulder.

Now screening what he saw before him. Sweeping it in, an ocean made of earth.

"Ready to head back?"

"Ready," enchanted, contented.

They came down through the gathering crowds, just about every station wagon, every RV, every motorcycle giving them a wave, both of them in the official stuff.

They got out at the Tower Fall store to quell a "That's my parking space" uprising.

Down on the flat just before Roosevelt Lodge they stopped to let the history go by.

Paul just shook his head. A stage-coach with full stage-coach team came lurching out from the corral at the lodge, tourists on top and inside, cowhand and sidekick at the reins, snapping the reins, convincing the six horses, controlling the six horses.

The very, very early tour bus headed out into the brush, bouncing in behind a hill, gone, dust.

"All in a day's work, Barnes."

"I guess."

His work day began.

CHAPTER

It began with a turn through the small campground, up on a rise above Tower Fall.

The usual. Here, Mr. Ranger, touch my son, make him whole.

Hey, Mr. Ranger, someone took my spot! Here, Mr. Ranger, have a burger. Hey, Mr. Ranger, we're from Arizona!

Most everyone was gone from the campground, out in the park, enjoying themselves--hopefully.

The visitors were beginning to get a bit uneasy now. Where are the animals? Demanding to know now. Not just bears, but all the elk, moose, bison and coyote now. "Up in the higher meadows," didn't quite satisfy them. Mr. Ranger Barnes found himself explaining the balance of things to a lot of out-of-towners.

He made a turn through the parking lot down below at the Tower store. He made sure of the directions he gave out to fifteen different parts of the park. He made sure of campground capacities around the park over the radio.

The radio. He really enjoyed it, casual, fairly formal, always laced with each individual voice, each individual area, each individual accent, each influenced by the park's personality.

He was following a fire lookout following the spark of a fire; following a trail crew returning from a few days in the Lake back country; following a report of a car that had been broken into at Old Faithful.

He drove across the confluence where the Yellowstone allowed the Lamar River to join it. He had a specific spot in mind to park and get some business noted.

Two paper-white trumpeter swans--in a pond about the size of a backyard pool. The pool floated in a green, burnt-gold clearing, green and golden reeds swaying, wrapped around the pond and its swans.

Not a bad spot to check up on all his fishing regulations.

Let-the-games-begin had begun.

The clouds floated like the white swans, a photographer with a tripod and a lens, like something from the bridge of a ship, taking pictures from a safe distance. The photographer fit. Like a fly fisher? Paul asked himself. One photographer anyway.

Swans mate for life, he reminded himself. Rachel. Back tomorrow night. He sang some lyrics. "I'm gettin' hungry, hungry for your love ..." incredibly out of key. Beach Boys? Laughing at himself, he continued on patrol.

No doors to check, no flashlights into back seats, no sirens.

Lower parts of Specimen Ridge, like young women reclining on their sides, elbows, the grass dry, the upper of the ridge still green, still snow on Cutoff Mountain like a Himalaya out there to the east.

He pulled out above the Lamar River, active, creative under the two-lane bridge. The river reminded him of fishing. He turned back to head for a favorite hole.

He knew the Lamar Valley was just, just up the empty road. He turned back to head for the favorite hole.

His binoculars could find elk across six meadows. He trained them on the favorite spot where the Lamar flowed into the Yellowstone. Couple of trucks, couple of cars parked above the rivers.

He trained the binoculars on the river. Is that somebody giving me the finger, blown up in my binoculars? He took them away from his face to blink, to check, to see with his own eyes the figure down on the river.

He put the glasses back. Sure enough, the fishing figure was like a statue that gave the bird, fishing with one hand, saying "fuck you, ranger," with the other.

Paul focused. He didn't need to. He knew who it was. It was Gary Delling, looking like a cross between a native brave, a gypsy and a rag picker. Shirt off, hair in braids, a cutthroat trout on a piece of cardboard at his feet, that finger still in the air.

Paul smiled. He understood. He knew Gary Delling would have a license.

So, you're out here too. So, that felt O.K. in a way.

Flaming arrows? Paul checked with the binoculars one more time. Yep. "O.K., bub, I'll be seeing you."

CHAPTER

The horses being loaded in the trailers woke him, the corral just behind the window of his bunkhouse room.

Right up in bed, right away glad for the morning. I'm going out to Lamar today. Why am I so glad? The horses weren't particularly glad to be leaving the barn, the hay, saying so.

Paul showered and dressed and joined the rest of the station at the corral.

He sat on the rail fence and tried to learn a bit. Horses were still new to him. Concrete had been a lot of his life back across the Mississippi. Cabs were horses.

"How long?" he asked Dan Carter, spurs, boots, hat, chaps, a mile-wide smile.

"Four days," absolute relief in his voice. Out of the patrol car, away from Mr. & Mrs. America. He coaxed his mount and his mule into the trailer.

"I hear you're going out to Lamar today," smiling, knowingly across his sun-burned face.

"I am, right now." He climbed down off the fence. How would I look in spurs?

"Enjoy it!" Dan yelled at his back.

"You, too! I know you will!"

There was a dead elk some bear had chewed on out where Dan was going, up on the Buffalo Plateau, across Hell Roaring creek. How would I look in spurs, galloping away? He dug his spurs into the gas pedal.

Across the Lamar River, past the nesting swans, only 8: 30 a.m., past the gravel entrance to Slough Creek Campground, into the short, bouldered canyon, the Lamar River pounding through. He pulled into a turn out and listened to it.

It wasn't a roar, it was a reminder of high waterfalls and white water, power, assurance, reassurance. Ahead he could see where the canyon and the boulders became meadow and forest again.

A valley.

He checked his equipment. Larry's coin in pocket? He rubbed. Yes. He checked the side mirror for animal, vegetable or visitor and pulled out.

It wasn't long before he pulled over. He had to. The Lamar Valley.

As if nature had conspired, aspired to make this valley thus, so, like this. Mountain and grassland, cliff and river, hills and aspens, hills and pines, flatland and cottonwood, bison and elk.

Specimen Ridge ran out into the long, open, ample valley, making it a valley from the right, up across from the flat, turning, curving Lamar River.

Bare rolling hills, bare but for the wheat burnt grasses, rolled down from the tree line along the right and left flank of it. An enormous sky stretched across it.

He'd come upon a secret place, secluded. A Brigadoon that could only exist when you stood here, outside the car, scratching your head, feeling tranquility like a drug.

What did Larry say of India, the mountains? A beauty near to pain? A pain that he would gladly die from? Paul never felt so alive. All oceans, all sunsets, all of his life was here. Perhaps that was the pain, the ache of living, feeling, knowing something totally, clearly, completely.

This place is for me. This place.

Specimen Ridge. Ridge didn't do its softness justice: green, brown, gray, green again. He followed its length. Its length took him to two matched peaks under the far edge of the enormous sky.

Paul ached. The ache that a woman gave you. This place wasn't mother nature--it was his woman, nature, his lover, nature.

His love, his bride, nature. He went to her.

CHAPTER

He let the car almost coast, down into the shallow valley.

I'm going to marry Rachel and settle down in here. He had the house already picked out.

It stood on a rise, rail picket-fence around its brown logs.

His dream house had its windows on the valley, quiet, secluded, a few intruders.

He'd put it right here where a brown log house with a rail picket-fence already looked out over the Lamar River and the aspens, the cottonwoods, the ridge line, the velvet meadows.

One of the ultimate coups as an employee of Yellowstone National Park. A place of your own. A house. A residence. An identity. A personality.

This ranch house was the nutshell of it all. I'm going to marry Rachel and live right here. He drove up a dirt driveway up into the settled complex: a John Ford, log barn, wood plank bunkhouse, a cottage-size house, and a big house out on a peninsula of rich ground above the road. A generator rattled in a rattled down shed. Two horses poked around in a stockyard wide corral. A mailbox on a rail post. Home. I've come home, Larry.

Someone was coming out of the log home. Someone tall and trim, with a military cut for a haircut, a green backpack, park service uniform of gray, short sleeves, green khakis, hiking boots.

The backpack looked packed for a few days.

He was as tan as leather, ranch hand in the face.

"Hiya," Paul said to him.

"Hello," and he kept on walking.

Paul sat and watched him, delightfully puzzled by him.

A pale-green pickup truck came down the road from the north and stopped. The tall, trim fella dropped his pack in the truck bed, got in the cab; the truck turned, drove away, disappeared behind the two mounds of a hill.

Paul followed it. Now who in the hell was that? He gave up his guessing at the leathery figure because two goliath bison were taking their time climbing up from a stream, onto the road shoulder and on across the road, big as you please.

"Please, let me live here," he asked of them.

"Please let me live here." Here in these cottonwoods, here where the Lamar made a deep, wide bend, a deep wide hole, a picnic table and a latrine; a fishin' hole. Paul sat quietly and watched one lone fly caster work the river. "Yes, you can live here in my valley."

His valley opened up where Specimen Ridge came down to meet the valley floor. An enormous expanse of Yellowstone spread into the distance. A quick-running creek ran below the road bed. He followed it.

The creek took him past the sun-burnt flora, the remaining fauna, the low-level hills, the distant forests, into an enormous turnout for an enormous view of what had been concealed behind a curve and a curtain of hills.

"I will live here!"

Take every color required in nature, take every detail that made Yellowstone--the mountains, the rivers, the earth, the planet, the Adam, the Eve, the Eden, the privilege.

Blue and white sky, golden and emerald valley floor. A deep brown ridge rising straight up. Follow that ridge to a fudge brown mountain, jagged as a castle keep. On to the north of that peak a higher peak, black as charcoal, gnarled and weathered by every storm that ever came across northern North America.

Lower down, green-leafed aspens swayed, two swollen creeks made some wetlands. A deep-grooved hiking trail crossed a wooden footbridge and off into the great unknown.

Paul drove a short distance to get a better view of it all.

The better view of it was from atop a defunct geyser mound, round at the base, chalk white funnel to its top like a miniature volcano.

He got up on it four jumps and sat down. Sulphur smell, the thermal not quite finished. Bison skull stuck in the mud below.

He turned, a light illuminating itself. "Holy fuckin' shit!"

He yelled it for all this world to hear. Two elk, two bison over there in the aspens were the only other living creatures who heard. They didn't look up from their preparations for winter.

He climbed down and continued on.

Continuing on was wide open and then closed in on both sides, narrowed and flat, tall and craggy. There were two jeeps in a turnout, a deep, worn trail switching back up a hill, into the fir trees. Must be fish up there was his thought.

Must be a campground, cooking smoke twisting up between the pines, voices in echoes, a dog barking, wood being snapped into fire pieces.

Pebble Creek campground on a well-named creek with black, gray and smooth white stones in the creek bed, the creek running shallow and swift.

Civilization, nomadic type. Tents. A family with a teepee, lodge poles locked at the top. A couple in a one room RV. An encampment stuck back in the trees, off the road, up against the rising of the ground; up against the canyon wall where the creek fell from above. Far up above these was a rock ridgeline cut like the blocks of a castle wall. An absolutely perfect place to camp, stay, live, work. Paul was convinced.

Black clouds lumbered into the sky. The temperature dropped ten degrees. It got dark. He looked up the road to his left.

I'll leave what's left of this for another time.

He turned right and headed back to Tower. The black clouds moored themselves to the valley's peaks. They unloaded their cargo.

Hail, beaded curtains of it as big as your thumbnail, pelting the road and the running surface of the Lamar River. He had to turn on his headlights.

The sun came out so hard he had to shield his eyes from it.

The sun came out. Rachel was waiting for him under the U. S. flag at the Tower ranger station.

"Hello, stranger," he said to her.

"Hello there, ranger," coming to the driver's window.

Paul wore the biggest shit-eating grin in all the western states. The taste of her kiss added to it.

"I've been there, Rachel." She knelt down on a knee beside the car.

"Out there, Lamar?"

"Uh-huh," a numbness, a starry-eyedness in his answer.

She put her hand on his shoulder. "Good for you. Good for you."

"Uh-huh, uh-huh," wonderfully silly with it all.

"Will you let me come visit you?"

"I'm not there yet, but I'd love to, I love you," hurried in right after "I'd love to."

"And now you've got Lamar on top of everything else," was her answer.

Any answer but "drop dead" would suffice for today.

"Where's your truck?"

"Up at the corral. They told me you were out east."

"Hop in."

Dave Ellison waved him down. "Come see me in a bit. Got an assignment for you."

"Sure. Rachel, Dave."

"Sure, I know Rachel."

"I'll be right back, Dave."

"Just come on in the house."

He dropped Rachel at the corral. She jumped up and sat on the rail fence. Paul walked back down to the house. Dave Ellison waited at the door.

The black sky from Lamar came with the hail. Rachel ran and stood in the shelter of the tack room, staring out at it, everything sharp and cold as it passed over and left everything silent.

"Yahoo! Yahoo!"

Someone was yelling "yahoo!" Rachel stepped out from the doorway. That someone yelling "yahoo!" was Paul Barnes, running up the road, waving his arms.

"Yahoo!"

If he had a ten gallon hat he would have flung it in the air.

A red-tail hawk in the sky would have caught it. "Yahoo!"

Rachel stood with her hands on her hips, a smile like a knowing mother, a knowing woman behind the man.

"I got it!" he yelled, grabbing her, whirling with her, loving her, loving that she was here to share it. It. Lamar Valley.

"What, what?" she screeched, giggling. She knew. "Stop grinning," giggling.

He caught his breath. "Yahoo!" a coyote, a ranger in heat.

"Man, yer lookin' at the new Lamar Valley ranger."

"Oh, Paul." She held him like they'd both won, like everyone who worked in Yellowstone had won.

"Come on, let's go to Gardiner and celebrate." She grabbed his hand.

"Yeah, yeah. Oh, wait, I've got to work. I've got a shift."

"Well, let's go to your room and celebrate."

He was about to run, pulling her by the hand. He let everything settle in.

"No, it's too daylight and too small, too close to everyone."

"I don't mind."

All of a sudden he did. "No, this has to be perfect."

"Perfect? Out in Lamar?"

"Yes. I'll be living at the ranch. As of tomorrow night."

"Tomorrow night then?" whispering it in his ear, holding him tight, tighter than any time before.

Paul felt that, wondered what the extra need was. He could only wonder what it would be like to love her out there.

"So, we are agreed?" he asked her.

"We are."

"Come on, help me pack."

"Oh, sure, we can't make love, but we can haul your junk."

"Yahoo!"

It took them about a half an hour, his junk amounting to the back seat and trunk.

She kidded him. "Today Tower, tomorrow Lamar."

"Mañana then?"

"Mañana."

CHAPTER

Mañana. No stars, no moon, ceiling zero. A storm found the elevation to its liking. Snow at the higher elevations, tar paper black lower down.

The Yellowstone ran black, deep and fast, cold, run off, white caps breaking across rocks.

Gary Delling wrapped his ponytail with a rubber band and pulled the wet suit hood over his head. All in black now.

Not a sound but for the running of the river.

Not a light but for a pen light he held in his teeth, checking the waterproof pack, his gear. Satisfied he snapped out the light.

He took a coil of nylon line from around his shoulder. One end went around a tree trunk, the other around his waist. He slipped the pack on and secured it with a strap across his chest.

He stepped into the edge of the Yellowstone.

He scooped it up and rubbed his face with it. He lowered himself in and let the current take him, fighting it to his left, his left, his left, across to the cottonwoods on the other bank.

He played out the line, keeping himself tight, kicking hard, letting the river take him, letting out the line, letting the current throw him into the low branches hanging into the river. He gulped some of the river and caught hold.

He was across the river, holding on against the current, the current pulling at his pack. He held on and tied on to a heavy root, pushing himself between two heavy rocks.

He didn't wait to catch his breath. Up on the bank, belly down in the short grass.

He could see at night. He'd learned how in the pitch that was night in Vietnam. He could see what he was looking for--a tall dark hulk in the dark. A drilling rig on a truck bed.

Steam from a thermal vent on the river bank blew across him.

The drilling rig was here to punch a hole through the ground, to get at the thermal heat, the steam, the power, the electricity for the ranch, the residents, the worshippers, the flock, the faithful.

He could see the rig in the dark.

Headlights on high beams beamed across the landscape and turned away to the left down behind two hills.

He got up and ran, pack pulled tight at the chest, scuba boots soft, silent on the ground.

He got to the rig and got himself flat between the cab of the heavy diesel truck and the flat bed with the raised drilling derick. He laid there and held his breath.

The high beam headlights came back, the faithful on patrol, armed patrol. He tucked himself in among the wires and cables, just a black shape.

The high beams drove away towards the lights of the central buildings.

He got up on his knees and went to his business, quickly.

He found the fuel intake on the big generator. He had three water bottles wrapped in black tape. He got the caps off.

He poured the sand in first, then the slow maple syrup.

Quickly, he jumped down.

A long, thin, flexible length of metal. In through the truck cab's vent window. He searched for it, keeping himself steady, his hands sweating.

He got it. The driver's door popped open.

Quickly, he reached in, found it, popped the hood open, easy, bracing for the sound. Quickly, he lifted the hood just enough to unscrew the radiator cap.

Two water bottles from the pack. Syrup and sand.

He spit, closed the hood, locked the door, knelt beside the rig. Darkness, silence, ceiling zero. A coyote yelled in agreement. He sprinted for the river.

The cold of the water on his face shook him good. It felt good.

He tied the line around his waist and let go into the river.

He floated down river. He pulled in on the line, pushing, kicking for the other side.

The line swung out, tightened, swinging him like a pendulum towards the other bank.

He banged into the rocks, the scrub brush, across, exhausted, holding on.

Slower than quick he made sure he was unbroken. He got the line from around his waist.

Rested a bit he moved quickly, recoiling the length of the line back up river to where he'd tied it on.

He coiled it over his shoulder, laid on his stomach in the grass.

Gary Delling spit, got up and ran.

A coyote yelled in agreement.

CHAPTER

Lightning. The storm scraped along Specimen Ridge, throwing sparks along the length of the ridge. The storm woke them.

Paul and Rachel had front row seats, front row rail fence around the ranch house.

No one around for miles. Paul wore nothing, Rachel in his bathrobe. The rain and the snow were beyond the ridgeline.

Electric white fractures of lightning. Compound, compounded fractures of it.

"Aren't you cold?" She left out the "sweetheart," but you could almost hear it in there.

"Never," and he snuggled up behind her, warm against the terry cloth.

She felt him hard against her. "Mmmm. Gimme him." She faced him. A roll of thunder like the coming of creation.

Like the coming of a man as she jerked him, jerked him, jerked it, held it, pulled it, jerked it, jerked it, jerked, jerked, jerked.

Like the moaning of a man, shivering from the jerking.

"You got it all over the bathrobe."

"The hell with the bathrobe," gulping for voice on her shoulder.

"I love you, Paul," deep and rich, puzzling.

He heard too much in it, in there in it. Sounded like some excuse was in there in it.

The storm was passing. He let it pass. It passed very slowly, but it passed.

"So much for the light show," he said.

"What a world out here, Paul. Your world. A privilege for me to be here."

"What's mine is yours."

"I know," tickling him where it tickled best.

"Now I'm cold. Let's go in."

A kitchen, white and simple, four rooms, about four pieces of furniture, oil burner for heat, a mattress on the floor for a bed, some shelves, a closet, a park radio on a table, a rack of elk antlers, a battered rug, windows all across the side of the logs, Lamar Valley and Yellowstone everywhere you looked. Home.

He heard her get up twice during the night.

CHAPTER

He heard her in the kitchen in the morning. A bison, rubbing off its decaying winter hide against the side of the house, was his alarm clock.

"Hiya. I didn't want to wake you. You looked too content.

I've got to run. I forgot I was so far from Gardiner. Easy to out here."

"Stay here," he said, joking.

"Wouldn't I love to. I made you some coffee," making ready to run.

Were you going to leave me sleeping? was sort of a nasty question forming in his mouth, but . . .

The big brown bison walked by the kitchen window, its back as big as a compact car. How could he be nasty.

"Call me?" she asked.

"I will."

She came to him.

"Congratulations. Your life begins out here." She hugged him, strength, joy. She hugged him longer than Paul thought was necessary.

He asked her, his lips in her hair. "Everything all right, Rachel?"

"Not here, Paul, not now."

"Something?"

"No, nothing. Leaving here makes Gardiner a major urban city.

Too many faces, places. Work. Ugh."

"Come back soon then."

"Soon then," kissing his cheek.

He now wore the bathrobe. It smelled of life, like his own buffalo robe.

"Come on, I'll walk you out."

Deep summer here was like early fall in other places, other elevations. You came to life quickly in your groggy morning, bracing, embracing.

Paul shook his head. Knock wood disbelief, belief. "You look great."

She did, black, high top Converse sneakers, white socks, dungaree jeans cut to shorts with the denim fold, the denim cuff just right, white T-shirt scrubbed pure white, a black leather vest and a broken-in New York Yankees cap, the official version.

She tugged the vest like a Gentleman Jim Corbet. "Miss Lamar Valley?"

"What's your talent? Uh, what's your other talent?"

"Rowing a raft down the Yellowstone. And I better get going." Kissing through the driver's window. "Larry, your friend, would be proud, Paul."

All was all right. Questions needed no answers.

"Yeah, I think he'd approve."

"I've got a place to take you to out here."

"I approve."

She drove out of the valley.

CHAPTER

Paul drove into the valley, full uniform. Someone had left the patrol car during the night. Someone drove up. Someone drove away.

Once upon a time there was a fairly handsome prince. The time was 2:00 p.m. A shift would be to 10:00. He was on his way to meet his boss, Lee Whitson.

Sick was Dave Ellison's description of him. Too long in the woods. Wants the ocean, the Keys, the scuba, the light of it, the no snow of it. Can't get it. Got a jug around most of the time.

A good man, just tired.

The radio told him what the two and a half million acres were up to.

He wasn't doing much so he pulled over. A fly fisherman, knee deep, where Cache Creek multiplied itself into four fast channels, cast his line, cast his line. Paul pulled over.

What is it, Paul? The fly tier cast his net. That's it? Like he was casting a net, in an ancient river, in the ancient manner--civilization, early on, easy on the source.

Paul could see Larry. Not with rod and line, but on the bank, sharing the time with the one casting the net. The official stamp of approval.

Something on the fly line, Paul following as close as he could out the window. Fly fishing. What did that bus driver from Missoula call lure, bait fishing? Bowling for fish? Ha, right.

Then it happened. A bear, a grizzly bear. Blood, flesh, the flesh and blood of a human, a visitor, over the radio. Paul sat up straight.

The ranger, breathing hard over the radio. The Pelican Creek trail. You could hear it in his heavy breathing--what he was reporting.

Someone beside the trail, about seven miles in from Fishing Bridge. Someone a grizzly bear had been at. A human.

You could hear him gulping, reporting it. They'd been looking for her. She'd been late coming out from a back country campsite.

She was alone. Looked like she had an illegal campsite beside the trail. Looked like she was dead.

The ranger began to describe her condition. Shit, shit was in there in his description of her neck, her arm, her back.

Someone came on the radio and told the ranger to switch channels. The car radio went blank, just static.

The radio stayed blank until someone had the nerve to come on with some local traffic, some simple stuff like campground reports.

Business was unusual in Yellowstone, in the wild.

Ranger Barnes got out of the patrol car. Pelican Creek was in another ecosystem, far across and beyond the valley. He stood in the turnout and looked up and down the valley. Serene, like they first tried out serene here.

He could feel the fear of a wild animal, deep, ancient within him. He felt absolutely, totally alive. A dead hiker. Eaten. Wild.

He wanted to howl like a coyote, a wolf, in mourning, in glory, in sorrow, in exhilaration.

He shut up and took it in stride. It took some doing, but he got in stride with the enormous event, the enormous hoop.

He took it in stride, some of the Pebble Creek Campground residents practically bowing as he drove through, checking up. He was thinking, I know something you don't know. Boy, do I know something you don't know. I guess you'll find out. It'll make the hair on the back of your neck … He drove out of the campground.

Now, come on, Paul. You know who it reminds you of. You've been to school. Think. Which artist? Baronett's Peak, on his left, followed him along the road. It was some sort of medieval city in the sky, a civilization of advanced cave dwellers. Adobe cliff dwellers, wet sand castles on sandy beaches too. Or, or? Who is it, Paul? Spanish? Right.

Got it. Gaudi.

Like a potter's wheel in an abstract hand, used to mold this peak, this abstract, undulating version of a cliff face, the face weeping tears of thin cascades, thin snow melt.

It undulated away into the spruce, the pines, the fir trees closing in on both sides.

A narrow canyon, narrow curves, sweet water current in a sweet creek, verdant rolls of grass, verdant air of the high altitudes.

The road eased higher, easing to a stop just below the alpine logs and the shake-shingle roof of the Northeast entrance, backed up with traffic.

CHAPTER

Rachel checked for traffic in the side view mirror. She checked the boat trailer in the rear view mirror.

The gray raft was plenty secure. Traffic picking up. She signalled and bounced into a picnic table turnout. She was bringing the raft back up from Livingston.

A good float from Gardiner to the railroad city. Just about fifty miles of a group from the Audubon Society. All day. No complaints, questions that made sense.

She was going to make some sense of why she was pulling over.

Charley. Charley Gates. That Charley. Her Charley--once upon a Charley.

He was across the Yellowstone, in that house now. Now, in that house.

Everyone knew that house, wrapped in the cottonwoods, smack in the Paradise Valley, smack on the river, smack on the map of the art world; the three story ranch house with the pagoda studio on top.

It was the home of Carlyle Stevens, painter, sculptor, one of the Paradise Valley's favorite sons, favorite artists; one among the many who made Montana their studio.

Rachel knew. A postcard trail from Paris, from Charley.

Charley, and she smiled a wise smile.

Charley meets Carlyle Stevens in Paris. Carlyle Stevens is seventy-eight years old now, in need of some assistance. Charley Gates has a gift for it. Charley has a collection of short stories published in New York. Charley gets around. Charley needs a place to live. He gets Carlyle Stevens to take him on. Cook and bottle washer, free rent, free space. Charley knows Yellowstone. The bargain is sealed.

No postcard could tell her all this. Charley Gates told her.

The postcard trail was bringing him west from New York. A bookstore in Bozeman, Montana. Surprise, somewhat.

"Hello, Rachel."

"Well, hello, Charley," chestnut hair, shoulder length, thick, parted down the middle, a blond beard and moustache always to a stubble growth, green eyes, browned skin, assurance all over his lean face. Good teeth, crows feet outside the green eyes, a little touch of marijuana red in the whites of his eyes, boots and jeans and a shirt from either the Seminoles or from Guatemala. An Aztec pendant on a silver chain hung from around his neck.

"Charley Gates," Rachel said. She found herself sharing a beer with him. Now here she was with a pair of binoculars scanning the famous house.

Rachel, what in the hell are you doing? This guy says he's going to take a hike without you, and here you are. She set the binoculars on the front seat. She could hear the chopping of wood carried across the river. She picked up the binoculars.

"Shit ...

There he was, chopping wood, without a shirt, sweat, Montana all over him.

"Shit." Paul Barnes, Pauley. That made her feel better. She got Carlyle Stevens in her glasses, out on the porch, walking with a cane, brittle, like an old bone, his work like Frederick Remington and Charlie Russell meeting Paul Cezanne.

Paul Cezanne. That made her feel better.

She pulled out and kept the big house in the mirror.

"Shit." She carried that with her for a few miles. A few more miles and she was above the Yellowstone, across the river from her religious neighbors.

Her righteous neighbors were busy around a drilling rig. Busy with a deputy sheriff's car.

That's right, she remembered. Somebody screwing around with their drilling equipment. Her short smile said, I think I know who's been screwing with them.

That smile made her feel better. Paul will get a kick out of this. Paul. That made her feel better.

CHAPTER

Nothing could make Lee Whitson feel any better. Key Largo, Florida maybe.

Thank goodness we had the bear attack to talk about. Ranger Barnes sat on the edge of the extinct volcano, the Soda Butte thermal. He had a map spread out on his lap.

Lee Whitson had been as Dave Ellison described. A bit distant, disinterested, biding his remaining time, stuck up out of the way in Yellowstone's northeast woods. Count your blessings, all your blessings was Paul's opinion.

They talked of the bear attack, then into Paul's duties and boundaries and that was that. Could the woods do that? Paul stared; without the deep circles under his eyes and the cigarettes, Lee Whitson could have once been a kid, like me? He met the two college kids and the retired Philadelphia fire fighter who ran the entrance station and that was that.

Now he was the law in Lamar. Now he needed the map to get a better lay of the law. Lee Whitson had promised some backcountry patrol come September, come the hunting season outside. He patrolled the back country on his map.

Features had faces, names now. The great black peak right here was the Thunderer, 10,554. Abiathar Peak to the northeast nearby, 10,928. Mt. Norris, 9,936.

Well-named Saddle Mtn., north, up the valley, beyond the valley. He looked for the sharp alpine peaks, above everything up at the Northeast entrance. There and there on the map. Meridian Peak, 10,538. Republic Pass, 10,000. If heaven could be found in the clouds, well ...

Water. Creeks. Calfee Creek, Miller Creek, Cache Creek, Cold Creek. Back in there, in the back of this country, Yellowstone's back. Where that fella I saw at the ranch house must be.

Lee Whitson warned him. He's a pure loner.

I understand. Sitting there alone, Paul began to understand.

He wasn't alone. He watched it but he wasn't quite sure he was believing it.

A blue Chevy Bronco pulled off on the narrow road shoulder.

A father got out. A young son followed. The father and son unloaded a small dirt bike from the back.

They wouldn't, Paul thought. They did. The young boy jumped on and drove out into the sage and elk thistle, whining, blowing blue exhaust smoke.

Paul rubbed his hands together. I spring into action. The law of Lamar.

He pulled up in the patrol car easy like, the father waving hello, like "hey, how about that boy of mine? Ain't this park great?"

He didn't like what Paul had to tell him. He took it in his manhood; all Iowa farmer, manhood of him. Paul didn't like his tone. The law.

He wrote him a wonderful citation. The guy truly deserved it. He'd fucked with Yellowstone, with Lamar. The father's son only wanted to touch the ranger.

The father left tough guy skid marks in the gravel.

Ahhh. Paul was prince of all he surveyed. He surveyed the last days in June.

CHAPTER

A meteorite shower for Paul's birthday, July 10th. He and his guests at the ranch, Rachel, Mary and her guest Jason, were sitting on the shaggy lawn, watching the colored stones flash across the universe, across the great black sky.

"Candles on your cake, Paul," Rachel told him.

"There's one!" Jason cried out.

A long green trace across the black, between the white stars.

They sat and waited. About an hour's worth so far.

"I'm cold."

Paul bundled up with Rachel.

"Maybe that's the end of it." Mary stood up. Mary sat down.

A red, a red, a blue, a green, raced each other through the stars, into eternity. They all applauded.

"Let's go in?" Paul pulled Rachel to her feet.

Warm, and warm coffee, with a shot of Jack Daniel's, everyone seated in the sparse living room.

Everyone would be staying the night, the night now about midnight, Mary and Jason heading out in the morning for Miller Creek. Bears. Take a look, take a sample, take a study, take a long, leisurely hike. Take care.

All of them comfortable on the battered furniture.

"Where's your roommate?" Mary asked.

"Mr. Davis? Sorry, I shouldn't call him that. Only fifty after all. Tom's out back somewhere out there. He'll be gone for a week." The Jack in the coffee felt really loose.

"Remarkable guy. A loner, like he invented it. Fed up with the human race I think. Ex-marine, ex-executive at Hughes aircraft, Princeton grad.

"He owns one spoon, one fork, one knife, one plate, one Nash Rambler. Chucked it all one day and took what he needed.

"Looks the ex-Marine part. A piece of rawhide with eyes." Rachel and Jason laughed.

"We're both glad we only see each other a few days a month."

"Feels good out here doesn't it, Paul, the solitude." Mary rocked in the rocker.

He didn't hesitate, ponder. "It does, Mary. I get the folks at Pebble Creek and that's enough. I'm looking forward to September when I get out of the patrol car and onto the backcountry a lot more."

"Important," Rachel added. "Get back in, remember exactly why we're here."

"Yes," Mary answered. "I'm taking Jason in to show him a big piece. Get him away from some pesky folks."

The young blond was old enough to drink.

"The religious folks nosing around?" Paul asked him.

"A bit," Mary said.

Jason spoke. "Quite a bit."

Jason opened the side door to the ranch house and stared into the dark.

"She's there now. Elizabeth the prophet." You could hear the dark in his voice.

"How do you know?" Paul asked.

"I know," with a narrow smile. "We all know." He took a sip of coffee. "She knows."

"Knows what?" Paul asked him.

"When the earth will end. When Armageddon will come. Those who will survive. She knows."

"Does she?" Rachel asked, sarcasm.

Jason smiled and shrugged. "Enough people think she does."

"What people? Who are they, Jason?" Paul found himself on the edge of his seat.

"Have you ever been to Los Angeles, Southern California?"

"No."

"Money, the pursuit of happiness. The getting of the money.

The pursuit of the happiness continues."

"The prophet finds you. Holds your hand. Takes you to a simple place. A place of you. You are the center, the only one.

"Rise up with me, survive with me. I am the chosen, I speak with the tongues. I have chosen you. Bring your wealth unto me and we the puzzled, the children of the will be one."

"One after another she finds the weak, confused, the groping, the fearful, the rich."

Rich.

"Come to the mountains. Let us leave Sodom and Gomorrah behind. Happiness is found among us, with me. Gather around me and let us speak of us, we. Let us dance and chant. Let us prepare. It is clear. I, we," and he ran out of breath.

Rachel spoke first. "Where does she come from?"

A coyote pack interrupted with a howl. The humans listened.

"From everywhere," Jason told them. "From the past, from the present. From the spoken word."

No one said a word. This person Jason was describing was right on the park boundary. What a turn of events.

"And you've gone from them, Jason," Mary said.

"I am," taking a deep breath. "Now, if they'll just realize it."

"Uh, Jason, how did you come to them?" Rachel wanted to know.

"Me? My mother. Mary's cousin."

"Small world," Mary added.

"My mother," Jason continued. "Thought I was a lazy beach burn. I was. So, she takes me with her one night. Elizabeth the prophet. In an empty hotel against the ocean." The three listening could see him remembering.

"Well, you had to be there. You could hear the surf. She, uh, well, she hypnotized me.

"She told us, me, of a world in the pure mountains, free of war, safe from the nuclear world, protected, for us. A place she meant to create, was sent here to create. Let the world kill itself. Come with me, believe in me ..."

"Some birthday present, Paul," Rachel whispered to him.

He didn't quite hear her, intent on the sound of that surf, that night.

"Anyway," Jason said, "we all wound up here. She did it, brought us safely to our mountain shelter. I love this place." He sat in an overstuffed chair, stuffing showing in a few spots. He went on with his tale.

"Got cold and dark out there. Us, we, them. Where are you going? When will you be back? Orders, obedience." He saved the worst for last. "Guns now. Protection from them, you," and he looked up to see their expressions. Their expressions were, Paul pissed off, Rachel pissed off, Mary quiet, private.

"And the bomb shelters." Jason paused. "First time down in one of those. Nuclear war? Made me sick, less than human."

"Your mother still out there?" Paul asked.

"She is."

"Any chance?" he asked.

"No," shaking his head no. "I'm going to stay, but not with them."

Mary knew, enough of this. "Maybe we should call it a night?"

"Some night." Paul breathed a sigh of "some night." He didn't know Jason well enough, he didn't feel wise enough to put a hand on his shoulder. "Good luck, Jason."

"Thanks. Hope I didn't ruin your birthday."

"Out here? Impossible."

They all said goodnight, good hunting tomorrow.

Mary and Jason got their gear. They rolled out their sleeping bags in the bunkhouse next door.

Rachel and Paul rolled in bed.

"What a story, huh?"

"Wicked witch of the west."

Rachel laughed. "Now, what else can I give you for your birthday?"

The truth about what's been bothering you. But not now, Paul, not now.

He whispered it in her ear instead, what he wanted.

"Do it, Paul," she told him.

A shooting star threw sparks, tearing across the black sky.

It crash landed somewhere in the Rockies.

Charley Gates pulled to the side of the road and watched it fly. He was out late. Gary Delling didn't keep regular hours.

Gary Delling kept him supplied--a little weed now and then.

They knew each other from back when; when Charley Gates had a place in Gardiner, with Rachel.

Charley Gates knew Gary Delling's reputation, knew the stories. He knew they were true. He knew he'd been an Army Ranger in Vietnam. He knew what had happened. He heard some stories.

Mountain man out of his time. Out of his head? He drove up to the small house, chimney smoke drifting up.

A coyote pelt hung on the door. Charley Gates knocked on its hide.

"Hey, Gates, come on in," indifferent.

"Been awhile, Gary."

"Yeah," sitting on the stone edge of the fireplace, the red logs warming his back.

Aren't you going to ask me where I've been? "Well, this place hasn't changed much."

No stereo, no radio, no television. No plastic, no vinyl, no plants. Nothing but the stove and the refrigerator to remind you of the 20th century.

The one living room was part tack room, part library, part teepee, part cabin, part lodge house, fully male, filled with bone and wood, blankets and tools.

Kerosene lamps lit all of it, lit enough of the wall to show Charley Gates a Carlyle Stevens print. He looked across at his mountain man host, his top knot and his face covered in hair.

Interesting cuss.

Gary Delling flipped up a wooden box worthy of a stage coach strong box and produced what Charley Gates had come for.

"How's that girlfriend of yours, Gates?" flipping him the small bag.

"Rachel?" taken by surprise. "Still around, still around."

"Got herself a ranger friend."

"Oh?" Gary Delling didn't add anything to it.

Charley Gates fidgeted with his belt buckle. It was the rounded nub of an elk antler, courtesy of Gary Delling.

Gary Delling lit a joint and passed it across. He actually struck up a conversation.

"Where you been?"

"Europe, Paris."

"You always were hot shit, Gates," staring him right in the face, bloodshot eyes from behind the beard. "How long?"

"About a year I guess," pulling in on the joint, warming up, settling in, 2 a.m.

"I see your neighbors across the river spread out a bit."

"Them?" Gary Delling spit into the fire. "Weaklings.

Squatters." He scratched his beard and laughed out loud.

"What?" Charley Gates asked.

"Nothin', Gates, nothin'. Nothin' you'd know." He took a deep pull on the weed.

"Got the money, I'm leavin'."

"Where you going at 2 a.m.? "Sure. Ten bucks?"

"Yep."

"Ever been in Europe?" he dared to ask.

"Nope."

You've been to Nam though haven't you? Where are you from? New Mexico? "You should go sometime," stupid as could be.

"Yeah, sure. Right now I'm headed out." Charley Gates left by himself. Down the hill he waited by the road. He didn't see Gary Delling leave.

Gary Delling was already out the back door, binoculars, bow and arrows. He needed some meat. He knew where he could find some elk.

Charley Gates asking him about his neighbors across the river got him up on a high rock so he could scan the complex with his binoculars.

He went from right to left across the trailer buildings. He held the binoculars at a point up river from his neighbors. The point was the black iron bridge across the Yellowstone to their estate. He held the focus of the bridge in the dark. He laughed out loud.

CHAPTER

"Do it! Do it! Ahh, shit! Uh, ahhh!"

Rachel shook him. "Paul, Paul, wake up!"

"Uh, oh, what?" rolling over quickly, snapping awake.

First she laughed a little bit. "What were you dreaming? Awful loud."

"Was I? Damn," wiping his face. "Give me a minute." A breath. "Must have been that dream again. Yeah. Some smoke, some fire, some explosion. Shit. Running the Yellowstone?"

She gave him a kiss. "Must have been Jason, from last night."

Tales from the crypt."

"Maybe. Phew. My little nightmare."

"You have a skeleton somewhere?"

"Me? Never."

"I bet."

Easing up, clearing away the smoke. Tightening up a bit. Now I'm going to ask. What's your skeleton, Rachel? The one rattling around lately.

He stared at the ceiling and let the dream fade away.

"Rachel? Now that I've escaped my little dream …"

"Yes, what?" knowing.

"Last night was a pure dream. Tasting you there, my tongue in there. Smokey, heaven."

She was pleasantly surprised. But she knew the other was coming.

"Mmm, it felt brand new, good."

"And, well, the other."

"Yes?" He rolled into her.

"There's .."

"There's what?"

Simply. "What's wrong?"

"Nothing, Paul. It's not much." Simply.

"Charley's here."

He rolled on his back and stared at the ceiling.

"Here in Yellowstone?" He knew what Charley she meant.

"Yes." Her breast sat on his chest.

"Not to worry, ranger. Not to worry"

"Your not too sure yourself, are you Rachel?

"Have you seen him?"

"Yes. From a distance." Lying to him Rachel? "How do you feel about it?"

"A little weird. Unexpected." Lying again? "Mean anything to us?"

"Nothing." Nothing Rachel? Shit, I don't want to have to deal with this, not now. He leaned up and licked her breast.

He didn't have time to think about it. Someone was banging on the front door.

"Ranger! Ranger!"

CHAPTER

Out of breath, out of breath. "Hey, hi, my name's Roger Timmons," a tall, trim fella with wire rimmed glasses and a blond Yosemite Sam moustache.

"I'm with a study group up on Specimen Ridge! One of our guys broke his leg! We need some help pretty quick!"

Paul Barnes got right to it. "Come in, come in," in his bathrobe, taking a seat at the in-house radio.

"Let me show you! Here!" His house guest pulled back the window curtain. "There, right up in there. I got down as fast as I could. Got my car from the trailhead."

Up in there, a gray gouge in the ridgeline. Petrified trees up there.

"Right in that gray," catching a breath, calming down, sitting down, Paul on the radio.

His message to the com center was the information and the directions. His request was a helicopter and a doctor. "On their way ..." was the response.

"We're from Washington State University. The petrified trees.

He fell. A leg, and maybe his wrist too."

"Let me get my pants on." He'd forgotten about Rachel.

"Big trouble?" leaning in the bedroom doorway, wrapped in a sheet.

"A bit. Somebody up on the ridge with a broken leg," wrestling into a work version of his uniform.

"I'll get out of your way."

"Sure, O.K. I'll call you. Thanks," kiss on the cheek.

"Come on, fella, let's get outside,. I'll use the car radio.

The chopper is on the way." He flipped on the auxilliary switch in the car and announced his presence to the comm center, the mike wire dropped out the window.

The comm center gave him the call sign for the helicopter.

He handed the researcher a pair of binoculars.

"I may not be able to spot them. They're just off in the tree line off the face."

"Can a helicopter get in to them? How many?"

"Two, one of them the one with the leg. I don't know about a helicopter."

They heard it coming. Paul got right to them, bringing the helicopter down the valley, in direct line with the ridge.

The gray gouge was easy to pin point. The pilot got the message, got the spot and turned, banked into it.

They watched the pilot hover into it. They heard him over the radio, "O.K. I've got them."

He couldn't land. Paul shared the binoculars. A rope dropped from the helicopter. Two rangers rappelled down it. A wire stretcher followed after them.

The pilot radioed they were down with the injured hiker. Paul got the pilot on the radio.

"Any more help required? I have one of the party here with me."

"10-4, 211 Barnes. I'll be down to pick you up."

"10-4." Rachel.

"Gatta go, Rachel!"

"Have fun!"

The helicopter covered the distance to the ranch quickly. It hovered over them, coming down on the lawn. Paul had to blink to remind himself that a helicopter just landed on the lawn in Lamar.

It was fun.

"Ready?" Paul yelled at the blond fella.

"Let's go!"

Woosh and they were high in the air above the Lamar, Rachel's truck a miniature as it moved out of the valley.

CHAPTER

This pilot knew his stuff. These weren't two smoke jumpers in his chopper. He hovered, balanced, swung the veteran bird right against the gray slash. Paul and the professor jumped out. It was fun.

They scrambled across the shale and rocks, the first two rangers in behind a couple of pine trees, doing their business, silent as Marines on a mission.

"Good, you two can help carry him when we get down on the flats. Joe, Arkansas, about 1858, flintlock, tomahawk and all. Sam, Maine, about 1758, flintlock, tomahawk and all. They had a plastic cast on the left leg, had him wrapped in a blanket, ready to lift the bearded fella into the stretcher. A young woman, young enough to be a student was as calm and collected as the fella with the busted leg.

Joe and Sam said "lift." The three of them got him up into the stretcher.

Joe and Sam knew ropes like rodeo cowboys know ropes, getting the stretcher down the face of the ridge, through the trees. They worked with coils of green climbing rope.

Quick as sailors Joe and Sam got the stretcher roped in, through it, over it, around a stiff pine trunk then around another pine further down, Sam skidding down to it. It was fun.

Sam let everyone know over the radio. An ambulance would be waiting below at Lamar picnic area.

The blond professor asked a question. Why don't we use the helicopter? Sam, like John Wayne wished he looked, gave him a look. You try dragging this stretcher out onto that shale. He left out the stupid. He did say, "and we like it this way…" The way down went in short drops of a few yards and a few trees at a time, Joe and Sam letting the heavy line run through worn leather gloves, enjoying every minute of it.

Paul and the professor and the student stayed out of their way, sliding alongside the stretcher, making themselves almost useful.

Everyone on the radio heard their progress. Paul knew they were scoring major points with the ranger corps. A mountain rescue. Daniel Boone, Davey Crockett, Jim Bridger, Erroll Flynn.

The ridgeline leveled out at the edge of the treeline. Joe and Sam undid the ropes as clean as longshoremen. It was Paul's turn. He got one side, the professor the other and the student up front.

The flat ground across was soft and green. They carried, rested, carried. An ambulance and two patrol cars waited across the river.

How are we going to get across the Lamar? Paul wondered.

No problem. Five rangers were already knee deep across the swift bend in the river, roped together--a chain across.

By this time the body in the stretcher was embarrassed by all the attention, laughing, embarrassed.

Joe and Sam couldn't resist. They waded into the river too.

"Bring him on!" Joe ordered.

A silent "yes, sir," Paul with a smile.

Like a boatswain's chair between tossing ships the wire stretcher went across. A little strain, a little pain, the chain of men pulling itself back across once Paul, the professor and the student had been passed across.

Everyone stomped their wet boots, everyone content in a good job. Joe and Sam even said, "good job," to Paul. High compliment.

Paul leaned, sat on the picnic table under the cottonwoods and watched them all leave the valley.

He felt nothing but nothing. It began to rain. Heady stuff.

CHAPTER

Heady stuff, meeting Carlyle Stevens.

Rachel felt the strength in his work hands, both of them holding hers in greeting, squinting up from his chair, from behind his wide body dark glasses. He was out on the deck, warm sun, early August sun.

"I'm glad to meet you, Rachel. Charley's mentioned you."

"Well, thank you. I've admired your work."

"Thank you. Charley tells me so."

Charley. He would be here, here with the, what was it, the Cezanne of the west? Yes, that's close.

Charley. Oh, Charley, taking a seat next to the Cezanne of the west.

She could see some of his sculptures through the broad window.

Rodin versions of the wrangler types she knew from the K-Bar.

Carlyle Stevens. He looked a bit like Virginia Wolf and Frank Lloyd Wright.

Charley was sitting inside with Robert Ford, the blondest, tannest man in Montana. The winner of an Academy Award, writing and directing.

Heady stuff. Rachel was swooning, soaking in it, self-assuredly, finally, settling into it. She knew Charley. She knew how to handle all this. She was pretty sure she knew.

The Yellowstone ran flat and full. Rachel could have thrown a stone in it from her chair.

"Your river, Rachel?" Carlyle Stevens asked.

"Partly. We point out your house on our floats?" like a request.

"Just don't bring them ashore" with a laugh.

"Never, never," returning the laugh.

Charley came out with Robert Ford. Rachel enjoyed their beauty, felt intoxicated, light hearted, sure-footed with all the male notoriety. Charley included now. He'd just sold a story to Hollywood. A film perhaps. A check, without a doubt.

"Shall we all go in to lunch?" Carlyle Stevens proposed.

"It's all ready." Charley was cook as well as bottle washer.

"Can I help you?" Robert Ford offered Carlyle Stevens his arm, in reverence. Rachel could see it all over him, all over them.

Lunch was a round table of laughs and opinions, politics and the arts. Rachel did pinch herself. Robert Ford on producing films. Carlyle Stevens with a tale of Joan Miro, about meeting him. Charley Gates with scenes of Paris. All of them with scenes of Yellowstone. Rachel held up her end of it, listening and talking, telling and sharing.

Out of the blue sky Carlyle Stevens asked her about the valley Lamar.

She went right to it. She went right by Paul. She went back to him, and paused. She went right back to Robert Ford asking Carlyle Stevens about a specific piece of his work.

Charley nodded a nod to Rachel. It meant business. Business between these two luminaries.

"We're going to take a walk," Charley told the other two men.

"We'll see you later then," Carlyle Stevens answered.

"Maybe not me," Rachel told him. "I have a float trip later today."

"Come back then," he told her.

"Glad to meet you, Rachel," Robert Ford getting up from the table to shake her hand. I'll take your float some time."

She almost yelled, any time! but kept it graceful. "Please do. It was a pleasure meeting you."

Charley walked her to the gate, to her truck, the warm sun sparkling through the cottonwoods. They kissed.

CHAPTER

"Well, that's another one ya can kiss goodbye," out of the side of his mouth, over and around the snuff stuffed in his lip.

Ranger Jerry Combs and Paul.

He was up in Mammoth to get the patrol car serviced, get his paper supply resupplied. He had that moderate mountain rescue on his resume now. He was invited along.

Poacher kill. They stood over a young male elk, still bleeding, eyes bulged out, a ham shank hunk off each flank, its fresh meat cut away, neatly, cleanly. A dry wind blew dust around them.

They were up on Deckard Flats above Gardiner and the Yellowstone, just at the boundary. Not so far off, a well-beaten track-- elk around here, around the humpbacked hills up above. One less elk.

Paul could smell it, from the carcass. Something wild on the wind. Something wild on the wind, in the dust. Something wild all around-- man and beast, beasts.

He smelled some change in the weather, the way of things.

Completed business around the elk with a few photographs and coordinates, and a few random assurances that they were going to get this son of a bitch. This son of a bitch who knew damn well how to use a bow and arrow.

They dragged what was left of the elk into the brush. The coyotes would come to it at dusk.

Paul left Ranger Combs to the business back at Mammoth. He drove home, that scent he smelled a taste on his lips.

But the drive home washed it all clean. Each turn, each thing green, each thing wild helped dilute that odor in the air.

He turned to Lamar at Tower, park visitation at its height, families with maps unfolded on the hoods of cars. He tried to make the patrol car invisible, run the gauntlet.

No one waved him down. Too lost to notice me? So he went on patrol through the valley, up through it slowly, stopping at the Lamar picnic area. Check a fishing license, two families from New York. They shared their accents.

Up the road, out of the car, a short, quick switchback hike into Trout Lake. Round as a coin, compact as a pocket watch.

Rainbow trout the size of sailing-pond sailboats. A fisherman out in his wading inner tube. His professionally broken-in bush hat meant Paul didn't have to check for the proper I.D. He shoved his hands in his back pockets, feeling his coin against his wallet.

The air smelled of pine, of clear water, of a moose dipping its broad snout into the shallows across the lake.

Up the road, Pebble Creek Campground was a living community now, always full, full of questions and answers. He emptied the metal tube with the day's camping fees.

He drove up to Warm Creek picnic area, just below the Northeast entrance. You'd have to be looking for it to find it.

Secluded, he sat by the creek and added up the campsites and the receipts.

That done, he went shopping. Out through the log entrance, honking to the duty gate rangers. Up the road cut between the pines and the firs.

Silver Gate, Montana. A handful of houses and buildings. A stage-coach stop on the 20th century trail.

Private homes in the trees. Extra homes for those who could afford it, appreciate it.

Cooke city, Montana. A town that boomed on the visitor business. A town, a one-street cluster of log and sheet-metal homes, in behind the pancakes and eggs, the motels, the ski rentals, the film shops, the wild western general store like a wood frame church without the steeple, without the religion.

Paul did his shopping, creaking down between the dry goods on the hard wood floors.

Lacy and Harry, two Los Angelians holding onto the remnants of their hippie lives, owned and operated, swapped stories with Paul, Harry all haired-out like a younger Walt Whitman, Lacy all over tan, lean, short hair like a younger Amelia Earhart.

Harry and Lacy stayed the winters, stretching what they earned from the season. Paul listened. Winter began to register on him. Its enormity, its divinity.

With his bag of groceries he headed home, daylight heading to its home. The temperature dropped.

Winter? Yes, I'd like to stay the winter. Shack up with you know who.

He drove past the ranch corrals and pulled up to his door.

Two of the guys from the tour buses were there to greet him. Jack Cummings with a six pack and his fishing gear. Free room and board and fish the Lamar. He was glad to have them, dinner in the grocery bag.

CHAPTER

Dinner. Gary Delling laid the chunk of red meat on the frying pan. The gamey smell of elk frying filled his rooms.

He turned up the volume of the Mozart on the cassette player.

He flipped the steak. He added raw onions and raw peppers. The juice of the meat sautéed it all. The meat was a developed taste.

His developed taste was barely brown, barely not red on the inside.

He added a splash of Olympia beer to the mix and turned off the burner.

He sat on a stool on his porch, the tin plate on a log splitting stump. Night and day were finishing the ritual changeover.

A chunk of meat, a mouth full of beer. Life was perfect.

The siren came long and low from across the river. The faithful were being called. Gary Delling stood up and listened to it. The call to prayers.

He took a slug of beer. He could see the serious lights on their new piece of drilling equipment, reaching down into the earth to get at Yellowstone's thermal boiler.

He took another slug of beer. "Kaboom," like a whisper, like a secret.

"Hello," like a Whisper, like a secret. Down river, Rachel, greeting her dinner guest on her front step.

"Hiya," Charley Gates standing still, listening to the nearby moan of the siren. Then it stopped, then it was silent.

"Eerie," he said.

"Eerie," Rachel didn't have a lot more to say.

I brought wine and he held up the bottle. "From Paris." Rachel invited him in.

CHAPTER

August could see September. You could see a slight change in the park. A slight one.

There were a few less cooking fires at night in the campgrounds, a few less visitors falling on their faces, a few less days of real warmth, a few less days before school would begin again, out in the cities of America.

Americans, packing up and going home. Rachel's raft had only been half full. She was hosing it off on the street in front of the Gardiner office. She was in a hurry. Paul. His fourth phone call finally found her. Yes. I'll be out this afternoon. I've got something special for you.

For you, Paul, was her thought. I need Lamar. I need you. I do. I do. I'm almost sure I do.

Everything done she checked in and checked out.

Up to Mammoth. Past the superintendent's stone house, past the stone chapel and she was checked out.

Across the high bridge over the Yellowstone; the bustle, the hustle, the tussle with the tourists, and Charley Gates disappeared into the sheltering pines, the rocky meadows, the bodily curves in the road, the hawk-on-the-air currents, the bison shapes in the clouds, the road junction at Tower.

She showed a smile like a close friend, come home again.

It was easy to remember Carlyle Steven's home, and all the rest. It was easier to feel this, a sandhill crane, like something Egyptian, near enough to the road.

The narrow gap between the boulders opened up and there was Lamar, like the first day on earth. Calm, cooled, all the earth's wealth collected. A friend come home again. She drove down to the ranch house.

Paul, hey, Paul, come on, put down the binoculars. He laughed out loud, too serious about watching for her.

He got away from the window and went outside, trying his damnest to remain Gary Cooper cool, foot up on the fence.

Rachel honked and waved from the road. He gave her a cool Gary Cooper, his wrist almost breaking from the strain, from the strain in his guts.

He sat on the fence, collected in a vice grip of I'm cool, it's cool, she's here, I'm here.

I'm back. It's good to be back, Rachel, pulling up to the house. Back with my man, my ranger. One of my? came and went.

"Welcome back," he told her.

"Good to be back," letting him lead her into the house with an arm around her waist.

They said their serious hellos in the kitchen.

"Ranger Barnes," in his ear, making him catch his breath, his equilibrium.

"Yes?"

"I have a treat for you today."

"Oh?" moving onto the living room couch.

The warm sun had warmed the cushions.

"Willing to do about five miles today?"

"Sure, where to?"

"Slough Creek. A favorite place."

"Of course."

"The fishing crowds will be down. But we'll go up above them anyway."

"Then what?" lips on her neck.

"How long has it been since my last visit?"

"Few months."

"No, no, come on. A week?"

"Eight days."

She had to kiss him. "So, I owe you."

"O.K.," just a tiny bit puzzled, hoping, knowing? Some business talk. Patrolling the Lamar, rafting the Yellowstone, bar talk, weather reports.

"Oh," Rachel remembered. "I saw Mary in Gardiner. Wanted me to tell you that Jason's gone from Yellowstone. Pressure she said.

From you know who. Gone to Europe, Paris. Then on to India? Searching, still, she says."

"Good for him. Clear out, clear it up."

"Up you go, ranger. Let's go with the warm sun."

"What do we need?"

"Not to worry, I've got everything. Not to worry today," and she meant "today," not "tomorrow" or the next days.

CHAPTER

The day was why you could never leave Yellowstone.

Enormous, everything. The colors of the grass, the silver of the river, the glacial boulders, the cry of the raven, the sail white clouds, the woman beside you in her barroom shorts, her barroom-soft ball shirt, blue and gold, No. 6 on the back, tucked in behind a fine-tooled brown and silver touched belt, a Pendleton shirt tied to her backpack, soft-soled, gripper climbing boots, and a raw silver pin like a bucking bronco from the mind of Picasso.

"Where'd you get that wild pin?" reaching over to touch it.

"From Carlyle Stevens," absolutely beaming, absolutely forgetting what all that might mean to Paul, to her, to them.

"Do you know him?" she asked.

"A bit. From being here. Out in the Paradise, isn't he?"

"Yes," biting her lip.

He took them down the dusty road to the trailhead. He didn't ask any more questions.

Three mule deer, frozen like figures on a frieze, posed for them.

It was later in the season. Less folks meant more of this, more elk, more deer, more snow higher up, more of the enormous cycle of things.

Rachel said the right thing. "Now I have a pin to match your coin."

Paul pulled to a stop just above the secluded Slough Creek Campground. If you listened, and he did, you could hear Slough Creek rushing by the campsites.

"I wonder."

"Wonder what?" she asked him.

"Your Carlyle Stevens. I wonder if Larry could have possibly known him. I read something about the artist in Paris." He listened for the sound of rushing water.

"It seems like Larry was across all of time. Like he was present at all things."

Geez, he's beautiful, wonderful. Listen to him, she thought.

"I have a present for you today."

He heard her voice from where he'd gone. "Well, let's get to it then."

Three other cars there with them at the trailhead. Three separate states, three similar ideas. Fish, fish and more fish.

Paul locked up and Rachel led out up the extremely obvious trail.

Between the Douglas Firs marmots greeted them, scurrying out onto a warm rock, scurrying back, shining in their shining overcoats.

An elk skeleton, some hide still attached, a gray jay on its skull. A narrow wagon trail for a trail, a ranch for the somewhat well-to-do dudes out beyond the park.

They stopped where the trail reached a crest and leveled off.

"Look, Rachel. No surveys, no reports, no impact studies, no administration, no politics, no numbers, no disagreements."

"Bureaucracy getting to you, Mr. Ranger?"

"No, no," laughing. "You do get a bit of Yellowstone's flip side don't you?"

Through the Aspens it was a silver silk scarf that Slough Creek laid on the ground, the ground the warm colors of your favorite sweater; a black battlement rock wall and young hills swollen with the last warmth of summer completed it completely.

"God, it feels good to get out of the patrol car."

"I bet it does," putting her chin on his shoulder.

"Soon you'll be up on Wolverine Pass. Up Pebble Creek."

"Right. Once hunting season starts outside."

"You'll be the bureaucracy on the park boundary."

They laughed their way down the wide trail.

There, you could see Slough Creek down through the trees.

They were still back up the trail, looking down on part meadow, part wide curve of flat water, and part Cutoff Mountain, a part of the Rockies, a good day's hike away.

"Slough Creek," Rachel announced, with pride.

Two guys in bait and tackle came up the trail from below them-Slough Creek's certification.

Three "howdy's " and one "hello ;" No one asked how the fishing was. No one said how the fishing had been. It was understood.

The view said it all.

Rachel and Paul hiked down to it.

It wasn't the middle of nowhere. It seemed to be the middle of everywhere. It wasn't isolated; it was absolutely quiet, Slough Creek motionless, a lariat loop of water through a golden green stretch of ground. Only two people on the well-used track.

"I love it, Rachel. Right now, right away. Right in my own backyard. Not totally off the beaten track, but. .."

A fly fisherman. He could have been a tree growing from the bank of the water.

"Come on, we've got a bit to go yet."

He followed, obediently. Slough Creek, in varying shapes was always there on their left, one meadow away. Warm enough so Rachel could pull her shirt out of her shorts, Paul with his shirt open, unbuttoned.

"Up a ways still."

The wagon trail went up, just barely, Slough Creek just barely visible between a rock face and an Aspen stand. Then it was gone.

"When we see the Creek again we're there."

He kept after her.

"There," Rachel pointing down to it, the full flow of it, the lazy curve of it, flowing right to left, down from its source in the high snows.

It went out of sight beneath a rise of ground, beneath a singular ring of black and white Aspens.

"Come on," and she took him by the hand, the dry grass cracking under foot.

"Holy shit," Paul standing on that rise of ground, a fifteen foot drop of black rock to a deep groove of slowly moving water.

The groove, the curve was deep enough to make a deep pond. A gravel strip of the other side was level and dry.

The Aspens were perfectly still, standing on the rise with him. He turned to tell her what he thought, what he was thinking.

Rachel stood there, naked.

"Welcome to paradise, ranger."

He went for her, but she held him at arms length. He felt her arms in his pants, in his throat.

"Watch," she told him.

She stepped to the edge of the fifteen feet of raised rock.

She stepped down a foot and dived.

Breasts and arms and ass and thighs. She dived to the pond of it, cutting it cold, clean, her thighs and ass clear to the gravelly bottom.

Kicking hard back to the surface, blowing out the pure water. Swimming easily, powerfully, freely to the sandy bar.

Paul stripped like a comic in a silent movie. He braced himself for the cold of the water.

Rachel was a mound of flesh and dripping pubic hair, lying on her back on the warm sand.

"You look like evolution!" He yelled across to her.

She opened her legs, spread her arms. "Sheena, queen of Slough Creek. Come on in, the water's fine."

How could any man resist? A deep breath, a plunge, the sweat on his back iced over, the depth of the cold water covering him.

He stayed down, feeling it naked, feeling it ancient, feeling it evolution.

The surface was warm and cold. He backstroked, kicked his legs, submerged, surfaced, performed for her, crawled out on the sand next to her.

His finger loved her until she was good and wet, the sun drying the rest of them.

He was blind with it. It was Rachel, but it was woman, it was man. Man woman man woman man woman, until woman yearned for more man, more man.

He rolled between her legs. His manhood felt the tickle of her woman's hair. He felt the edge of it, the moist lips of it.

"In me, Paul, get in me."

One assured shove and he was.

Animals. The paragon of animals. Animal sounds. Mating sounds. Lusting sounds.

Colors. Purple and reds, blues and whites, purest light, brightest light, flashing light, lighting light.

"All right!" He emptied himself. He filled her.

Sweat and slowing down, coming back, coming back, feeling the earth again. Feeling her breasts again. Hopelessly her's again.

"Rachel. Jesus Christ, Rachel," laying on the sand, his cheek on her curly hair.

"I think I'm the one who got the birthday present," touching his hair.

He rolled next to her and rested his head on his forearms.

"Let's build a cabin here?"

She didn't answer. She was up and diving into the water, swimming across. He watched her, riveted on her.

She climbed out, up the short level of rocks. He watched her backside go into the Aspens. He was too weak to follow.

He woke from a dream of a white bear, white snow, a cold cloud of breath.

Where is she? Naked, he walked down the bank. The ground leveled with the creek. The creek narrowed, churning white between the boulders. Up to his chest in white water he waded across.

The ground felt perfect under his bare feet, cool in the Aspen shade against his flesh.

There she was. Oh, brother. Stretched out full, asleep on her back on a great grandfather rock, Slough Creek dropping into a shallow canyon, watery mist, radiant sun.

I can't ever lose this. I can't. He leaned bare-assed against an Aspen for support.

He went down to her and woke her by licking her between her legs. She spread her things and came awake.

"Hmm, Paul."

"Yes," then quiet with his tongue, eating of the stuff he would hate, hate to ever lose.

The moon was a small pearl, pale white in the big blue sky.

A shaft of cold shade cut across Paul's back, Rachel in the late afternoon sun with her hands in his hair.

The mist from Slough Creek was cold on them. The weather paid no attention to them.

Clouds, big as locomotives, barns, steamships, formed in the sky.

They were still warm enough. Heat, Paul over her face, his red and purple meat beating in her mouth, finishing the warmth, this day, this spot, this beating in her mouth.

Then it was cold, instantly, the mountains again as they really were.

Paul dressed slowly, photographing it all with his memory, etching the scene, the scenery, the sensuality, the inevitability.

The cold wasn't the summer. September would be here, soon.

You could hear it on the park radio, read it on the park calendar, sense it across the environment. The end to the season.

The time to leave. The time for decisions.

The co-ed plans were clear--school days. But, if you wanted to stay in the mountains you had to find a way, a job, to stay.

If you wanted to stay. Bigger world beyond the Yellowstone? Paul was sure on this side of the Yellowstone.

He watched Rachel tug on her shirt. Slough Creek didn't say a word.

I wonder if she'll be staying? Rachel didn't say a word but for a kiss on his cheek. She offered him cheese and bananas.

The round, three quarter moon showed against the cold, diamond-blue sky. Rachel led them away from Slough Creek.

CHAPTER

The bright moon hung on the coal black night. A lamp to light his way.

He'd been traveling all day. In behind Electric Peak. To get in behind the enormity of Electric Peak took all day. Across Swan Lake flats then up into the enormity, the sanctity, the secrecy, the hospitality--the shimmering Aspens were changing leaves, a light, light green before the gold.

Gary Delling didn't stop to enjoy the hike. He stopped enjoying a hike around the age of nineteen.

The bright moon allowed him to get around and past the base of the mountain. From there he bushwhacked his way, further down, further down. Then he stopped, above the cult's encampment.

He could see their lights below. He wanted to see something for himself. He wanted to see one of their bomb shelters, for himself. Maybe see what he could do to it, by himself.

He stretched out on his stomach and ate a pear. A Billings newspaper had furnished him a photo of a cult bomb shelter. His own logistical skills furnished him with its coordinates.

He lifted his face to the bone-white moon. He bathed his face in it. The same moon used to hang over New Mexico. The high desert.

His high desert--a trekker, a canoer, a dirt biker, an eater raw of the high desert life. Content.

The Army got him at seventeen. He ate bootcamp raw. They noticed. He ate where they sent him raw. Ranger school--advanced warrior, willing to die for the cause, the nation. He was eighteen, what could he know? He knew Vietnam. 1966. Assassinations, positions overrun, ambush, explosives. It was fucked, from the get go. He fought, he killed, he hiked. Vietnam drove it into his skull, into his blood.

Politics. What the fuck did he know about politics? Personal danger, period. I've got to kill, fight my way out of here. That's what this is.

The "is" stayed with him. He came home. He had a Silver Star because he kept himself alive one night when a lot of the Vietnamese who were trying to fuck with his rotation date got in his way.

A boy of action. He left the Silver Star in an attic. His blood kept the action.

He was waiting for the moon to get in behind the nearest peak.

No fear, no anxiety, child's play compared to what they once made a child play at.

There, the moon was gone. Early morning, still dark enough to cover his movements.

He moved down, between the serious rocks, soft on the broken stones, then soft on the ground where the slope leveled off.

He knew where he was. He'd spent a day studying the wide cut in the slope. Back in there.

He knew he was above it. He just had to feel his way down the cut until there were signs of their civilization, construction equipment and a tall, white metal entrance into the ground.

He listened for a bit. He took off his blue watch cap and wiped his face. He made his way down in the graying dark.

CHAPTER

The heavy white door gleamed in the darkness. He was just above it, on the right wall of the slice they'd dug out of the slope.

Construction work was scattered around. No one but him.

He dropped down to the entrance to the cave and ducked in behind a cement mixer. He could hear a dog barking, a truck shifting its gears.

He could do with a buck knife anything a Swiss Army knife could do if there was a lock on the bomb shelter. In the silence you could hear the big knife snap open.

He checked his back and dropped on a knee at the metal door, twice as wide, twice as high as any home's.

No lock, just a metal bar shoved through the handle. He opened it quick, holding tight, holding it from squealing. He was in, the door delicately closed behind him.

He snapped on the flashlight, just the size to fit in his palm.

Cold and white, a narrow hallway, with metal cabinets on one wall, an empty gun rack against the other side.

He checked behind him, listened. He moved on. Boxes of C Rations piled in a narrow room. Metal doors. He was moving deeper into the hill side.

The hallway opened wider, metal benches in a row along both walls. The light from his palm found a light switch. He figured he better not. He could feel all the earth on top of him.

Shovels and pitchforks, fire axes neatly stacked. A door halfway open. He felt like he was scuba diving in deep water.

His light only lit a patch of it. Ahead it looked like the hallway, the tunnel ended. He wondered where the air came in.

He pushed open the heavy door. His light found an enormous, bare room, low ceiling. His light covered it in narrow points.

The what? he asked himself. The inner sanctum? He didn't laugh much, ever.

He found himself in the center of the room, his head just below the ceiling. He felt what it was for. For nuclear bombs.

He felt that. He knew something about that.

He went exploring. A door in a wall. He had that check-things-out-careful-like Vietnam DNA. He did almost laugh. It was a bathroom, a pile of cots stacked up in a corner. His light found all the parts: toilets, sinks, showers.

Showers? He licked his lips. I wonder. He stopped to listen. Quiet as a tomb.

He turned the shower on, just barely. Rusty, brown, then clear water. Well, well, well. I found my scent, now I can mark this fuckin' place.

The place was a bomb shelter under Montana. That pleased him, not the fact that he was inside it.

He whistled some little tune. He turned the three showers on full. Why not? He turned the sinks on full. He allowed himself a smile.

He allowed himself a few more minutes to get back out. He kept the light off. He let those old eyes from the orient adjust to the pitch.

O.K., go easy. He felt his way out. He felt the water level going up behind him. He felt a smile on his face.

He felt forward for the entrance. He found the split between the metal door. Now easy bub, easy.

He pressed his cheek against the metal, cold. He listened for any sound on the planet. Gray light sent a gray shaft across his chest. Morning was on its way.

But he wasn't done yet. He'd left his mark; now he wanted to leave his scent. He took off his day pack and peeled a hide, a pelt from inside it.

A coyote pelt. There was the scent of urine, human.

One deep breath and he was outside in the purple gray of morning, his back against a corner where the bomb shelter met the hillside.

There were hooks and nails all over the work area. He got a house nail and stuck it into a hinge on the door, bent it down. He hung the pelt on it by its head.

A truck was coming. He was going, scrambling, disappearing up the hillside, the mountains gobbling him up.

CHAPTER

Morning in Montana, and Wyoming, and the Yellowstone ecosystem, all systems, the totality of the system, all aglow in a mountain of gold.

September was upon them. A change was in the air. Change was the air. A few less cars parked outside the motels. A few more empty seats at the lunch counters.

Paul Barnes felt that September glow. An enormous breakfast at the Town Cafe in Gardiner. Feed the fall fever.

Wipe up the yokes of five eggs with five pieces of buttered toast. Nothing to do today, but nothing. So, I'll do that. I'll finish my coffee, go surprise Rachel. All aglow.

Departures far outweighed arrivals; but there were still people arriving. Arriving in time, in the time of the big herds moving back down onto the flat land again. The time of snow back in the cycle, back higher up where the herds had been. The time when all the herds were migrating, in America, Europe and Asia.

The time of those retired, with the time to arrive now. The time of those with the good sense and the good fortune to arrange for the Yellowstone system when you could park, walk, breathe, camp, learn, share, understand, relax.

Relax, Paul, she'll be home. He was in the line of campers and cars pulling up their tent stakes, pulling out of town. Empty tour buses were coming back from the Bozeman airport. They'd fill up the Mammoth Hotel. Paul honked at a driver he knew.

Rachel's pickup wasn't in front of her place. He stared for a long time before he left.

Her truck and boat trailer were parked at Carlyle Stevens house, between two versions of two English Land Rovers. Charley Gates and Miss Carolina Keefe.

A busman's, an oarsman's holiday for Rachel. Company raft with the company's O.K. Just the mention of Carolina Keefe. Writer, author, novelist, heroine, Floridian, National and Pulitzer book awards. The guest of Carlyle Stevens.

The four of them filled out the raft, Rachel letting the Yellowstone take them to Livingston, taking it easy, taking them carefully on the oars.

A box of cold beer and ham sandwiches. Someplace to stop and get off. Then Livingston for a drink. Then Bozeman for dinner and a movie. No one could say no to that.

That feeling of working the river took control. Rachel felt a lot better. There was Charley, Olympia beer, bare toes trailing in the river. There was Carlyle Stevens in a wide straw hat, Olympia beer, sitting in the sun. And there was Carolina Keefe, looking like Amelia Earhart at above sixty. Tough as tree bark, soft as a woman, a blue bandanna around her forehead, her hair almost gray, her calm brown eyes staring off at something, wearing a shirt a Seminole had bestowed on her, a pair of straw and leather sandals a Mayan woman had left her, a pair of faded bib overalls with a small conch shell brooch pinned to her breast pocket, and a cold beer.

The 'Blue Heron'. An Everglades idyll. An Everglades under fire. An Everglades in the deep, cracker south. The passion in the weather, in the heat, Rachel as passionate for it as The Blue Heron's reviews. Now Rachel had an autographed copy, by the author.

Carolina Keefe's life was public, in the papers now and then, from her home in southern Florida to the New York Times. Her husband had died, after a long illness with liquor. She was here at Carlyle Stevens' invitation, friends, associates, artists, residents of a communal Carmel California twenty years ago.

Rachel steered them under four overhanging cottonwoods. The raft scraped gravel. Charley and Carolina Keefe jumped out and pulled the raft up out of the river. Charley helped Carlyle Stevens climb out. Lunch.

Rachel secured the oars. Charley came over and kissed her neck. "I love you," was his message.

"Thanks," was her answer.

There was no answer on her home phone. Paul hung up, again.

He had a beer for lunch.

Lunch under the trees with Carolina Keefe, with tales of her latest novel, "The Atocha." Spanish treasure, Key West, Spain, Key West, the Caribbean Sea. "My James Michener," and she laughed.

"You'll have to come to Florida, Rachel. I'll repay you for this with a canoe trip on Lake O'Cachobee, and an airboat on the Everglades.

"Can I come tomorrow?" and everyone laughed.

I love you for this Charley Gates.

Carolina Keefe wanted to know. She knew alligators, cottonmouths, water moccasins, coral snakes, diamond back rattlers, bobcats, Florida panthers. "What about the grizzly bear, uh , grizz?"

Lunch on the Yellowstone. Grizz. Each one of them told her a story. Carlyle Stevens when Yellowstone was younger, Charley and Rachel when Yellowstone was just a year and a half ago. The bear joined them to right now.

Carolina Keefe paid attention.

They picked up the beer bottles. Charley helped Carlyle back into the raft. Rachel kissed Charley on the shoulder. Carolina shoved them off.

Rachel and the river steered them to Livingston. Autumn's leaves, Aspen leaves, turned to gold, floated along with them.

Dinner. Paul was eating alone. Pizza for one, the K-Bar. A pitcher of beer for one.

There was one other table occupied. Pizza for one, a Budweiser. Gary Delling.

Paul's attention was diverted, to him. His attention got Gary Delling's attention. They shared a stare.

Paul held the stare. He found himself saying, "how you doin'?" What are you doin'? What am I doin'?

"All right, ranger. I'm doin' all right." He went back to his meal.

"My name is Paul, not ranger," at the side of his head.

Gary Delling looked up and almost smiled. "O.K."

I think I'll get up and go on over and sit down. You fascinate me, bUddy. He thought twice more about it. He thought better of it.

He got the bartender's attention. "Give me a Bud?" he asked her.

She brought it over to him.

The juke box played Willie Nelson.

"It's for him," Paul told her.

"All right." She took it over to Gary Delling's table.

Paul got up. "That's from me," for Gary Delling's information.

Gary Delling raised the bottle and tipped the top against his forehead.

"O.K.," and he went looking for Rachel's truck.

Rachel sat next to Charley, Carolina and Carlyle, filling up a table at Bridger's Restaurant, the building in red brick, joined at the bricks with the Greyhound station.

Steaks, with Charley's leg up against her's. Potatoes, with Carolina Keefe's genuine laughter. A pitcher of beer, with Carlyle Stevens and Carolina Keefe swapping stories, honestly, openly, each encouraging the other, straight up, straight through, generous and egotists, Charley and Rachel pitching in with Carolina Keefe's introduction to Yellowstone, Charley secure, Rachel a bit unsure, in up to her ears, not quite over her head.

"What will you do for the winter, Rachel?" Carolina Keefe didn't make small talk. She wanted to know, to learn what goes on here.

"I'm not sure yet. But I better hurry. I may be able to work at the cross country ski shop at Old Faithful."

"Oh? And what's winter like?"

Rachel answered quickly, assuredly. "An overwhelming beauty. Everything here up close, slowed, um, rewound?"

"Rewound. I like that."

Charley Gates moved against her leg. "We met in the winter."

"And you, Charley, you'll be in Los Angeles with Carlyle?"

Rachel felt Carolina Keefe's question.

"Yes," Charley answered. "A studio bought one of my stories.

Looks like I'm going to get my hands on a screen play. And with Carlyle's show, I'll be warm this winter."

Los Angeles, L.A., screen plays, museums, American writers, painters. Rachel swooned in her beer.

"How cold, Rachel?"

She heard the American writer's question. She heard herself answer.

"Fifteen, twenty below."

"Poor little one, Florida girl. I don't know if I could."

Rachel's smile was understanding. "But if you see the bison deep in the snow, deep in Hayden Valley the cold goes away. The scenes are set in the cold, permanent, history."

"Can I quote you, Rachel?" and they all laughed.

Rachel swooned in her beer. Bozeman, Montana, Florida, Los Angeles--a long way from Gardiner, Montana.

Mary Gregor was taking an evening stroll through Gardiner.

Paul needed a stroll. They met under the Roosevelt Arch under the night's endless constellations.

"What brings you to town, Paul?"

"Rachel. Seen her around?"

"No. I'm just back from a few days on the trail. In near Bridgers Lake on the thoroughfare."

Some of that was still Greek to him. One thing though was permanent. "Grizz?"

"Grizz."

They were quiet, reverent for a moment. They walked along the road, towards the entrance station.

"I got a card from Jason." Mary picked up a rock and threw it.

"Oh? How's he doing?" indifference there, his mind on the constellations and the girlfriend. He corrected his indifference.

"Really, how is he doing?"

"Fine. Gone from Paris. Now he's in Istanbul. Getting ready for India."

India? Don't I know something of India? Don't I? Don't I have something in my back pocket to remind me of India? I've forgotten it. I have. He retrieved it, it in his pocket the way your wallet always was.

Automatically. Larry's coin felt good and cold. I think I'll go out there tonight, where Larry was. Where Rachel was. Yeah, I think I will.

They stopped at the entrance kiosk.

"I'm going to walk a bit more. Care to join me?"

"Not tonight, Mary. I'm going to take a ride."

"Good night then."

"Yes, good night." The night sky was silver and pearls, diamonds and silver dust.

The road to Old Faithful out of Mammoth was empty. His headlights would be seen from space. Space and time. Right now he didn't know any, have any, anything but a destination. Firehole River, Mound Geyser, Larry, Rachel, Yellowstone.

He got as far as Swan Lake Flats above Mammoth. The night sky. It filled, flooded the windshield. It swamped him. He pulled over, Swan Lake, shallow, flat as a coin.

He got out and laid on the engine hood, back and neck reclined against the windshield. He sighed, he thought, he considered.

Fountain Flats Drive will be closed this time of night. No access to the Firehole. The sky understood everything. The sky was everything. He lay there, his flat coin held like an ice cube against his forehead, against a headache.

I am that star stuff up there. All the cities of the earth, Paris included, would be just one pace across the universe of light he gazed into.

Light as a feather on an engine hood. What shall be has already been determined, Paul. He wasn't so sure that Paul was right.

I don't think, therefore I am relaxed. He laughed out loud.

Like a nap, like consultation. Refreshed, rewarded like 5:00 on a Friday.

He drove home. Twinkle and shine, I wish upon these stars.

I wonder where she was tonight?

CHAPTER

She was in the back seat of a Bozeman cab. Back to Livingston, back to Carlyle Steven's house. Back to reality? She didn't know from anything but a reality of imagining herself in a cab in Montana, rubbing elbows, knees, shoulders and toes with the stars. Stars in her eyes, ears, nose and throat.

"What a night," Carolina Keefe with her head out the window.

The lights of Livingston, compact, awake, asleep. They stopped to make sure the raft was back in Gardiner. They rode home through the stars, across the valley, over the rivers and between the wooded mountains, full of food and beer and a day of each other.

Rachel rested her head on Charley's shoulder. She thought she heard Carolina Keefe say something softly. Something like, "she's beautiful." She could feel Charley's nod of approval.

She could feel Charley's nudge. "Wake up, Rachel, we're home. Come on, I'll drive you home."

"Fine," still half asleep. She woke up. "My god, what a night. Look."

The four of them stood in a circle, the heavens above them.

"Every star ever, Carlyle." Carolina Keefe held his hand.

"Want to go?" Charley close at Rachel's side, knowing her answer.

"Yes."

"Good night to you, Rachel. I'll remember all this. I envy you. Comes the winter ... "Carolina led Carlyle into the house.

Charley Gates followed Rachel home.

Charley Gates led her up her front steps.

Rachel led him into her house. She didn't turn on the lights.

The stars were in her eyes.

CHAPTER

A bison running, foaming at the mouth, stampeding, lightning strikes, breaking its leg in a gopher hole, an explosion, a grizzly feeding on human flesh, a red flame, the clank of metal.

A dream, a dream, a dream, a dream. Come on, it's a dream Paul! Wake the fuck up! It's a dream, a dream! Awake, still wild awake with it, the blank walls of it. The Rachel of it. Where in the hell is she? Where in the hell am I? I'm in the Lamar Valley. It's September. I'm O.K. I'm going to figure this dream some day. I'm going to get hold of Rachel today. Today? Today I get out of the patrol car. Today I begin to get up on the boundary. Today I leave the roads and the campground. Today I climb. Today I sweat.

Today I sweat it out of me. She, me. Today I sweat it out of me.

He got himself up. Today was after the last of it--a week beyond Labor Day. Lamar was the first to know their absence.

Silence on the road through the valley. A long stretch of silence.

No explosions, no lightning strikes, no clanking of metal. He got dressed quietly.

Quietly, he strapped on his revolver. This was hunting season. This was serious law enforcement. Serious enough to make him concentrate on the business at hand.

Upper Pebble Creek. Up to Wolverine Pass. Along the boundary, the ridgeline, alone.

Elk, high powered rifles, outfitters, hunters, poachers, professionals. One lone ranger against the hordes. The business at hand.

He left the patrol car at the Warm Creek turnout. The engine shut off, no man-made sound, none.

He made man-made sounds on the hand radio. Someone from the entrance station would be down to get the car. He snapped the radio to his belt. He pulled his official ball cap down across his forehead. He adjusted his day pack. He adjusted his gunbelt. He crossed the road and entered the forest.

The sunlight, the shade. The sunlight, the shade, the well worn trail. It took him in.

He switch-backed to his right. He began to feel the climb in his legs, in his lungs. He felt the privilege of today's duties.

He felt better.

She felt great. She said so.

"Charley, I feel terrific." She held her face in the cold morning sun.

"What was it Carolina Keefe said? The work of an artist, a writer? The truth become a dream? I feel like that."

"Well, keep that good thought. I'm driving Carlyle to Missoula in the morning. We'll drop Carolina at the airport in Bozeman. I've got to get everything ready." He took her hand.

"Think about your winter plans, won't you?"

"Yes, I will. I will. How long will you be gone?"

"Three days."

"Oh. Thanks." She embraced her lover. "See you soon."

"Yes. A few days. Bye."

"Bye. Tell Carlyle I said hello."

"Sure."

Listen to me. Tell Carlyle I said hello? The truth becoming a dream? She watched Charley Gates in a Land Rover dust cloud disappear over the rise and down the road.

Now what, Rachel? A cup of coffee at the kitchen table, her chin in her hand, staring off into the distance. The distance was Southern California, the city of angels. Los Angeles, California.

I wonder. I wonder. Wonderful? What would I do? Are there rivers there? Are there mountains, like these? Who would I meet? What would I do? What would I find out? The stars.

Rachel, Charley Gates dumped you and left for Europe never entered her head.

Maybe I could write something. She laughed. Maybe I could. Maybe Charley could help me.

Maybe there's a world out there. Maybe I'm going? Maybe.

She finished her coffee. She heard the painful moan of the siren call from across the river. Maybe I should go.

CHAPTER

Paul followed some small talk, some park talk on his radio.

A stop for a gulp of water. A stop on a yellow elevation, an avalanche of broken rocks, a broken cliff, the broken rocks hard enough and large enough to build a castle keep. He sat on the battlements.

The view was part Lamar Valley, part alpine, part forest, part narrow road, part way up the trail. A bleached elk rib lay in the groove, the trail. He tossed it down on the rocks. Its sound carried for miles.

He adjusted his pistol. He adjusted his pack. The climb carried him to a level plateau. He felt his legs favoring its flat, forest floor. Cold and dark. It felt like wolves and bears.

It felt great.

Look, there's a wolf. No, no. He made a shadow, a shape, a wolf. "Youuuhhh!" out loud.

He heard it echo. He stepped from the trees into this earth's own amphitheater.

Amphitheater of a ridgeline, gray and earth brown, across the quietest place, the quietest meadow on this earth.

One lone man in the middle of a raw, wild place, a worn track in the ground, and the game trails like veins on the ground.

Ancient caravans, ancient rituals.

Pebble Creek was full of large stones, right up to its banks.

He checked his trail map. Bush-whack up to Wolverine Pass. He turned right from the amphitheater. A moose, suddenly. It, she stood in his way, ash black and unreasonable.

He was scared, he was exhilarated, scared, glad. He backed up, backed up. The moose stood, in control, in tune. He backed, backed back and around, around, around, slipping on the rocky ground.

He watched back over his shoulder for the wild animal. So was he, bush-whacking, pulling, pushing himself up, Pebble Creek cascading down a lot easier, a lot faster than he was going up, everything around him scoured, burned, rubbed raw by the raw winds that brought winter over the pass above him and into the lives of everyone, everything for the next four hundred months.

Paul needed to be scoured, rubbed raw. He climbed, winded.

He could see the level height above him, steep now, all alone now, trying not to get hurt as he hand held, foot held his way across the rushing creek. There, he could see a boundary stake above him.

The ground was gray with immortality.

Hands and knees, hands and knees, crawling, clinging, a fish evolved out of its water.

A little more, a little higher, a little higher. Stand up, straighten out.

Stand up straight, feel the ache. Walk, feel those knees.

Feel the absolute edge of Yellowstone National Park. Feel the level parapet.

Drop dead, drop to your knees. Drop everything you were thinking, everything you ever thought. Look out at this.

Swiss chocolate with whipped cream, about four hundred servings. A table full of a mountain range, arranged like individual servings of serenity, intensity, majesty, simplicity, eternity, impossibility.

He knelt in a flopped down sitting position. He was the one the others would climb up to. Tell me, tell me the true meaning of life. He could tell them. This, and a woman. He concentrated on this, this, this ...

The woman Rachel soaked herself in the hot soak of the hot pot on the Gardner. She related her elation to her pal Cindy soaking next to her.

"He's in Missoula for a few days."

"So, he spent the night?"

"He did."

"Well, it is the rutting season."

They both laughed.

"It is, isn't it?" Rachel laughing out loud.

"Who's the bull and who's the cow?"

"Hmmm . I don't know. I feel, I feel … well, I feel dominated by him."

"Him who?" hinting at the two men she knew Rachel knew.

"Charley. A bit. I mean a bit still, dominated? With the additions to his life. I get a big feeling of it. He's important now, I think."

"Important?"

"Better?"

"You tell me. He's the one that took off once upon a time."

"Yes," and she didn't say anything more, dunking her head under the hot water, sticking her legs into the ice cold rushing by.

"Will you get me Carolina Keefe's autograph?" she was asked when she surfaced.

"Sure, any time, kid," sharing the laugh of it.

"So, the winter, Cindy. What have you decided?"

Right away, right at it. "Alaska," like a wind of fresh air.

"Big winter."

"I know. Silence, solitude. Too many tourists this summer."

They were the only two soaking.

"And you might pick L.A.?"

"All the people in the world?"

"Yep."

"I haven't decided. I've been invited."

"None of this in Los Angeles," wiggling her toes in the hot pool.

"Maybe that's it. I need to find out?"

Cindy put her face down level with the water to nearly mask what she had to say. "Learn much out in Lamar?"

Rachel said the words "Los Angeles," testing the sound of it.

"Oh, what, Lamar?"

"You know, the Lamar Valley."

She did know. She did. She had other things on her mind.

She did know. She did. She dunked her head under the rush of warm water pouring down from the river bank.

She stayed under for a long time.

CHAPTER

Paul dropped his binoculars on the cord around his neck. He rubbed both his eyes with both hands.

He checked the lenses on his binoculars like a silent movie comedian.

He was on his way out, back to the road, a thousand miles away-- his knees felt that way.

What a day, solitude but never alone, full with the darkness of the deep shade on the high skyline. Full with the cowboy make believe heft of his heavy holster on his hip.

He raised the binoculars to be sure. Yep.

Wolverine Pass dropped down into the Gallatin National Forest.

The hunting season was in full swing, in full view down below on a flat and worn parking area. A gnarled and rutted logging road led up to it.

An outfitter was getting ready to go in--a muscled truck and a horse trailer. Four mounts stood with two mules, packed with those worn canvas covers from every pack trip that ever was.

It was him, Gary Delling on one of the hard-working mounts.

Paul felt silly all of a sudden with his little holster and pistol.

Gary Delling had a Winchester, its stock showing from its leather case under his saddle bag. He had a high powered something with a high powered scope showing some of its high power from a leather sheath across his saddle horn.

He looked like Tom Horn, the real one, tall in the saddle.

His trail boss could have been Tom Horn's father, his real one.

Two tender feet, tender hands, tender faces, tender careers were going to try for an elk, an adventure, an endeavor.

Looks like they've signed on with two of the classics. Are their eight Gary Dellings, Paul? Believe me, I wouldn't want to meet them in a dark ravine. I wouldn't want to meet them in a sunlit ravine.

The sun was six o'clock. He stood exactly on the boundary.

A white stake said so.

Gary Delling's pack train started into the hunting grounds.

Paul followed them in, into the pine forest, and gone. I feel sorry for any elk in their path. Any elk? Me against them? I don't think so. Have fun guys.

Coming down was easier than coming up. A day full of satisfaction, pure, positive distraction.

Lee Whitson was waiting for him in the patrol car.

Lee Whitson was absolutely oblivious to everything Yellowstone. He'd been hired, Cumberland Island, Georgia. It wasn't the Caribbean, but it was water, water everywhere. Wide, open space. His shit-eating grin was his conversation back to the Lamar ranch.

"Ready for Republic Pass?" was some of his shit-eating conversation.

"Whenever," Paul told him.

"Whenever," with that grin.

Paul lost his grin when he picked up his telephone. He dialed her number.

CHAPTER

It went all right. All right Paul, don't force it.

All right Rachel, here we are in the middle of this.

Some hemming, some hawing. Some information, some interest.

Some anxiety, some questions. Some patience, some news, some gossip. Some spontaneity, more spontaneity.

Some plans. Tomorrow evening in Gardiner. No, come out to Lamar. "Fine. No wait, I can't. Come into town?"

"Fine."

"Good, Paul. I'll meet you then."

Some anxiety. Some snow, like dust on the valley floor. Some business first. Pick up Bob Davis at the trailhead.

Some sight, Bob Davis coming in from two weeks of it back there. One lone human on the landscape. Paul watched the figure coming his way, still a way out across the flats, across Soda Butte Creek.

One lone figure on all that landscape. Paul waited patiently, Bob Davis coming in closer, in focus, big square pack on his back.

If he were French it would be Hudson's Bay, 1750.

Paul sat on the hood of the car and waited. An elk bugled its challenge to every male elk in existence.

Bob Davis crossed the wooden footbridge over the creek. Paul could almost touch the French fur trade.

Now here he was coming up the trail to him, face as tan, as leather as a whaler's, sweaty and tired as a ditch digger, mud splattered and wet hiking boots.

"Welcome back, Bob."

"Thanks," and that was all he said.

"Thanks," was all he said at the ranch house, unloading his pack.

Some character, Paul. Another character--Charley Gates. Paul Barnes meet Charley Gates.

264

CHAPTER

Meet Rachel Cramer.

Monday was becoming evening. Yellowstone was becoming patches of New England.

The K-Bar was becoming Monday night football.

There she was, in the middle of the howling, the hooting, the beer glasses, the guys and the gals.

My gal, Rachel. You think so Paul? He waved to her, like a stranger. She waved back, smiling, getting up, a big wool sweater over bib overalls.

They met around a televised touchdown. He, they didn't know whether to kiss, hug, embrace, shake or nod.

"Hi," warmly.

"Hi," warmly.

"Let's take a walk?" practically yelling it in her ear above the sound of the instant replay.

"Sure!"

Montana was as quiet as a church. Church was empty.

So they walked.

"Oh, look, Paul," lifting her heavy sweater. "My new look," showing off the shoulders of the bib overalls. "I picked it up from Carolina Keefe."

"Oh, yeah, Carolina Keefe? You know her now?" almost sadly.

Rachel wasn't sad. "I do, I do."

He wanted to put his arm around her, gladly. He didn't, couldn't.

"I did my first boundary patrol." They were at the edge of town.

"You did? What a relief from the patrol car?"

"It was."

They were walking away from town, alone, with the park boundaries all around them.

"It's great to see you, Rachel. Seems like a long time."

She didn't say a word. They walked on the gravel road. She said some words. "I'm glad you could come in." Those weren't exactly the words he wanted to, needed to hear.

He stopped and sat on a glacial boulder. "Have a seat." They shared the glacial boulder.

What else could he say? "So, Carolina Keefe, and Carlyle Stevens?" What else could he say? "And Charley Gates?"

If you listened real easy you could hear the Yellowstone.

Rachel listened real hard. It was hard. "Do you know Carolina Keefe?"

"I know of her."

Night began its descent, down the slopes, down the slopes, across the land.

"Charley Gates?" Rachel asked.

"Believe me, Rachel, I don't want to ask. But, you know, I guess I've been asking for awhile now."

"I know," turning her face to him. The darkness made it easier. "Yes, I know him. I've, uh, been knowing him again."

"Uh-huh," with an Adam's apple as large as the rock they sat on.

She took his hand. "But I know you, too."

His heart got as big as the rock. "Listen, Rachel. I know I don't have any, uh, I know claim's not the word. Listen, you know how I feel about you."

"I know, Paul, I know. What I feel for you is wonderful. Wonderful for me, us."

"Won't you stay with me this winter? Here?"

The stars lit her face. "I don't know."

"Uh-huh," manly, cowardly, sincerely, carefully, courteously.

Careful, Paul, careful.

"There is something, Paul."

"Yes?" looking away from her star lit face.

"Los Angeles? Maybe?"

"Oh, boy," puzzled, forgetting that there were still places beyond the Yellowstone. "City of lights, stars?"

"I don't want to surprise you with it. I don't want to kick you in the shins."

"You're not kicking me in the shins." Not much you're not.

He took her hand. "I love you, Rachel. A winter here with you would be …" and he didn't know.

She did. "I know. Can you imagine that I could love two men? Can I imagine that I can love two men?"

"I can't be Los Angeles. But it can be Lamar."

"Thanks." She leaned her head on his shoulder.

"Oh, look, it looks like the Aurora Borealis, the northern lights." She sat up real straight.

Thick, wide bands of orange and red and yellow against the black and white sky.

Paul stood up. "It's a big fire."

They stood together. The fire lit up Montana across the river. Something down river, up off the road, was burning up, filling the night with flames.

They could see down river from the fire's yellow light. It wasn't Rachel's trailer. It sure wasn't the cult's compound. It was across the river, across the road.

"It might be." Rachel stepped forward. A fire horn blew, loud as judgement day. The tall flames danced with each other.

"Might be what?" stepping forward to join her.

"Gary Delling's place."

"Yeah, could be," a ranger on the case, imagining images of, of what Paul? What do you think is going on? "I think it is."

"Me, too." They held each other, an eerie sight, suddenly a very eerie night.

"Take me home, Paul?"

"Sure, sure."

He felt her and she felt him, and they felt each other. They felt for each other and they fell into each other.

The fire horn blew like judgement day.

In the morning the remains of the fire were bone dead, burnt to the ground, to a crisp.

The black frame and the black rubble showed no signs of life, each item of someone' s life desecrated on the ground--a melted cassette, an empty chair, a blackened set of dishes, everything covered in a glaze of frost from a busted pipe.

Paul and Rachel stood with the other bystanders on the service road just below the former house. They were both glad for the distraction, glad for some distraction from the hemming and the hawing of the morning in her trailer.

Some distraction. Just a few others with them. There were just a few others left in town now. You could see your breath now.

"I wonder where he is?" Rachel asked.

"Delling?"

"Uh-huh," buttoning her down vest."

"I saw him," eyes fixed on the fire's victim. "Out in Wolverine Pass. I saw him packing into the Gallatin." I saw this fire in my dream, that dream? He didn't share that with Rachel.

"I guess he won't know then."

"I guess not. It didn't look like an overnight trip in." He blew warm air into his hands.

"I wonder how it started?"

Paul turned around. They were high enough up the road to see across the river to the cult's campground. White trails of smoke rose up from the trailers, obvious against the cold, cooking fires, content, composed.

Paul shoved his hands in his pockets and stared across.

Rachel turned and stared at him.

"What is it?"

"Nothing, I guess, nothing."

A sheriff's car came up the road. Paul left it at "nothing, I guess. Let's go."

She held her gaze across the river. "Sure," following him away from the fire.

The hemming and the hawing from earlier continued.

"Where to now?" he asked her.

"Drop me in town. At the shop?"

"Want me to drive you back home?"

"No thanks, I think I'll walk."

He looked back at the burnt out building in the rear view mirror. Rachel looked back in the side mirror.

"When will I see you again?" coming into the wooden buildings of town.

"I don't know, Paul," softly, a little irritation. "Soon."

"Soon enough," crossing the Yellowstone over the Gardiner bridge. Rachel looked out her window, far down the river.

He pulled to a stop in front of the raft company. Her work place was empty and shut, the summer absolutely over.

"I've got to do a few things. Tomorrow I've got to go to Bozeman and begin the unemployment."

"I'll go with you?" absolutely, instantly sorry he said it.

"Not right now. Understand?"

"Sure. I think." I shouldn't think. He did. "When do you see Charley Gates again?"

"Not right now, Paul. Understand?"

"Sure, sure."

"Thanks," squeezing his hand.

"Call me, or I'll call you?"

"I will, I will." She got ready to get out.

"An eerie day," he said.

"Yes, it is, it is." She got out.

CHAPTER

He was alone at the buffalo ranch now. Bob Davis had disappeared, gone for the season, disappearing. Only one guy from the road crew now. He came out to the ranch from Tower, spending his days stabbing snow stakes into the shoulder of the road. The folks from Cooke City and Silver Gate had to find their way once winter became their entire life.

Winter was already the entire life higher up. Higher up-that's where he was going. Republic Pass.

No contact with the world outside the Lamar Valley for two days now. Now he was going to spend two days climbing over Republic Pass and down into Cooke City. Boundary patrol, up at over 10,000 ft., winter.

Cache Creek was running white and quick, shallow. He splashed across, pack, pistol on his gun belt.

Golden light on a golden meadow, icicle frost on the ground, and then right into a tunnel of trees, sopping wet trail, mud, cold, shade, shade, dark, cold, muddy, going up, up where grizzly bear stories had their origins.

One man among it all. Daunting. He felt it. Daunting. The whole place of it.

The daunting felt good, heavy, serious, important, necessary.

He sat on a stump and took a drink from the water bottle. "This is the forest primeval ... " The dark forest didn't answer him. He listened for an answer. Nothing, not even the sound of his breathing.

He sang some songs, out loud. Oh Mr., Mrs. Grizzly, I'm coming.

Sunlight coming through the tops of the trees, never reaching the slippery trail. There was a dry cabin waiting for him. Not too far, not too far now as he slogged up, up, up the trail. A coyote appeared and vanished into the bramble of fallen branches.

Oh Mr., Mrs. Grizzly. A wide wall of sunlight up, up, up ahead. He slogged up to it, and there he stood in a thick panel of warm sunlight on a narrow ridge, the dark tunnel of trees behind him, a cup, a bowl, a scoop of a sunlit clearing beside a silver, quick creek, a small brown log

cabin somehow sitting in the middle of it all below him. Not daunting-
-welcome.

He adjusted all his straps and belts and buckles and wandered down the dry trail to it.

It was a light in the forest, a forty acres and a mule in the forest; a homestead, settlers, squatters in the forest. It would be good to squat here in the clearing, in the cabin. Squat down for the rest of the day, over the pass in the morning.

Cache Creek kept him company. He had a few letters to write.

He had shelter for the evening. Plenty of fuel for the lamps, plenty of stores, plenty of water, plenty of daylight.

He checked the hardness of his hard bed. Perfect. There were two books on the hard pillow. Bob Davis? Paul took a peek. Now, who is this? The Moon and Sixpence? Cakes And Ale? By, who is this? Don't I know this? Somerset Maugham? Who is this? I know this. This is, is… It's Larry.

Didn't he say something? Yes? Yes, yes… something about knowing him? Knowing him in Paris? In Paris? I think so.

He pulled out his coin. He held the books, the coin. He held the books, the coin. Fine, good. Good. He had plenty to keep him company. A light, a night in the forest.

CHAPTER

Headlights in the night, the only light, powerful and clear.

Gary Delling shut off the engine and left the headlights on.

He got out of the jeep and surveyed the wreckage, his place, his wreckage, all eerie and white, black and white in the high beams.

He walked over and poked at a charred plank with the toe of his boot, the blackened pile of his possessions flat to the ground.

He just stood there a bit, thumbs hooked in the pockets of his jeans, hat brim covering his eyes, the moonless night covering any expression on his face.

He kicked a blackened pot and got back in his jeep. The headlights led him away from the remains. He drove back towards Gardiner.

He pulled over and stopped, above the Yellowstone. He turned off the headlights and adjusted his sight.

Now he could see it down there, the bridge, across to the cult, short, spider black, stretched across about thirty yards of the Yellowstone, iron, straight up and stiff like some nuclear insect from the 1950's.

Gary Delling hummed a little tune, surveying the scene below him. No other cars on the road. The little tune he was humming was Ghost Riders in the Sky.

He got going again, his headlights searchlights in the dark.

This ghost rider noticed everything, everything, Vietnaming.

He noticed there was more than one vehicle at Rachel Cramer's residence. The social life of Gardiner, Montana. He never took part, but he noticed, he noticed. The side of his mouth smiled.

He knew whose vehicle it was there at Rachel's residence. He knew who's vehicle it wasn't.

He noticed the Yellowstone, like a blue artery in the earth's arm, pumping along, slower, lower, losing the summer's pulse.

He made his plans. The side of his mouth smiled.

CHAPTER

Paul Barnes hadn't planned on snow. He should have.

It snowed during the night. A night of a lantern and a few letters, a few pages of the books Bob Davis had left behind.

The lantern dimmed, so did he. Pitch, pitch black. Deep, deep sleep.

Now the sun was the lantern, an inch of perfect white snow on the ground.

He got ready to go, bare feet on the cold wooden floor, steaming coffee, cheese, orange, apple, crackers, peanuts, M &M's, raisins, the cabin door open--a doorway full of yellow sun, welcome, come on in.

Now he was ready, stomping his boots on the floor, leveling off all the gear. He turned on the radio on his belt. A mountain of gray clouds was larger, grayer than the sun. He knew there was snow in the gray. He knew there was wind in it. He knew he was going higher up, into it. He made boot prints in the snow like the first man, ever.

The sun came and went. The trail was obvious and easy, the tops of the pines swaying in the weather.

Flat and easy going, going between the pines like through an audience in a museum, curving and turning, gliding, quietly, easily, the sun now and then from the skylight overhead.

Then he turned and there was scat in the trail, alive, smoking, indicating, marking the trail. Grizz? He looked for tracks. He looked out for his backside. He should have yelled, a warning, but he remained silent, alive, breathing.

He was going up to 10,000 ft. It began. Then there were no trees, no shelter, plenty of wind, nothing of the sun, the trail more a guess than a certainty.

Snow on the ground, packed against the jagged rocks, against the scrub pines. A jagged groove in the ground ran like a shallow fault line. He got in it and started up, the cold wind slanting into him.

More snow, more wind, more elevation, more bear scat, smoking fresh on the fresh white snow. Bear prints like a helicopter with claws had landed. He tried not to notice. He tried to see the summit. No chance.

He could see his next objective--a squat tree trunk and its tree top right out of fiction, fairy tale, phantasmagorical, gnarled and twisted and lumped like some royal wizard, all of it swept to the east, swept by the eternal wind, branches like arms extended, casting a spell.

I'll rest a spell up there. He gained each foothold in the rock gravel ground, slippery with snow.

CHAPTER

There, I'm almost there, almost there, blinking in the snow and wind, and there, there in a yard of snow, like it was cast in stone, a paw print, a bear's paw print. He looked up quickly, checking for a reality check. Here I am and I'm pretty damn sure this print is a grizzly bear. Reality was pretty god damn real.

The tree trunk, the tree trunk, the tree trunk. Grab hold, hang on, get on the windward side. Reality check. I'm still in one piece, sitting, back against the wizard, sheltered from some of the growing weather.

Something else had been to the tree. He could smell it.

Could it smell him? Then he heard something. The something that had been at the tree? It sounded like a yawn, if this was Olympus and one of the gods had yawned.

I have to see this. Who said that? I said that. All of this said that.

Sheets and slants of snow, wind. Is that the summit? One boot ahead of the other, all white, all the way up to where the steady incline rolled down into a narrow bowl before the climb leveled off, flat, with nothing but gray sky beyond.

The wind stopped. There were prints, heavy in the snow, down in the bowl. Up above, he heard that god yawn.

Paul Barnes chewed the inside of his cheek. He moved to his right, making room for the thing that made those prints.

Up out of the bowl the wind was blowing snow off the peak like dust in a sand storm. He squinted his eyes in the dust.

There, what's that, that? A shape of two shades of gray, ash and blacker ash, silver and ash at the neck and shoulders? Paul squinted and the wind changed direction, clearing the dust, and there it was, large as a car, black and ash, silver tipped, black snout shoved in the snow, then up and sniffing the wind, on all fours, all fours big as two-by-fours.

Big as a car it turned to look back from where it had come, a face as blunt, as powerful, as ancient, as perfect as something cut from Mayan stone.

The winter wind came up and blew across the high elevation-nothing but dust devils of snow. Paul didn't dare proceed.

He didn't dare breathe, one of the wildest, noblest, most dangerous creatures alive was ... was where? squinting in the force of it up here at 10,000 ft.

He got to his feet. He felt it in his knees. His feet and his knees moved him forward, his own prints in the snow.

The wind yanked his sleeves out like sails. He braced. He stood over a gouge in the snow. A gouge like a tractor's blade.

Whatever it was, it was gone, the snow blowing across its tracks.

He felt it rushing up behind him. He turned to defend himself, to die. Nothing.

Get the hell down from here. What in the hell am I doing up here? Who in the hell would be poaching up here? Up here a few feet and he could see about ten feet in front of him, about five thousand feet beneath him, not a trace of a trail, bare ground, snow, tree tops, snow, rocks, brush, snow, a rocky gray creek bed far below.

"Rachel! Rachel!" for all the world, for all his effort to hear. His echo called her name.

He started down, groping, grabbing, below the summit, sheltered from the wind.

Ankle deep in the snow, then clear; hip deep in snow; grabbing a branch, a stump, a rock; twisted ankles in a clearing of rocks, sliding on his butt, cold red hands, cold red cheeks, hot blood heart.

That gray, rocky stream bed. That gray, rocky stream bed.

There it is, there it is. If I have to I can follow it down, down through the pines, the pines becoming a forest, a flat forest at the base of Republic Pass.

Holy mother of nature, a trail, its gouge dropping right into the gray stones, into the shallow gray stream.

I'm saved, I'm saved, and he splashed across, on terra firma, drinking his water like champagne.

This was the forest primevalest, dark and deep, home to whoever, whatever that was up there. He looked back up there. It looked back, wild and indifferent, still wearing its storm, etched, chiseled, frozen into his memory.

The trail felt like a carpet. He kept his eyes, ears, nose and throat open.

The trail opened into open sky and open spaces, civilization and some of its discarded junk: rusting machines and rusting tools around a discarded cabin, smoke rising from its rusting chimney.

Even Cooke City was too big for some folks.

Rusting cans and rotting food--a mound of it. Civilization.

The city's dump. Free lunch for him or her from back up there, with a ring of abandoned refrigerators like picnic benches.

Suddenly there was a road, then a car, then french fries and burgers and grizzly bears in store windows.

I need a drink. I need Rachel.

CHAPTER

The Aurora Borealis. Dame Margot Fontaine, Fanny Brice, arctic foot lights. May Day banners unfurled across the darkening sky, orange and blue, red and gold, purple and breathing, heaving, growing, sliding, fanning out across the sky like tropical flocks across tropical skies.

It's a sign, Paul. For the past two days everything was a sign. She's staying, she's staying. Even her flat phone call was a sign. She's going to surprise me.

He bathed in the beauty of a chilled tropical night, arms folded across the rail fence at the buffalo ranch, his chin on his arms.

Rachel sat on her porch, elbows on knees, chin in hand, eyes on the sky, wide, wide open. Charley Gates echoed in her ear: "Malibu, Beverly Hills, Santa Barbara ... " Wide, wide open. But the sky, the sky. She stood up and held her face to it, bathing in the banners, in the coral sea.

Gary Delling stopped digging. No one could ignore the sky.

He jammed the shovel in the ground and leaned on the long handle like a range hand layin' in a fence line.

He took off his hat and wiped his brow, content with the blue and the red and the orange and the golden sky. Enough. He went back to digging, around in behind a hill, three hills up from the charcoal of his cabin.

The sky cast all sorts of light. Two, three dainty antelope appeared in it, disappeared in it. Gary Delling took notice.

His shovel hit something solid, something wooden. He got down on his knees and scraped away the remaining dirt. A wooden ammo box.

Dainty, wiry as an antelope, he stopped to listen, look, taste, smell. He yanked the box from the ground. It fit squarely in a canvas sack. He stuck the shovel's blade in the hole, deep, stiff. He got the heel of his boot locked on the handle, listened, tasted, smelled, then snapped the handle in half. All of it went into the hole, quickly, pushing the dirt back in on top. He shouldered the canvas bag. He disappeared like the antelope.

CHAPTER

Paul Barnes looked for signs along the road to Mammoth. The morning mist, the camouflage of Camelot, rising up from a wide and shallow pond, two swans entering and exiting through the mist? Or the breath of the bison? The solitary road? The frost on the fallen leaves? Two Canada geese in union in flight? The cold river? Rachel sitting on the steps of the visitor's center?

Mammoth Hot springs was closing down, obeying the seasons.

The elk had the run of the place. Paul honked at her and she waved. He felt the tension and the ease of the order all around him, them.

"Hiya."

"Hiya."

He hugged her. She hugged him, all in their denim and down coats.

"Tell you what," she said. "Mammoth Terrace?"

"Sure," not saying a word, trying to gauge the hug, the reason for the Mammoth Terrace.

One of the reasons was simple. The thermal terrace was a great layer cake of egg nog and vanilla, brown sugar and blue icing, white powder and tapioca pudding, basted in the sunshine, left out to cool in the steam of the morning air.

Paul drove them up, some minor league chit-chat about some minor league matters.

A station wagon dragging a trailer pulled out of its spot and left them alone above the layers of the cake, above some of their park.

Rachel got out. A cloud of steam blew across her. She reappeared. Paul was next to her.

"What a morning," as far as the eye could see.

"We're lucky, Paul."

"We are?" snapping off the question mark.

"Yes, you especially."

"Me?" He didn't resist. "If I have you Rachel I am."

"What if you just have all this?"

"I already do."

"Especially you. And you'll have it this winter."

The steam from the thermal pools warmed his cheeks. He blew warm air into his cupped hands.

"And you, Rachel. Will you?"

"No, Pauley."

He cried immediately. Not a sob, or a whine, or a sound, just tears welling in his eyes, spilling onto his cheeks.

He licked them off his lips and turned his face away.

"You're leaving?"

"Yes."

"Where?"

"Los Angeles."

He coughed, and coughed again wet with tears.

"Not exactly sure. Growth, interest, activity, curiosity?"

"Charley?"

"Yes, Charley too."

He stepped away from her and stared out across the great plateau. She came next to him.

"Can he give you something I can't? I love you deeply, Rachel. Deep as all this."

"I love you too, Paul, Pauley. I do," resting her head against his arm.

"You love two men?"

"Can't I? Can't I?" softly against his arm.

"But you have to leave one of them."

"I know."

"That means me I guess. I guess I can't compete," wiping his eyes, sniffling his nose, coughing the despair out of his throat.

"It's not competing. It's what I need now, Paul. What I feel I need."

"I need you too, Rachel. More than Los Angeles does."

"What would your friend Larry say?"

"Larry who?"

"Larry who?" nearly in shock.

He came back to reality, all the way from sandy beaches to sunlight sparkling on the emerald and ivory thermal pools. He could almost feel the heat, the magma plume boiling beneath his feet.

"Larry, yes, Larry," he said. "He'd say stay," still not strong enough to turn and hear all this from her lovely face.

"He'd say go, if going was what you felt."

"I don't know, Rachel. Larry's not here. I am. I want you to stay," absolute resignation, resigned to the painful order of it all.

"I can't, Paul. Don't cry," the impossibility of her halfhearted request all over her resignation.

"I won't," he told her, "after a couple of weeks." The laugh between them bumped over a rutted road.

He finally turned to her. She was leaving Yellowstone.

"I guess this Charley Gates is really something. Maybe ... I'll leaving it at that. He looked around him. "What a way to go."

"Will you stay the winter?"

Shrugging his shoulders, head down.

"I do love you, Paul. Pauley." Her kiss could taste the tears on his cheek. "I have to get going."

He wanted to wail like a coyote.

"Sure, I, well, I…"

"That's enough now. I know where you'll be. I'll know.

Goodbye, ranger. I'll always." Her hand slipped away and she started down the wooden stairs, down the terrace, in and out of the steam, across the road, across the lawns, through the elk, into her truck, and gone.

He followed her closely. He cried.

CHAPTER

He cried for several days. Two days. Then two more days, waiting for her at the Lamar ranch. The road was empty, the valley crusted with frost. There was snow on Specimen Ridge, white as an altar boy's surplice--just as perfect, just as holy.

Paul Barnes hardly noticed. Frost on his innards, around his heart, around his hope. Not broken, just numb.

Dumb, too. He told them he wasn't going to work the winter.

Think I'll take off for awhile. Next winter, next year? I wonder what the temperature is in Los Angeles? He packed his bags. He packed the trunk of his car. He wiped his nose. It was cold, in the thirties. The minus 10's, the minus 15's were on their way, close by. The whole sky, the whole earth was heavy, enormous with it.

He said his goodbyes. "Goodbye." The weathered corrals, the barn, big as an ark, the creek, the hills, the ground, the log house, his home. "Goodbye." He drank for several days. He got the cliche, the norm--he got drunk.

He got a motel room in Gardiner. He looked around for her.

She didn't show up.

Jack Daniel's, Olympia beer, Jack Daniel's. He got drunk.

The word got around, around Gardiner, almost empty now. It took one night, after two nights of him sitting in the corner of the K-Bar, picking at a pizza and a pitcher of beer. She didn't show up.

"You all right, Barnes?" from a concerned bus driver soon to evolve into a snow coach driver as soon as his winter fur grew in.

"Yeah, sure, thanks, Barry."

"Stayin' the winter?"

"Nope."

Mary Gregor tried one night.

"Paul?"

"Oh, hi, Mary."

She sat down. "Are you feeling all right?" pulling off her wool cap, her wool scarf, her wool mittens.

"No."

"Want to talk about it?"

"Yes, with Rachel."

"Oh," and she replaced all her wool. "Hot chocolate and a willing ear when you're ready?"

"Thanks, Mary," with a swig of Jack Daniel's. "Not right now, O.K.?"

"Sure. Don't drink too much."

"I won't."

CHAPTER

He did. He switched to the Blue Goose, cigarette smoke like steam off a geyser, pool balls clicking, three locals sitting at the bar, Paul Barnes wallowing in it at a table. Wind and snow blew in through the front door. Gary Delling blew in with it.

He said a few things to a few of them at the big slab of the bar. Paul saw him in the long mirror, in the rows of bottles.

Gary Delling saw him back. Was that a smile or a grimace? He got his drink and walked to the back room. Paul thought he heard spurs, gunslinger spurs.

But Gary Delling wore fleece-lined Sorrell boots and a sheep skin coat, bulky as a bomber pilot's, weathered as a Basque sheep herder's. He sat down alone at a little round table for two.

Paul was tipsy enough, numb enough, lonely enough. I think I'll join him. I think I will? Yeah, I think I will. So he did, no spurs a'jingling.

He didn' t know what he was going to say. Then he did, standing at the table, Gary Delling with a clean-shaven face, younger than Paul imagined, still much older in the face than Paul.

"I was sorry about your place burning down." He was.

"Yeah, me too," sipping a beer with a shot.

"Have a seat there, ranger," cordially?

Paul almost said, "don't mind if I do .. " He said, "sure," like obeying an order.

"Big storm coming," he said like a hick who'd invented the sticks.

"This ain't nothin', ranger." He eyed Paul up and down, parallel and horizontal. "You stayin' for the winter?"

"Uh, my name's Paul.

"You stayin' for the winter, ranger?"

"No, I don't think so." He thought he heard Gary Delling chuckle. But those eyes, confident and cold, squint lines like eagle talons. A chuckle?

"What about you? Are you staying?" Paul asked him, somebody in the bar yelling "god damn that eight ball!"

"Me? Maybe not," staring across a shot glass at Paul. "Maybe not."

It was warm in here, Paul was lonely. He was sad, he was drinking. He was warm in this blanket of it.

"How'd your place burn?"

Gary Delling put down his beer. "How'd my place burn, ranger? You really want to know, ranger?"

This blanket around him felt soft and warm. "I think I do know."

"Think so?" leaning forward in his chair. "You rangers been investigating?" Paul had to laugh at that, warming to his drinking buddy.

"No. Across the river, across the Yellowstone?" He waited for Gary Delling to plant a Bowie knife in the middle of the table. Just three beer bottles and a shot glass. Paul tiptoed forward.

"The cult? Elizabeth the Prophet and her bunch?"

Gary Delling leaned forward, closer. "You know, I knew your girlfriend, Rachel. Not much but I knew her," softly, quietly, privately, gently.

A Bowie knife right in the middle of the table.

CHAPTER

"What do you mean you knew her?" slowly, softly, quietly, gently, sadly. Across the river? What cult? What fire?

"I recognized her. I'd see her. You were lucky, ranger."

"I was? Yeah, I was. I guess."

"You want a shot?"

"Yeah, I do."

He got up and came back with four shots, of tequila.

"Strong stuff," from behind clenched teeth.

"You can take it can't you, ranger?"

"Stop calling me ranger," the first shot glass empty.

"Sure."

Paul stared into his beer bottle. "Her name was Rachel. We'd lay in bed and listen to the cult across the river being called to prayers." Which brought him back to Gary Delling.

"She run off with Charley Gates?" Gary Delling asked.

"What? Yeah." Do you know everyone around here? "Never mind him. But yeah, she did. For Los Angeles? But never mind him, them," the next tequila fresh on his tongue.

"What about you, Delling. Huh? You the one that's been fuckin' with them? Ain't you?"

"So, you ain't stayin' the winter?"

"No. I want to get away now."

"Well then rang," and he cut himself off. "Yeah, I've been fuckin' with them," so only the two of them could hear. There were only four of them left in the place.

"Yeah?" caught up in the local tale of it, the reality of it. "So they burned your place?"

"You figure it out."

"Why?"

"Why what?"

"Why fuck with them?"

No hesitation, no indecision, no nothin'. "I like the action. I don't much care for them. They're fuckin' with my home," softly, quietly, sadly, gently.

"Your home?"

"Yeah, my home."

"No, no, I understand, I understand. Yeah, but don't you poach the park," the tequila giving him strength.

"Everybody tell you that?"

"Yeah, everybody."

"I take some elk, some meat. On their turf, their terms."

Paul wasn't any official capacity of the park service. "I see." He didn't.

"Now it's the antelope."

Paul thought he heard Gary Delling say "now it's the antelope. " He knew he saw another beer and another shot on the table.

"Antelope? What antelope?"

"Our visitors across the river. Building fences. Cuttin' off the antelope. Cuttin' 'em off."

"Feeding, migrating?"

"Yep."

"Yeah, I thought I heard."

"So, you're not stayin' for the winter?"

Paul didn't answer this time. He waited for Gary Delling to tell him. He didn't have to wait long.

"Me neither. But before I pack up I have some business to finish."

"What business?"

"You want to leave with a bang?" tequila wet on his lips.

"I could use a bang," right in Gary Delling's face. "What sort of bang?"

"Bang, boom. Their bridge across the Yellowstone."

"Who's bridge across who's river?" knowing damn well, but being damn well drunk and damn well in the reality of it.

"You know who."

"Yeah, I do, I do. Holy shit."

"Yeah, holy shit."

288

Holy shit. Paul said "how?" impossibility in with the possibility.

"I'll tell you a little secret. Vietnam vet magic. We can do anything. Magic. Any cliche. You name it, we can do it. We can get the blame for it, or the pity, or the praise. Or, the satisfaction of giving them across the river one royal ass pain in their butts. Vietnam style. Magic. Black magic."

Paul heard that "magic" part.

"It's my dream," dream like.

"What dream?" puzzled, pissed-off like.

"My dream, my dream."

"This ain't no dream, cowboy."

Paul was studying the blank wall, with a blank stare, a head full of flashing lights and burning bridges.

"You hear me, cowboy?"

"I hear you, I hear you." He came back from the wall. "Yeah, a good bang will do it."

"Make you forget your girlfriend," without a trace of sarcasm.

"Forget? Maybe. Maybe not. Let's find out," elbow slipping off the table, trying to get sober all of a sudden.

"How?" he asked his new partner.

"Black magic. Come here," closer across the table. "You know anything about explosives?"

"Uh." He was going to tell him he'd been in the Coast Guard, but not this guy, not this night. "No."

"You know how to hand things up to me?"

"I do."

"From a float tube, under a bridge, at night, on the Yellowstone?"

"Wow, the dream. It is."

"Well, do you?"

"I do. Float tubes?"

"Yeah, you've seen 'em. Inner tube and hip boots, to fish, to float."

"Right, right. On the river?"

"I'll take care of you, don't worry," with a wide grin.

Paul was surprised by how wide the grin was.

"Explosives though. I don't want to kill anyone," sobering up real quick.

"I can make that magic too. Nobody gets hurt. You'll be my look out. Bang, boom, their bridge is in the river."

"Sure, why not," the liquor and the dream talking.

"We're going to have to leave Gardiner and everything."

"I know," sadly, gently, quietly. "Where will you go?"

"None of your business."

"Sure. Where will you get explosives?"

"From my Vietnam vet guide book to the great outdoors."

"I see."

"Well?"

"Well. You trust me?"

"I trust you."

"O.K. then."

"O.K. then."

They shook on it.

CHAPTER

The plan. To meet at the hunter's access, in the turnout above Yankee Jim Canyon. About 2:00 a.m. Get back above the bridge, "about where your friend Rachel used to live.. " Get in the river, float down under the bridge. Blow the bridge up. Float away, get in our cars and leave.

"When?"

"Tomorrow night."

"Tomorrow night?"

"Yep."

"How do we get back up river without the cars?"

"I've got a trail bike."

How do you have a trail bike? wasn't asked.

They shook on it.

Paul walked back to his motel room, slowly, very slowly. He emptied his pockets on top of the dresser in the room. The coins and the paper clips and the keys, and the spare button splashed across the slick surface. Larry's coin slid against the mirror.

Paul Barnes flopped on the bed, more sober than drunk now.

He slept. He dreamed. Not of bridges but of soft rolling waves on soft sandy beaches. Then a river and a city. What city? Just a river and a city. Mountains. Distant mountains. Far distant mountains. A city. What city? A city without an ocean.

A river, a river, a river. Tequila. Sleep.

Tequila. Awake in the gray day light, the gray in his mouth, between his ears, in his eyes. He rolled over, still in his clothes. Snow, soft and fluffy, pretty in the window.

The gray in the mouth tasted like shit. He remembered, slowly. Bang! Yeah, tonight? Yeah, tonight, reminding himself in the mirror, gray around the eyes. Why not? It's the dream, come true.

He took a shower and felt a hell of a lot better. Brushed his teeth, combed his hair, got ready to blow up a bridge.

The car was already packed. What time is it? It was two in the afternoon. I need to walk around a bit. He started to refill his pockets. Pennies, nickels, a paper clip, a button he discarded, his keys.

I'm missing something, patting his pockets.

Of course. Of course as soon as he touched it, as soon as he held the coin in his hand. A river up his arm, a river in his blood, soft waves on soft sandy beaches in his nervous system.

Of course not, holding the coin like a hand shake. Of course I'm not going to blow up some bridge. Not that I wouldn't like to.

Not that I don't want Gary Delling to. But of course I can't. I couldn't, Larry.

My dream? Just a dream, Paul, just a dream? Yes and no? Yes, Larry, yes, softly, gently, sadly, gladly.

Outside, a brand new version of the weather--a low ceiling of gray, running out of snow while up above part of the gray had parted, leaving an enormous deep blue dose of radiant sky and radiant sun. That part of the sky opened wide like a view down into a desert canyon or a tropical ocean from a seaside cliff.

Paul walked around under it, conscience clear, wondering where in the hell he was going to go. Some river, some city? There was snow on the ground. Just on the ground, the road from the Roosevelt Arch to the entrance station still black.

Just enough snow on the ground. Someone was out early in the season, seasoning their cross-country skis, on the flat ground, gliding, effortlessly. Paul glided along on foot.

Where in the hell is Gary Delling? He checked the clock at the entrance station.

CHAPTER

Twelve midnight arrived. Gary Delling was in the willows, under the cottonwoods, on the Yellowstone, below Rachel's residence, snow on the roof, on the porch. The snow was wet on Gary Delling's tongue, catching it coming down, fat and flat as flap jacks, dainty as doilies.

Let's see now. Explosives in one inner tube, me in the other, the explosives and the deflated tubes under a camouflaged poncho.

There wasn't a third inner tube for ranger Barnes.

There wasn't a star in the universe that wasn't in the sky.

The snow stopped, the wind blew. Gary Delling leaned back against a tree trunk and enjoyed the view, biding the time.

The time now was a half an hour past midnight. Paul Barnes had run out of bars. No Gary Delling. Nobody.

On the streets of Gardiner he could smell the town's wood smoke. Cold, with a few neon signs sparkling in it. He stood on the bridge above the Yellowstone. The river made no sound, like the power of a ballerina, or an athlete in mid air.

Where in the hell is he? Now calm down, just drive out there and let him know that you're not going to be able to assist him in the big bang. If all of it had hit him at once all of it would have knocked him cold. What time is it? One, in the a.m. Gary Delling got ready.

The inner tubes were really small rubber rafts, with wading boots attached. Slide into the boots, slide into the raft, waterproof at the waist--wade or float. Gary Delling would be floating.

The river. He knew it. He knew it would take him fast. He didn't have far to go. He could see some light from the pre-fab part of the compound on his side of the river, at this end of the bridge. Lights were going out, after one a.m. now.

He could hear the river the way you hear the wind. A hand pump the size of his hand and the two rafts were inflated. There were only a few thousand people left in all of Montana. None of them heard him.

He tied the rafts together with a length of powerful climbing rope. He scooped river water into the wading legs of the lead raft.

Weighted down he lowered the two rafts into the river, the climbing rope secured around his waist. He used the camouflage cover to cover over the leg holes in the lead raft.

He laid a sleeping bag cinch sack, dry inside a waterproof bag, on the cover. The cinch sack was full of TNT explosives, tapioca blocks of TNT, as long and solid as church candles, a perfectly round hole at the end to slide in a blasting cap. The blasting caps were in a fly box, each one where a hatch fly would be; each one wrapped in cotton, the box in a plastic bag in the pack on the ground. The detonator cord was in with the explosives.

He put on the pack, carefully. Carefully, he tied his rope end to an exposed tree root. Carefully, he slid into the legs of his raft.

He splashed his face with ice cold water. He had a canvas water bucket. He tied a length of rope to its leather handle. He tied the rope through three of the hooks and clips on the raft. He laid the bucket in his lap. He made sure the explosives were ready to ride, patting, friendly like. He was ready to go. He untied the line and let go.

CHAPTER

Ranger Barnes was at the pre-arranged spot. No Gary Delling.

No willis Jeep, no trail bike, no nothin'.

I better get going. Where? I don't know where. Anywhere but Los Angeles.

But maybe I'll stick around for awhile. I know where he is.

I bet he knew I wouldn't show. I bet. And I know what he's going to be doing. In all of Montana, only two people knew.

Paul walked across the road. The iron guard rail around the big turnout was ice cold. He sat on it anyway. He couldn't see Gardiner now. It was gone. Where in the hell am I going? The Yellowstone flowed out of the park, calm as you please.

Calm, so no kayaker would fear it. Gary Delling didn't, the river running shallow and pebbly, deep and thoroughly, taking him to the bridge.

He knew where the bridge would be. Gary Delling had dreams too.

He kept an arm in the river for balance, for direction. He didn't make a sound, the river treating him right.

A white light up on a pole, a preying mantis shape across the river. He threw out the canvas water bucket behind him and yanked the rope. A sea anchor, filling with water, slowing, braking the two rafts.

There wasn' t going to be much to grab onto; part of the bridge piling, part of the rocks, part of the scrub growth. He let the bucket sink, taut on the rope. The bridge was coming at him, taking shape.

He got one arm in the river like a rudder. Here was the bridge, and the rocks, and the scrappy brush.

The first raft bumped the concrete bridge piling. Gary Delling cut the rope to the water bucket and grabbed at the bush, a hand-full for an anchor, the front raft trying to get back in the river, bumping the piling.

He got hold of a rock and some branches, ice cold on his wet hands. He got the remains of the rope from the sea anchor and got it tied around a slick wet rock.

There. He caught his breath. There he was, not quite under the bridge. He caught his breath.

He made sure the rope was tight. He reached forward and moved the explosives. He splashed more water into the open leg holes.

The front raft stayed level.

He started to squirm up out of his raft. Slowly, delicately, carefully, he took off his pack and set it in the raft. Slowly, carefully, like a UDT ready to go over the side he lay belly down on the two rafts, the climbing rope coiled around his waist. Half a wet suit, shorts and rock climbing booties.

The bridge was a web of black metal. Toe holds and hand holds up the brace above the piling. Tie on the rope. Toe holds and hand holds back down to the rafts.

Tie on. On his belly, let go the anchor rope. The rafts spun into the river and under the bridge, held in the current by the tie on. No metal banging against any other metal. No sound, no alarm.

No one expecting him under the bridge. He didn't waste any time.

He went right to work.

He'd done it all before, in the dark. In the woods and swamps of the Carolinas. In the woods and swamps of Vietnam and Cambodia.

CHAPTER

Quietly, softly, sadly, he climbed up under the bridge, plenty of hand holds and foot holds, the metal all bumpy with bolts and braces like the skin of Nimo's Nautilus.

He crouched in a joint of the beams, took off the pack and wedged it, carefully. He blew some warm air into his hands. He went to work, night vision like any nocturnal creature.

The metal supports that carried the bridge were carried by railroad logs, by iron joints, square and as strong as a robot's shoes--a giant robot's shoes. Another beam ran straight ahead and bolted itself into the railroad logs driven into the river bank.

Masking tape, blocks of TNT. Masking tape. The TNT taped in place around the ankle of the robot shoe. Another four blocks were taped to the joint where the straight-out beam joined the logs.

Now came the combat, the live combat part. Gently, carefully, slowly, again blowing on his hands, he extricated the blasting caps from the pack. He laid the fly box on the beam.

The detonator cord. He rolled it out, dropping it down off the bridge until the end of it was just above the raft, bobbing on the Yellowstone. With his buck knife he cut two lengths of it.

Now. He went to the overhead beam first. A piece of cotton from the fly box. A blasting cap in his cold fingers. He pulled in the slack of the blasting cord. Carefully, calmly, he inserted the cord in the blasting cap. Now he had to crimp the end of the blasting cap. He did it with a Swiss Army knife, its flip-out scissors, squeezing, carefully, calmly. The back end of the blasting cap was snug around the detonator cord.

He reached up and slid the blasting cap into the hole of the explosive block, the cotton he'd used to pack the caps in place and a piece of masking tape to hold it all in place.

He got two more blasting caps and just ever so gently, slid them into two other blocks.

That done he crouched and listened. He ate a banana. He got back to work.

The TNT in the shoe joint got the same treatment. He worked carefully, professionally, his second, third and fourth nature.

He thought he heard something, up river. He crouched and listened.

I guess not. He got on with it.

CHAPTER

Down river. Paul Barnes snapped awake, back in his car, too boring to stand out and wait.

Something, something across the river. Something. He got out of the car and went to find out.

Across the river, in the compound. A quonset hut, big enough for a basketball court. A door banged open, corrugated metal against cold corrugated metal. The hum of a hundred, two hundred, three hundred human voices, like the hum of locusts, came out through the open door.

The light from the open door was something like fire, cloudy and razor bright in the dark. A shaft of it.

Elizabeth the Prophet stepped out into it, a dark cloak against the night, the hood thrown back off her head.

Tall, taller than the two men standing in the light behind her, the hum of the voices filling the quonset hall.

Across the river Paul Barnes listened. The sound of car engines.

Two Chevy Blazers pulled up into the light from the quonset hall. A driver jumped out of the lead Blazer and held the passenger door open.

The two men in the doorway went first. The tall woman in the cloak waited patiently in the light and dark.

The two men stood at the passenger door. She lifted the hood of her cloak over her head and went to the back seat of the Blazer.

The two men jumped in next to her.

Two more men came into the light. They filled up the second Blazer.

An arm came into the shaft of light and drew the door back in, shut. The voices inside were muffled.

You could hear the car engines in Jackson Hole.

Gary Delling heard them. He finished his business quickly.

He could hear the cars coming.

He played out the roll of detonating cord. Two lines of it dangled above the two rafts.

All his gear together, he climbed down off the bridge.

Rocking, on his knees in the raft. The Blazers were coming.

Calmly. After all, it was only some religious kooks, not the North Vietnamese who were coming.

But this all had to be neat, clean.

All the loose gear he dropped in the front raft. He sank it with his buck knife. The Yellowstone ate it whole.

The kooks were coming, up above the river, four-wheel drives on a gravel road.

Calmly, with a twenty-nine cent lighter, he lit the fuses. He let his raft go. The river didn't waste any of his time.

The fuses burned up to the explosives.

For a moment, a few moments, the Blazers and the raft were horizontal, the Chevys above the raft on the river below, headed in opposite directions. For a moment, the river faster than the engines.

The fuses hit the blasting caps.

CHAPTER

Bang! Like the Yellowstone ecosystem and all its creation.

Bang! Like the tolling of time, of eternity, judgement day.

Paul jumped out of his skin, and ran for his car.

A gray cloud, the gray of a heron's wing, rose from the bridge. Some of it settled on the windshields of the Blazers. The four-wheel wheels skidded to a stop, about a hundred yards from the bridge.

It wasn't pretty, and it wasn't heroic, but it sure as hell was efficient. A crimp in anybody's plans.

Half of the bridge snapped off, limp as a broken arm, as a broken wing, snapped away from its moorings, flopping loose, the current in the river tugging at a section of it, all of its snapped-off weight tugging at the opposite moorings. You could hear the bridge moaning under the strain. It was done for, judgement day.

Four, five, six, eight of them out of the Blazers. The bridge was done for. They noticed, at the edge of it. All the lights in the campground were on. Cult members on the other side of the bridge were out in the dark, in their bathrobes.

The one in the hooded cloak remained in the lead Blazer.

The one in the raft on the river let the river put some more distance between him and all those lights.

The river took Gary Delling. It took him, spinning onto a soft, grassy bend in the current.

The buck knife, and the raft was gone under the current.

With his pack secure on his back he moved away, quietly, gently, sadly. Into Montana and he was gone.

CHAPTER

A river. A city.

The river was the seine, the city was Paris, France.

February in Paris, France, the river Seine flat and gray, silent within its stone canal, the city tall, ornate and gray.

Paul Barnes too.

He sat by the river, by the great, aqua-green Charlemagne, his bronze statue too long in too many Februaries.

Charlemagne appeared to be in battle with Notre Dame Cathedral, tall and gray, post Yellowstone.

Paul followed the barges on the river. It wasn't the Yellowstone but it would do.

He was doing all right. He'd been in town for a few weeks.

Why Paris? Why not? Why Paris? Larry Darrell of course.

He couldn't speak the language, he couldn't get her out of his mind. He thought he saw her once, at the Louvre. Come on, Paul, you're in Paris. Get a fuckin' grip.

He got something of a grip on the city. Shakespeare & Co., the famous bookstore, was on a short list for today's American in Paris. American tourist. It was his turn to ask, excuse me, ranger. The locals weren't quite as courteous.

But the city, it had manners, dignified and proud.

Shakespeare & Co. was right across the river. He could see its sign board. All those from the 20's and the 30's wouldn't have seen it from where he sat, but there it was, now.

He got up and crossed the short stone bridge over the Seine.

He felt that big bang from not so long ago in the soles of his shoes.

He could feel the left bank, the rive gauche, in the soles of his shoes. In his soul? Not quite. But he was there looking for an author. Larry mentioned? I've read him now. Somerset Maugham.

That's him.

Shakespeare & Co. faced the boulevard, tucked not too neatly into a corner, sort of slanted at an odd angle into its allotted space.

The rows of book stalls along the river were opening for business. The wrought-iron gate into a Parisian pocket park was open.

There were book bins outside of Shakespeare & Co. Paul browsed a bit, the windows of the bookstore moist and gray, winter breathing on them.

He went in. English was being spoken by the early customers and the employees.

Hard wood and neatly ramshackled. Narrow and cosy.

Books. Fiction. Alphabetical. Neat and cosy. J, K, L, M.

Paul ran his eye along the authors. MA. MAUGHAM. There were several. Then several more. Paul wasn't choosey. This fella may have known Larry.

He pulled out a thin, hard back, black dust jacket with white letters. 'The Razor's Edge'.

O.K., this will do. How much? $15 American. He noticed he wasn't in the paperback section. He noticed this book wasn't brand new.

He was about to replace it, but the title. The title struck him. It struck him again. He had a pocket full of travelers checks. This fella may have known Larry.

He did his business with an American who could have passed for an American mule skinner, past his mule skinning prime.

Paul took his book to the river.

On a stone bench, older than Napoleon, he took a seat. The trees around him were bare. He reached in his pocket and took out the coin. He set the book on the bench and set the coin on top of it. It all went well with the grand river.

He flipped through the book. He flipped to the very last chapter, the very last page.

Something caught his eye. That something the way an elk among the pines, an antelope crossing a stream, an osprey leaving its nest catches your eye.

This is the end of my story. I have heard nothing of Larry, nor indeed did I expect to. Since he generally did what he proposed, I think

303

it likely that on his return to America he got a job in a garage and then drove a truck till he had acquired the knowledge he wanted of the country from which he had for so many years absented himself. When he had done that he may very well have carried out his fantastic suggestion of becoming a taxi driver; true, it was only a random idea thrown across a cafe table in jest, but I wouldn't be altogether surprised if he had put it into effect; and I have never since taken a taxi in New York without glancing at the driver on the chance that I might meet Larry's gravely smiling, deep-set eyes. I never have. War broke out.

He would have been too old to fly, but he may be once more driving a truck, at home or abroad; or he may be working in a factory. I should like to think that in his leisure hours he is writing a book in which he is trying to set forth whatever life has taught him and the message he has to deliver to his fellowmen; but if he is, it may be long before it is finished. He has plenty of time, for the years have left no mark on him and to all intents and purposes he is still a young man.

He is without ambition and he has no desire for fame; to become anything of a public figure would be deeply distasteful to him; and so it may be that he is satisfied to lead his chosen life and be no more than just himself. He is too modest to set himself up as an example to others; but it may be he thinks that a few uncertain souls, drawn to him like moths to a candle, will be brought in time to share his own glowing belief that ultimate satisfaction can only be found in the life of the spirit, and that by himself following with selflessness and renunciation the path of perfection he will serve as well as if he wrote books or addressed multitudes.

He had to stand up.

He had to gulp for air. He had to re-read what he had just read.

He had to clutch the book to his breast. He had to get up and walk.

He followed the river, a slow moving barge for company.

He walked far down along the river. There was still plenty of river up ahead.

Paul Barnes stopped and stared down the length of it. The page of what he had just read was marked by the coin. He removed it and held it. He knew.

"India," softly, gently, quietly, gladly.

Made in United States
Troutdale, OR
08/30/2024

22440971R10192